# A FAMILY FOREVER

This Large Print Book carries the
Seal of Approval of N.A.V.H.

# A FAMILY FOREVER

## BRENDA COULTER

**THORNDIKE PRESS**
*An imprint of Thomson Gale, a part of The Thomson Corporation*

THOMSON

GALE

Detroit • New York • San Francisco • New Haven, Conn. • Waterville, Maine • London

THOMSON
———★———™
GALE

**LIBRARY OF CONGRESS CATALOGING-IN-PUBLICATION DATA**

Coulter, Brenda.
  A family forever / by Brenda Coulter.
    p. cm. — (Thorndike Press large print Christian fiction)
  ISBN-13: 978-0-7862-9706-1 (alk. paper)
  ISBN-10: 0-7862-9706-9 (alk. paper)
  1. Large type books. I. Title.
PS3603.O8863F36 2007
813'.6—dc22                                                    2007013770

Published in 2007 by arrangement with Harlequin Books, S.A.

Printed in the United States of America on permanent paper
10 9 8 7 6 5 4 3 2 1

Oh Lord, You are my God;
I will exalt You and praise Your name,
for in perfect faithfulness
You have done marvelous things,
things planned long ago.
— Isaiah 25:1

With X's and O's to my sister,
who believes in me,
and who doesn't hold it against me
that I was mean to her
when we were little.

# CHAPTER ONE

Staring in increasing revulsion at the mushroom-and-Swiss-cheese omelet on the plate in front of her, Shelby Franklin was distinctly aware of each cold, tingling bead of perspiration that erupted on her forehead. Whatever had possessed her to order eggs? Accepting this breakfast invitation had been dumb enough, but she'd reached the summit of stupidity by ordering eggs.

Her stomach endorsed that opinion with a rebellious squeeze. Breathing deeply through her nose, Shelby shifted her gaze to focus on the upside-down reflection of her face in the shiny bowl of her unused teaspoon. If she concentrated, maybe she could hold this back.

A sudden, sharp noise made her flinch, but she didn't look up as the clatter of metal on thick ceramic echoed through the nearly deserted restaurant. The realization that her companion had dropped his fork and must now be studying her with those alert, coffee-brown eyes of his caused Shelby's heart to plummet into the roiling cauldron of her stomach. Did he have to notice everything?

"Shelby?" Tucker Sharpe's deep voice rumbled like distant thunder.

She lifted both hands to deflect his concern. "I'm okay," she insisted, not daring to look up. Her mind spun in desperate circles as she struggled to think up an excuse, an explanation, anything that would prevent him from guessing what she wasn't ready for him to know. "I haven't been sleeping much," she offered, staring hard at the spoon.

Tucker would buy that. Judging by his haggard look when he'd greeted her earlier, Tucker hadn't been sleeping much, either, these last three weeks. He and his brother had been unusually close, and losing David had hit him hard.

Maybe almost as hard as it had hit Shelby.

"How far along are you?" Tucker queried softly.

Shock jerked her head up. *"What?"*

A muscle twitched in his angular jaw as his mouth tightened and his dark eyebrows slammed together, creating the remote, disapproving expression Shelby had come to know well in recent months. Her best friend said Tucker was great looking, and maybe he was, with that lean, wholly masculine face and that luxuriant chestnut hair that rioted in little waves and spikes on top of his head. But every time he looked at Shelby, his shapely mouth thinned into a hard, straight line and his dark eyes sparked with silent accusations.

"You heard the question, Shelby. How far along are you?"

Shame caused her head to droop like a rain-drenched garden rose on a weak stem. "Just a few weeks," she whispered.

She didn't need a doctor to tell her when it had happened. There had been only the one time, just four days before David's accident. Shelby hadn't felt right about it, not even when David had reminded her — as if it could have slipped her mind even for a moment — that their wedding was less than a month away. Catching her bottom lip between her teeth, Shelby bit down hard. She had broken God's rules, and now she must face the consequences.

She tucked her curly, shoulder-length hair behind her ears, then instantly regretted the nervous gesture because it exposed more of her guilty face to Tucker, the mind reader.

"You just found out." He released a heavy breath that sounded as though he'd been holding it awhile. "You didn't know on Sunday."

No, if she had known then, when she'd sat beside him in church, he'd have read her as effortlessly as he was doing right now.

"I'll marry you," he said quietly.

Shelby looked up, certain she couldn't have heard him correctly. "M-marry me? *You?*"

He nodded almost imperceptibly, then just sat there, tall and straight and silent as a lighthouse, watching her.

Tucker was a friend to everyone in town. He'd even been Grand Leprechaun at this year's St. Patrick's Day parade, a very big deal here in Dublin, Ohio. But it was clear he didn't like Shelby. She hadn't been good enough for his younger brother.

After David's funeral she had expected to be forgotten, but she'd quickly learned that straight-arrow Tucker would not allow his personal feelings to interfere with what he saw as his duty to look after David's bereaved fiancée. If she happened to sit down alone at church, Tucker would materialize at her side, grave and solicitous. He was constantly inviting her out for meals, inquiring whether her ancient car was running okay, asking if she needed anything.

Yeah, she needed something. She needed

Tucker to get out of her life so she could concentrate on rebuilding it.

Twisting the diamond ring on her left hand, she shook her head, declining Tucker's ridiculous proposal. Then because he still seemed to be waiting, she gave him some words. "No. Thank you. There's no need for . . . that."

His eyes widened in apparent horror. "But you're going to *have* the baby, aren't you?" He glanced over his shoulder as if afraid someone might overhear them, but it was late and the breakfast crowd was gone. He leaned forward and lowered his voice, anyway, his dark eyes urgent. "Please tell me you're not thinking about —"

*"No,"* she interrupted, shocked. "I could never do that."

His shoulders slumped and the vertical line between his eyebrows almost disappeared as the tension drained out of him. "Then marry me. You don't have to go through this alone."

Didn't she? She'd been alone all her life. Until six months ago, when she had foolishly allowed herself to begin dreaming of marriage and children. When she had accepted David, she'd thought God was finally going to allow her to taste happiness. But after dangling it in front of her, he had snatched it away.

"The baby deserves a father," Tucker pressed.

Why did he assume that having the baby meant *keeping* the baby? She couldn't do that, not without money or parental support, and she had neither. Oh, sure, Tucker was offering to marry her. But even if she could disregard that pesky detail about not being in love with him, she'd have to be crazy to sign up for a lifetime with a man who so clearly disliked her.

She knew what she had to do. On a violin teacher's salary, she had no other choice. But she pressed her lips together as her stubborn heart fought to override her common sense. From the moment she'd realized her body sheltered this little spark of life, Shelby had been gripped by a fierce, protective love that went beyond all reason. This was *her* baby. How could she ever put it into another woman's arms?

"You can't do it." Slowly tracing the rim of his coffee mug with a long, square-ended finger, Tucker watched her intently. "You can't give it up."

How did he *do* that? How did he look inside her, read her mind? He often finished sentences for her, but there was nothing endearing about it, as might have been the case had David possessed the ability. It frustrated her no end, being unable to entertain a thought without Tucker picking it up and saying it out loud.

But maybe, just this once, it was all right, because the turmoil inside Shelby was threatening to rip her apart. Maybe a full confession would assuage some of this awful guilt. And there was no need to worry about Tucker's good opinion, was there? Because she couldn't lose something she'd never had.

"It was just one time." She said it fast, before she lost her nerve. "I know it shouldn't have happened at all, but —"

"You don't have to tell me this."

"Yes, I do." She sucked in a breath and forced herself to continue. "I know what the Bible says, and I meant to honor God by waiting, but then I *didn't* wait. I felt horribly guilty afterwards, so we agreed —"

"You don't owe me this," he interrupted again. "It was between the two of you and God."

"But if I . . . *marry* you . . ." Had those words actually come out of her mouth? She had no intention of marrying Tucker.

He shook his head. "I want this child to have David's name and be brought up by the people who loved his father. Right now, that's all I care about."

That was *all* he cared about? Shelby swallowed hard. "Do you mean you wouldn't expect —"

"You need time to grieve." Tucker's voice broke on that last word and his thick black eyelashes dipped low, reminding Shelby that he, too, was grieving. She had a feeling he blamed himself for not preventing David's accident, but she knew as well as anyone how difficult it had been to talk high-spirited David Sharpe out of anything. He'd wanted to ride his motorcycle in the rain; what could his brother have done to stop him?

Tucker raised his eyes and pinned Shelby with a sober gaze. "We could have separate bedrooms until the baby comes. What happens after that will be up to you."

"But how could you be content with that kind of arrangement?" she blurted. "Why would you saddle yourself with a woman you don't love?" Or even like, she added silently.

From the way his mouth tightened, she knew he'd read her mind again. "We'll get along fine," he said.

Yeah, she'd believe that in about a million years. "Do you even like babies?" she challenged.

"I've never been around any." Above the collar of his black T-shirt, his Adam's apple took a long, slow dip. "But I'll be a good father. And husband."

"No." Shelby managed to gather her wits enough to give her head an emphatic shake. "I couldn't."

"Just think about it."

She sure would. The next time she needed a good laugh, she'd just think about marrying Tucker Sharpe. Wouldn't it be delightful, sitting down at the breakfast table every morning and being treated to that scowl of his?

He lifted his coffee mug with a hand that trembled slightly. "Have you told your parents?"

"Last night." Resenting the way his gaze roamed over her face as though cataloguing each of her hated freckles, Shelby turned her head and looked out the window next to their table.

A light breeze ruffled a sea of pink tulips on the berm underneath the restaurant's sign post. It was a perfect spring morning, all blue sky and cotton-ball clouds, and even through the glass Shelby could hear the sweet "cheerio" of a robin. The world was still turning, just as if David hadn't died. And it would keep on turning, no matter what happened to his baby.

"They won't support you," Tucker said flatly.

Shelby's gaze jerked back to his face, but she said nothing because he wasn't wrong. She loved her mother, and her stepfather was all right, but Diana and Jack Dearborn had never been the kind of people to make a stand as a family.

"So what are your options?" Tucker pressed.

David had talked about buying life insurance and naming Shelby as the beneficiary, and if he had followed through on that, she'd be okay right now. But all he'd left behind was the wrecked motorcycle, a flashy car that wasn't paid for and a couple of thousand dollars in credit-card debt.

She couldn't give up the baby, but how could she keep it? Just two years out of college, she was still paying off loans and existing month to month on her meager salary as a middle-school strings teacher in nearby Columbus. She had a handful of private violin students and she jumped at every opportunity to pick up her own instrument and perform with a friend's quartet, but she was barely making it.

Tucker lifted one of his giant hands and rubbed the back of his neck. "You know, there are lots of places in the world where this kind of marriage wouldn't even raise an eyebrow."

Shelby raised *two* eyebrows, then said with some asperity, "This is not one of those places."

He folded his arms on the table, nudging his plate away with an elbow. "Well, I don't know of any Bible verse that says a couple has to be 'in love' before they marry. So as long as we're both fully committed to providing this baby with a real family, why shouldn't it work out?"

There were lots of reasons. Shelby was just too upset right now to think of any.

"As a matter of fact," Tucker continued, "it could be a real plus, going into marriage without any foolish romantic expectations to trip us up."

So romantic expectations were *foolish,* were they? Did he honestly believe marriage could be reduced to a business arrangement? "That isn't enough, Tucker. Not for me." Shelby shook her head at him. "And not for you, either."

"This isn't about us. This is about a child."

Shelby looked down at the hands she'd clenched together in her lap. She turned the left one slightly and watched her three-quarters-of-a-carat diamond solitaire flash red and purple sparks. She could sell the ring, she realized. She could get a smaller apartment and give up regular haircuts and premium chocolate and those ridiculously expensive caffe lattes. If the pregnancy and birth were uncomplicated and the baby was healthy, she might be able to manage.

But would "managing" be enough? Didn't her baby deserve more than that?

"Did David tell you about his childhood?" Tucker asked.

Shelby looked up, startled by this shift to a new topic. "Not really."

On the night they'd become engaged, David had confided that he'd had a rough life before being adopted by the Sharpes as a young teenager. Since Shelby, too, had endured a painful childhood and preferred not to discuss it, the conversation hadn't gone much further.

"He was two years old when his unwed mother abandoned him to the state," Tucker said. "He was in and out of foster homes until he was fourteen. None of them were particularly good places, but the last one was a nightmare."

"He said your mom was his English teacher," Shelby hinted, hoping Tucker would skip over the troubled years and just explain how David had come to be adopted

20

by Tucker's parents.

"She was. She believed David was being abused, but he was too ashamed to admit it, and they could never pin anything on his foster father until —" Tucker pressed his lips into a hard line that turned them almost white.

Shelby couldn't stop herself. "Until?"

Tucker's eyes narrowed and glittered with barely suppressed anger. "Until the man decided his fists weren't enough anymore. He went after David with a hockey stick. Broke his jaw."

Shelby knew her mouth was wide open, but she still wasn't catching any air. She rubbed the goose bumps on her bare arms and tried to remember how to breathe.

"I'm sorry," Tucker said, looking abashed. "I shouldn't have spelled it out like that."

Shelby closed her eyes. If Tucker was trying to scare her away from the idea of adoption, he was doing an excellent job.

"Don't get me wrong," he said. "I know there are lots of good people waiting to adopt babies, and you'd have a say in placement." He shook his head. "But Shelby, you *want* this baby. No, you didn't plan this. Yes, you're shocked, and you're grieving — I get all of that. But it's no good telling me that you don't want this baby."

It was no good telling herself, either. "I want it," she managed in a squeaky whisper. She *wanted* it.

"Then let's get married."

As she bowed her head, a tear dropped onto the rim of her plate, making a soft *ping* before rolling down the slanted edge to collide with a thick slice of mushroom.

Tucker had loved his brother, and he was offering to protect and nurture David's child. How could Shelby say no to that? She looked up into the unfathomable brown eyes that watched her without blinking. "All right," she whispered.

He reached across the table to lay his large hand over her wrist. "We'll make this work, Shelby."

Tomorrow was to have been her wedding day. Just last night, she had pulled the protective covering off a dazzling-white satin gown and caressed with trembling hands the exquisite beaded bodice David would never see.

Let it go, she commanded her aching heart. Her own chance at happiness was gone. The baby was all that mattered now.

She jerked her hand out from under Tucker's and pressed it against her mouth to hold back a sob.

Tucker was no starry-eyed romantic, so it wasn't like he'd been expecting to close this deal with a kiss. Still, it was a little dispiriting to watch his brand new fiancée clap a hand over her mouth, shove her chair back and bolt to the ladies' room. He just hoped it was morning sickness that had made her gag like that, and not the prospect of marriage to him.

If his brother had still been alive, Tucker would have had plenty to say to him this morning. Even David's V-shaped grin, always so hard to resist, wouldn't have pulled an answering smile from his elder brother. Not this time.

A high-spirited charmer, David had broken rules and hearts with the same reckless abandon. But he wasn't unfeeling; he simply neglected to consider the consequences of his impulsive actions. And because the first half of David's life had been so hellish, Tucker hadn't been able to watch him suffer for his actions even when he deserved to. So every time David had stirred up trouble, Tucker had stepped in to make whatever apologies or amends he could.

Tucker sighed and stabbed his fork into

an untouched pile of hash browns. He was, as one of his former girlfriends — a psychologist — had pointed out on more than one occasion, an enabler. He wasn't proud of that, but he never could say no to David. At sixteen Tucker had sworn an oath to the skinny fourteen-year-old whose broken jaw had been wired shut. Nobody would hurt David ever again. Tucker wouldn't allow it.

He'd harbored some serious reservations about David's engagement, but he'd never voiced them, and that mistake would follow Tucker to his grave. Desperate to believe marriage would settle his brother, Tucker had risked the happiness of an innocent young woman who didn't realize that David couldn't always be counted on to keep his promises.

Now David was gone, Shelby was twisting in the wind, and Tucker's shoulders ached from the crushing weight of his guilt. The worst of it was knowing that if only he had stood his ground on that awful night, David would still be here.

With thunderstorms predicted for that early May evening, Tucker had tried to dissuade his brother from the nighttime ride. But when David had scoffed at his concern and threatened to go alone, Tucker had sighed and thrown a leg over his own motorcycle. He much preferred his custom-built racing bicycle, which he powered with iron legs and sheer determination, but David loved gasoline engines. So Tucker had bought a motorcycle, too, thinking they could share some road adventures.

He blinked at the forkful of potatoes that hadn't yet made it to his mouth, then exhaled hard and returned the food to his plate. He reached for his water glass and slugged down half its contents, but that didn't ease the ache in his throat.

On the night of the accident they'd ridden just five miles before the rain had begun. Minutes later Tucker had watched in helpless horror as David took a right turn too fast, swinging wide and skidding head-on into a pickup truck.

Aware that his breathing had quickened, Tucker spread his arms and clutched the corners of the laminated wood tabletop. But that was an ineffective defense against the flash flood of awful memories that tore at him and swept him away. . . .

*David hated to wear a helmet because he loved to feel the wild wind rip through his hair. But tonight his folly had been exposed and blood streamed from a gash on his scalp, saturating his fair hair in the dim, bluish light of the streetlamp. "Take care of her?" he gasped as Tucker knelt beside him in the cold, drizzling rain.*

*Tucker's mouth worked for what felt like several minutes before he was finally able to pinch an answer from his swollen throat. "You know I will."*

Tucker relaxed his grip on the table and drew several deep, calming breaths, then he turned to look out the window as he reviewed his sins.

He had known David wasn't ready for marriage, but he'd kept silent. Not only that, he'd loaned David $400 to help pay for Shelby's engagement ring. He had agreed to be best man and he had even been fitted for a tux. With every word and deed he had nudged David and Shelby closer to a future he didn't believe in. What he *should* have done was take his younger brother aside and ask, "Are you absolutely sure about this?"

They would have talked about it then, and maybe David would have agreed to wait awhile. And if there hadn't been a wedding in the works, maybe David and Shelby wouldn't have —

Tucker gave his head a determined shake. He couldn't change the past, so he was just going to have to deal with the present — and the future — that he had helped create.

Shelby was in trouble, and that was Tucker's fault as much as it had been David's.

Plain and simple, Tucker *owed* her.

She finally emerged from the narrow hallway that led to the restrooms. As she met Tucker's eyes across the empty dining room she stumbled slightly, but then she lifted her chin and squared her shoulders in a way he couldn't help but admire. She was grieving and terrified, but the girl had guts.

She was softer and rounder than was fashionable, Tucker noted as she walked toward him, but she possessed a natural grace that would have captivated any man. He also liked her hair. The untamed curls that brushed her shoulders were the color of an almost-new penny, coppery tending to brown. Her nose was a bit too large and high-bridged, her chin a little too pointed, but her eyes were remarkable. Under nearly straight auburn brows, sandwiched between sweeps of darker lashes, were a pair of irises so startlingly, brilliantly blue that the color really needed a name of its own. But *violet* came close.

As she reached their table, Tucker unfolded his long body and stood. At six-four, he probably had a good thirteen inches on her, and because he suspected that his size made her nervous, he hunched down a little, bending his neck to put his face closer to her eye level. "Feeling better?"

She met his gaze squarely. "I'm a little scared."

Tucker couldn't help smiling at that. If she was only a *little* scared, she was doing a whole lot better than he was. But he was fully committed to this course. He had failed Shelby Franklin once, and he would die before he'd do it again.

# CHAPTER TWO

"Sorry I'm just now returning your call." Rachel Dare spoke in dulcet tones. "After the gallery opening, Greg and I had a late dinner, and by the time I got home, I was afraid of waking you."

Shelby's hand tightened on the phone as cold, clammy tentacles of envy wound themselves around her heart and squeezed. A Scandinavian blonde with a Hollywood smile, Rachel was beautiful and clever, a glamorous travel agent and tour guide who led a charmed life. It just wasn't fair, the way Rachel got everything she ever wanted, while Shelby —

Amazed at the direction her thoughts were taking, Shelby blinked hard. Okay, she wasn't normally at her best at seven in the morning, but what was *wrong* with her?

"And I have bad news," Rachel continued. "Francine just called. She's come down with something, and you know I'm her backup for the France and Germany tours. So I have to leave for Paris at two-thirty today."

Shelby's rapidly deflating heart caused her shoulders to sink. She'd been counting on her best friend to get her through this, her would-have-been wedding day. "How long will you be gone?" she asked, trying not to sound as dejected as she felt.

"Six days." Rachel paused. "Look, I feel terrible about canceling our plans for tonight. I wish I could just —"

"I'll be fine." Shelby held back a sigh as she pushed a thick slice of whole-grain bread into her toaster. She didn't have time to be sad today. She was far too busy being sick and worried; sad would just have to wait.

"You're so brave," her friend said. "In your place, I'd be crying my eyes out."

"Yeah, well." Shelby forced a laugh. "The day is young." She slumped against the kitchen counter, propping her chin on one hand and casting a black look at the coffee-maker that had only just now started rumbling and steaming.

"Go out and do something," Rachel ordered. "Don't sit home all by yourself tonight."

"I'll be fine. Don't worry."

"I'll bring you some chocolate truffles from that little shop by the Eiffel Tower," Rachel promised. "And I'll cook something fabulous for us when I get back."

"Sounds great. Especially that part about the truffles."

"I hear you." Humor lightened Rachel's voice. "Anyone who says diamonds are a girl's best friend has never seen the two of us plow through a box of handmade French chocolates. Hey, I need to put the phone down a sec."

Shelby pulled her plain terry bathrobe more closely around herself and imagined Rachel's silky, flax-colored hair swinging over her slim shoulders as she opened a suitcase on her bed and bent to fill it with size-two outfits. Why was life so kind to slinky blondes and so cruel to chubby redheads?

Shelby scowled at her coffeemaker, afraid that if it didn't start dripping a little faster, she was going to lose her mind. Where was this awful mood coming from?

Sure, life was difficult. It always had been. But it was unproductive to whine, and Shelby had learned long ago to keep marching forward, no matter what. So was her current craziness a natural stage of grief, or was it related to the tide of hormones pregnancy had unleashed on her unsuspecting brain?

Maybe it was both. And maybe that was why she was having so little success fighting it off.

"So, you went out with Greg last night?" she asked when Rachel came back to the phone. She worked hard to inject a teasing note into her voice. "What happened to dreamy Dylan?"

"Dylan's history. I hated that he never opened my car door."

Shelby's amusement was genuine this time. "Rachel, you go to the gym five days a week and Dylan never lifts anything heavier than his laptop computer. You should be opening doors for *him*."

"A guy doesn't open car doors because a woman is weak, Shelby. He does it because he values her. And you know I always hated that Dylan didn't treat me like anyone special."

"You're right," Shelby admitted, leaning over the dribbling coffeemaker to inhale the fragrant steam. After the first couple of dates with David, she had assured him that while she wasn't a particularly athletic individual, she was capable of opening a car door. He'd laughed and explained that his father and Tucker would take turns pounding him into the ground if they ever caught him denying a woman that simple courtesy.

"Speaking of how guys treat women, Shelby, did you read Steve Tucker this morning?"

"Who?" Shelby's toast popped up and she hunched her shoulder, trapping the telephone against her ear so she could pick up a knife and slather apple butter on the warm slice. She had always loved the cinnamony aroma of the apple spread, but this morning it didn't smell right. Another weird effect of pregnancy? She picked up the smothered toast and took an experimental lick.

"The newspaper column," Rachel said. "You know. 'The Guy's Guide to Women.' Did you read it?"

Shelby fumbled her toast and watched in disgust as it landed sticky side down on her vinyl floor. "No, I didn't," she said irritably, ripping a paper towel off the roll next to the sink. "Steve Tucker is a Neanderthal," she added, bending to pick up the toast and wipe the floor. "He wouldn't open a car door if his ninety-year-old granny was on crutches."

"That's just his act," Rachel said mildly. "Hold on. You have to hear this."

As Rachel rattled newspaper pages, Shelby poured herself a cup of coffee, took a sip and waited for her foul mood to improve.

"Okay," Rachel said, and then imitated a man's voice. " 'Never ask a woman what's wrong unless you honestly want to know. If you ask what's wrong she will tell you, in excruciating detail. Is that really what you want, or would you rather catch the second half of the game?' "

Shelby drummed her fingers on the countertop. "Is that supposed to be funny?"

"Oh, come on," Rachel chided.

The coffee was a start, but it wasn't enough. Shelby put the cup down and leaned over her trash container to fish out the three Hershey's bars she'd dropped in there last night. Her bathroom mirror hinted that a "well-rounded" woman who was pregnant and therefore soon to become even rounder didn't need any extra calories. But this morning, Shelby didn't care. And at the moment she was desperate enough to sift through egg shells and coffee grounds to reach chocolate, so it was a blessing the bars had landed atop a fairly clean pile of junk mail.

Yes, she'd have to give some serious thought to prenatal nutrition. But this was not the week to give up chocolate.

"Listen to this one," Rachel said. " 'When your woman tells you about a problem she's having at work, just keep your mouth shut and do your best to look sympathetic. She is not asking for your advice. She just wants you to feel bad and hug her. When she wants advice she will ask her girlfriends, not you.' "

"I suppose that's true." Salivating, Shelby peeled off a black wrapper and unfolded the waxy paper liner to expose a chocolate bar.

"And funny," Rachel insisted. "They're *all* funny. Have you ever wondered what Steve Tucker's like in person? Happily married, probably, with three perfect children."

"No." Shelby advanced her own theory. "He's a serial dater. He can't handle commitment, so he dumps a woman the minute she starts talking about any future beyond next weekend."

Just like Tucker Sharpe. David had joked about Tucker's "flavors of the month," but Shelby couldn't see anything cute about a man whose razor blades lasted longer than his girlfriends.

*He's going to marry you,* her conscience said as she placed a square of chocolate on her tongue. *How's that for commitment?*

"Hey," Rachel said gently. "I know you're sad about David, but I think something else is going on here. What's wrong?"

Shelby closed her eyes. *Everything* was wrong. Was it even possible for her life to be any more wrong than it was right now? She doubted it. "It's nothing to worry about," she said, then wondered when she'd turned into such a casual liar.

"Have you been followed again?" Rachel demanded.

"No." Shelby managed a half-hearted laugh as she broke off another square of chocolate. "Who'd want to stalk *me?*"

It had happened a month ago, when she'd gone to pick up her dry cleaning. She'd turned into the cleaners' parking lot, then realized she'd left her checkbook at home. As she pulled back out onto the road, she noticed something odd. The red pickup truck that had been a couple of cars behind her, that had pulled into the gas station at the same time Shelby had entered the parking lot next door, was leaving without getting any gas.

The truck faded back, blended into traffic, and when she'd spotted it again a few minutes later, it was easing into a left-turn lane as Shelby prepared to turn in the opposite direction. So it had been nothing. She wasn't sure why she'd even bothered to mention the incident to Rachel.

"Women have a sixth sense about these

things," Rachel had said then. "When the hair stands up on the back of your neck, that's a signal to pay attention."

It was true that Shelby's heart had pounded a little faster that day. But that was nothing compared to the way it was banging against her rib cage right now. "Rachel," she began, croaking a little. "Are you still willing to do the maid-of-honor thing? Because I'll be getting married, after all."

Apparently, she'd shocked her friend into silence. Shelby twirled a springy auburn curl around her index finger. "To Tucker," she added with desperate nonchalance.

After several more seconds of dead air, Rachel managed a choked, *Tucker.*

Shelby let go of her hair and closed her eyes. "Yes."

*"Why?"*

Shelby squeezed her eyes tighter. "Because I'm pregnant."

Another long pause ensued, and Shelby congratulated herself on doing this over the phone and not in person. It was easier not having to see her friend's expression. "He feels a responsibility to look after David's baby," Shelby explained.

"You're *serious.*"

Shelby swallowed. "I'd like to have your support. It will probably just be us and a couple of witnesses, but I'd really —"

"I will," Rachel said quickly. "You know I will. But you just lost David. How can you even consider marrying Tucker? Shelby, what are you *thinking?*"

"I'm thinking I don't have any choice."

"There are always choices," Rachel said firmly.

"Not for me. I have to keep this baby." Shelby sagged against the counter and, in the bright light from the window over the sink, studied the sparkling diamond on her left hand.

"But how can you marry a man you don't love?"

Shelby rocked her hand back and forth, fascinated first by a flash of red, then a wink of blue-green. The colors were intense and beautiful, but they didn't last. Nothing good ever did. "I don't believe in fairy tales," she said. "Not anymore."

They were both silent for a moment, then Rachel sighed heavily. "That's sad, Shelby."

"That's *life,* Rachel." Shelby tugged the ring off her finger. "And it's time for me to get on with it."

In his father's garage, Tucker unscrewed the cap from a container of motor oil and leaned over the engine of his dad's aging

Volvo. As oil glugged into the reservoir, Tucker glanced over his shoulder at his father, who was looking tense and uncomfortable in the lawn chair Tucker had set up for him just outside the garage. "I had breakfast with Shelby yesterday," he said with studied casualness.

"I'm worried about that girl." Stephen Sharpe grunted softly as he shifted in his chair. "She didn't even cry at the funeral, did you notice that? You could see in her face how torn up she was, but she wouldn't let herself cry."

"She'll be fine." Tucker would make sure of that. "I thought your back was better today."

"It's not killing me, but it's not making me happy, either." Stephen smoothed down a wisp of thinning salt-and-pepper hair that had been ruffled by a light breeze. "Can't wait to get to heaven, where I can play golf again."

Tucker smiled at that image. His tall, athletic father had always been nuts for golf, but in the past few months he'd developed some back problems that were keeping him off the links. "You think there's a golf course up there?" he teased.

"Maybe not," Stephen said with a rueful smile. "But when we see our Lord, we won't be crying over anything we left behind here on earth." His smile faded as his gaze drifted across the quiet residential street to where the pale-orange disc of the sun had just touched the treetops between two houses. Tucker knew he was thinking not only about David, but also about the beloved wife he'd lost two years ago.

"It's getting late," Stephen said in a husky voice. He turned an expectant look on Tucker. "Didn't you say you were taking her out?"

Tucker shook his head. "She's having a girls' night with Rachel. One of those dinner-movie-sleepover things."

Learning about those plans yesterday morning had relieved Tucker. He'd figured on helping to fill Shelby's empty evening, but at some point he would have had to say goodnight and leave her alone with her grief. So he was glad Rachel meant to stay the whole night with her.

"That's good." Stephen nodded his satisfaction. "This has been hard on us, but imagine what it must be like for a young woman to lose her fiancé just three weeks before the wedding."

"Yeah." Tucker's voice cracked on the word. He swallowed hard and recapped the empty oil container. "Dad, there's something I need to tell you."

The worry lines in Stephen's forehead deepened. "Are you okay, son?"

No, he was terrified. But as he leaned over the engine to replace the oil cap, he forced words out of his mouth. "Dad, I'm going to marry Shelby."

He waited a couple of heartbeats before turning to face his slack-jawed father. "I have to." Tossing the oil container into an open trash can, he added, "She's pregnant." The plastic bottle hit the bottom of the empty receptacle with a loud thump that echoed through the garage, underscoring the announcement.

*"Tucker."* Outrage contorted Stephen's face as he gripped the arms of his chair and struggled to push himself up. "Are you telling me that you and Shelby —"

*"No,"* Tucker said quickly, not liking where that question was headed. "No. *David* and Shelby."

"Oh." Stephen settled back into his chair and exhaled wearily. "Please forgive me for assuming —"

"No, it was my fault," Tucker interrupted. It had stung, his father's thinking even for a moment that he could have betrayed David. But he attributed that lapse of confidence to the grief they were both suffering. "I

41

could have chosen my words better," he admitted, then vented his frustration by slamming the Volvo's hood.

"She isn't your responsibility," Stephen said quietly.

Tucker pressed his lips together. His dad was about to begin a lecture he knew by heart. Leaning one hip against the car and folding his arms, he lowered his gaze to the smooth concrete floor and waited.

"High-school high jinks were one thing, son. I always suspected you took the heat for David more often than not. Even in college, you were always bailing him out. But *this* . . ." He lifted his hands in a hopeless gesture, then let them fall to smack his denim-covered thighs.

"Dad," Tucker's voice came out strangled as grief gripped him by the throat. "He's *gone.* This is the last thing I'll ever be able to do for —"

"You don't have to *marry* her." Stephen's tone was firm. "I'll take care of her and acknowledge the baby as my grandchild."

"She won't take money from you," Tucker argued. "If you think that, you don't know her. And with no support, she'd have to give up the baby."

"But her parents —"

"Care nothing about her. They want her

to give up the baby. But that's not what *she* wants." Tucker shook his head. "If you had seen her face, Dad, you'd understand. She's scared, but she really wants the baby. What else could I do?"

"Pity's no reason for marriage, son."

"It's more than that," Tucker said, struggling to rein in his exasperation. How could he explain that he'd looked into her violet eyes and seen something that had branded his soul? But even forgetting all that, it wasn't just any baby she was carrying. It was *David's* baby.

Tucker snatched a lawn chair from a peg on the wall and set it up beside his father. "I need you to accept this," he said as he collapsed onto the chair. "I know it's the right thing to do."

Worry darkened Stephen's brown eyes. "Son, I'm not sure either of us is thinking clearly, not so soon after Dav—" Choking on his younger son's name, he squeezed his eyes shut, grimacing as he fought to process the pain.

*David.* Every bit as close to losing it as his father was, Tucker averted his face. How could anything hurt this much?

Stephen sucked air through his teeth and, with a visible effort, composed himself. "I don't know how to advise you, other than to say go talk to Pastor Dean. He'll know what's right."

"I know what I'm doing, Dad. This *is* right." Rubbing his thumb over the five-o'clock stubble on his chin, Tucker thought back over the past six months. Almost from the beginning, some instinct had told him Shelby and David weren't right for each other. Or at least, that they weren't *ready* for each other. They were just trying it on, the whole love-and-engagement thing. They'd been two foolish kids, rushing toward disaster.

"See what Pastor Dean thinks," Stephen urged.

"I will." Tucker didn't foresee any problem there. Once Pastor Dean understood Shelby's need and Tucker's solid commitment to her and the baby, he'd be firmly behind them.

"You'd be starting off with some real handicaps," Stephen warned. "You're both grieving, there's a baby on the way, and you're not bound together by love. But if this is the right thing to do, I know you'll do it right. You'll give it everything you've got, and then you'll give even more. Just like you do on the bike."

Exactly.

Tucker had learned early on that his body

was all wrong for his sport. Tall, powerfully built men, known in the cycling world as "Clydesdales," were hard-pressed to compete with the sleek riders whose narrow bodies minimized wind resistance. Big men had to work harder on hills, having more weight to drag up them. So even riders with less stamina and inferior technique had an edge over Tucker simply because they were smaller.

And yet Tucker had enjoyed remarkable success because after a while, even the strongest lungs and legs gave out. In the end, Tucker won races because he was an excellent strategist who was both disciplined and patient. And wouldn't those qualities make him a good husband and father?

He looked at his dad. "I'll need your prayers."

"Oh, thanks for reminding me," Stephen deadpanned. "Hand me a pencil, will you? I'd better jot myself a note."

In spite of the grief and worry that pressed his heart, Tucker met his father's twinkling eyes and laughed.

Diana Dearborn paused in the act of straightening the perfectly orderly stack of decorating books on her immaculate glass-topped coffee table to look over her shoulder at her only child. "That is the most ridiculous thing I've ever heard."

Too late, Shelby realized there was something worse than sitting at home alone on the night she was to have married David, and that was standing here in her mother's sterile living room explaining that she was going to marry David's brother. Diana's disparaging tone was bad enough, but her ice-blue stare made Shelby feel like a very stupid child. Why was her mother so impossible to please?

"I thought you'd be relieved," Shelby said. "I won't be an unwed mother."

"Relieved?" Fashionably svelte in an oatmeal-colored linen suit, Diana put up a hand to smooth her eternally perfect blond chignon. "I don't even know the man. How can I be relieved to know you're jumping into marriage with a perfect stranger?"

First of all, Tucker wasn't perfect. He wasn't a stranger, either. "I've known him for six months. And you met him at the engagement party, remember?"

Diana frowned, obviously not remembering.

"I'm sure you spoke to him at the funeral," Shelby persisted. "Tall guy? Dark-brown hair? Cocker-spaniel eyes?"

"Oh. *Him.*" Diana perched on her beautiful but uncomfortable Danish sofa and rolled her eyes in apparent disgust. "That big, awful bear."

Some of Shelby's tension dissolved into a chuckle. "That's Tucker." He *was* like a bear. He was tall and broad, and whenever he spoke from behind Shelby, that startlingly deep voice of his made her want to jump right out of her skin.

"I don't like him," Diana grumbled. "He reminds me of Phillip."

Shelby's amusement died. She gaped at her mother, who had just broken their long-standing, if unspoken, agreement never to mention that name.

Diana picked a piece of imaginary lint from the sleeve of her suit jacket. "He's big and handsome and charming. Change the eyes and hair, and they'd be twins."

Was that why Shelby was so uncomfortable around Tucker? On some level, did he remind her of her father? She shook her head, dislodging that thought. "Well, he's not charming to me," she said lightly. "He scowls at me all the time."

Diana pounced on that. "Why would he scowl at you?" She had never been the nurturing type, but she took it as a personal affront when anyone criticized her daughter. That was *her* job.

Shelby lowered herself into an elegant but hard-bottomed chair. "He doesn't approve of me. I wasn't good enough for David." She said the words as casually as she could, but the admission still hurt. Who was Tucker to make that judgment?

Diana's eyes narrowed. "Why does he want to marry you, then?"

"To preserve the Sharpe family honor."

"He said that?" Diana's voice dripped with scorn.

"Not in so many words. But that's his reason. He wants the baby to have David's name and grow up knowing about David."

"If he cares so much about David's baby, let him adopt it," Diana shot back. "Marriage is hard enough under the best of circumstances," she added with the air of one who knew. She turned her fine-boned wrist to check her watch. "I have a house to show in twenty minutes, so we'll discuss this later."

No, they wouldn't. Shelby stood, angry now. "I didn't come here for advice, Mom. I came to tell you I'm getting married."

Her mother didn't back down. "Then you're being selfish. Playing at marriage with Tucker is not in the best interests of the baby. That kind of marriage is doomed to fail, and you know it. Adoption is the only answer."

But what if something went wrong? What if the baby was born with some condition that made him or her unattractive to adopting couples? Or what if the baby *was* adopted, but not by good people? And even if a couple seemed nice, who knew whether they might end up in divorce court a few years from now?

Shelby tried to imagine what her pastor would say about that. Would he advise her to trust God and leave the baby in His capable hands? She couldn't. Although she was a Christian, she didn't trust God to handle the details of her life. Over the years she'd given Him plenty of chances to prove that she mattered to Him, and His unrelenting silence had spoken volumes.

She couldn't abandon her baby to an indifferent God and an uncertain future. There was only one way to know for sure that her child would always be safe. "I'm keeping my baby," she said firmly. "Whatever it takes, Mom, I am keeping this baby."

# CHAPTER THREE

Tucker tipped his head back and squeezed a jet of water into his mouth, then slid the plastic bottle back into the wire holder mounted on his bike frame. Glancing over his left shoulder, he eased into the Monday-evening tide of traffic on Bridge Street, Dublin's busy main thoroughfare, and headed east. He claimed a full lane as his own, easily keeping up with the car ahead of him at a respectable thirty-three miles per hour. Just after the river bridge he extended his arm to indicate a turn, then leaned a hard left and peeled through the intersection.

He was as wild for speed as David had been, but while David's tastes had run to fast cars and motorcycles, Tucker preferred to power his own machine. There was no feeling in the world like running right on the razor's edge of his anaerobic threshold, watching his front wheel grab smooth asphalt and pull it with dizzying speed underneath his body.

And Tucker was fast. Sponsored in part by Shamrock Bike Shop, the store he co-owned with his father and an uncle, he'd enjoyed four remarkably good seasons as a semi-pro cyclist. Last year he had won two important criteriums and finished third in a major road race, and every time he'd blazed across the finish line David had been there, fists high in the air, his head thrown back as he emitted a wild scream of victory.

It would never be the same without David. Racing required more than just legs and lungs, and Tucker wasn't sure he had the heart to go on. Not this season, at least.

But while he couldn't bring himself to race, he still needed to ride, so he rose from the saddle and flung himself into a recreational sprint.

He rocketed up the straight stretch of road, heading north on his "busy-day" loop, a quick fourteen-miler that took him up one side of the Scioto River and back down the other. He'd been late getting away from the bike shop and he had a full evening planned, but this short ride was better than no ride at all.

Sailing over a small rise, he spotted a rider ahead of him. In the game of bikes vs. cars that was played on the asphalt, all cyclists were teammates, so a friendly greeting was always in order. But this guy had no business on the road.

He wasn't anywhere near keeping a tight line as a minivan streaked past him, allowing only two feet of clearance. *Dangerous.* He was all over the road, just begging for a car to bounce him into the ditch, and he wasn't even wearing a helmet. Tucker scowled at the bare blond head and prayed that the Lord would protect this rookie from his colossal stupidity.

As he caught up to the rider, Tucker's annoyance was replaced by fury. Recognizing both the teenage boy and the brand-new bike, he clamped his teeth together to avoid yelling the rude words that ripped through his brain. "On your left!" he barked instead, warning the rider that he was about to pass. Three seconds later he blew past the kid, his mind on bigger problems.

At noon on Tuesday, Shelby took a deep breath and then yanked open the heavy glass door of Shamrock Bike Shop. When an obnoxious trio of brass cowbells announced her arrival by jangling against the top of the door, she winced. She hated unexpected noises.

She didn't much care for the rubbery stench of this place, either. As she walked past a long row of smelly new bikes, she tried breathing through her mouth. Much better.

She'd never been inside the unremarkable brick building that presented its narrow side to the street, so she was surprised to find that what she had assumed was a dingy little repair shop was in reality a spacious, bright, modern store. She advanced a few more steps, then paused uncertainly beside a large carousel holding Spandex bike shorts clipped to hangers.

A curly dark head swiveled in her direction.

"I'd like to see Tucker," Shelby said, smiling at the skinny teenager who wore a black T-shirt featuring a large green shamrock and the store's logo. "If he's not busy."

The guy grinned as he checked her out, his gaze making a slow sweep from her face to her leather sandals and back up again. Because he appeared to be all of seventeen, and because Shelby was nothing to look at, not in a limp blue T-shirt and faded denim shorts, not with her round body and her frizzy copper-colored curls, she was more amused than offended by his blatant perusal. "Oh, I don't think he's *too* busy," the wolf-in-training said, nodding in the direction of the cash register.

Shelby walked over to where Tucker was displaying an amazing talent for multitasking as he fielded a phone call, made change for a customer, shook his head at a man who wanted to know if the bike shorts were on sale and lunged to catch a ballpoint pen as it rolled off the edge of the counter. That he could manage all that while looking perfectly composed and devastatingly handsome was just plain annoying.

Shelby sighed. One of the many problems with pregnancy-induced lethargy was that it tended to make you despise energetic people.

Tucker's eyebrows lifted slightly when he spotted Shelby, and he held up one finger, silently asking her to wait. She watched as he closed the cash register, thanked his customer with a dimply grin, shook his head at the man who now wanted to know if the bike shorts would be on sale *next* week and ended his phone call.

She hadn't seen Tucker since Friday morning, when they'd decided to get married. She'd told him then that she needed some time alone, and Tucker had respected that, although he'd phoned on Sunday when she didn't show up for church. After she explained that morning sickness had kept her away, he had apologized for disturbing her. He hadn't called again.

"Thanks for waiting," he said now. His tone was polite, but the smile he'd used on his customers had evaporated.

The heat in Shelby's cheeks told her she was blushing, but that had to be better than the pale, sick color she'd seen in her mirror an hour ago. She tipped her head back, hating it that Tucker was so tall, looked him straight in the eye, and forced out the question she'd come here to ask. "Are you sure you want to marry me?"

"Yes," he said without expression. "What do *you* want?"

What did she want? She wanted David not to be dead. But she couldn't have that, so she focused on the only thing that mattered now. "I have to keep my baby."

"Then it's settled." Tucker's gaze drifted past her and his mouth tightened visibly. He blinked several times and looked profoundly annoyed, but he said nothing more.

"I'm giving you a chance to back out," Shelby explained.

His attention snapped back to her. "When I say I'm going to do something, I *do* it."

She stiffened. "And you'll resent me for the rest of your life?"

"No." His glanced away for an instant, then looked back at her, more irritated than ever, judging by the way his right temple flexed. "I had a choice and I made it. It's a done deal."

Her courage faltered and her gaze sank to the shamrock logo on his black T-shirt. "Mom says I'm being selfish," she admitted in a small voice.

"Like I needed this today," he muttered.

Why was he being so nasty? Getting married had been *his* idea. Raising her head, Shelby caught him looking past her again. But when she turned, all she saw was a slender blond boy of perhaps fifteen lingering beside a rack of cycling jerseys. The other customers had gone, and although Shelby could hear muffled laughter coming from the workroom, she and Tucker were the only other people in the sales area.

"Selfish?" he asked belatedly. "Why?"

"Because I want to keep my baby."

"That's not selfish." His tone had softened, but his alert gaze was again fixed on the blond boy.

Shelby plunged ahead. "Tucker, what if the baby could go to a loving home? Wouldn't you rather —"

"No." The word was crisp, decisive, but he was still looking past her.

"Why not?"

His eyes instantly shifted back to her face and he spoke slowly, deliberately. "Because no man on earth would take better care of David's baby than I would." His deep voice vibrated with an intensity that made Shelby's knees wobble. "So if you're sure about keeping the baby, then I'm sure about marrying you. I'm not comfortable with any other solution."

"I'm not comfortable with *this* one." Dismayed to find the tremors had worked up from her knees and were now affecting her voice, she looked down at the blue carpet, fixing her attention on a dark stain there. "But I don't know what else to —"

"Oh, please." Tucker groaned the words. "Tell me you're not that stupid."

Shelby's head jerked up, but she quickly realized he hadn't been speaking to her. "What's going on?" she demanded.

"Excuse me." Tucker's arm shot past her, making her flinch, but he only grabbed a bicycle helmet from a display table. He barreled toward the boy, who had pulled a red jersey off its hanger and was now making his way to the front door. "How's that new bike working out for you?" Tucker boomed.

The boy started guiltily, then turned. "What new bike?"

"The one you stole from here on Saturday."

Shelby felt her mouth drop open.

The kid tossed the jersey on top of another clothing rack, but it slid off and landed in a heap on the carpet. "I didn't steal *nothing*."

"You were eyeing one of our bikes on Saturday, just before it went missing." Tucker's long fingers drummed a threatening rhythm on the helmet. "Then yesterday, I saw you riding it."

Shelby's breath had quickened, and she felt lightheaded. Arguments and confrontations of any kind always unnerved her.

The boy tossed his head, flipping a tangle of flaxen curls back from his narrow face. "I bought my bike at a shop in Columbus," he retorted. "Last summer."

"Now that really interests me, because that model just came out." Tucker paused, and the brief silence seemed to crackle with danger. "How did you manage to get one last year?"

"Man, you don't know what you're talking about."

Tucker made a disgusted noise in his throat. "Kid, I know even more about bikes than you know about larceny. But I'll tell you what. You bring that bike in, and we'll compare its serial number to my records. If

I've made a false accusation, I'll give you fifty bucks and a sincere apology."

The boy's belligerent gaze drifted away from Tucker's face.

"Come on," Tucker prodded. "What have you got to lose?"

"I'm in a hurry," the kid mumbled. "Maybe later."

Tucker sighed. "Well, take this." He thrust the helmet against the boy's chest, not gently.

The kid backed up, refusing to accept it. "What for?"

"Let's just say I'm fanatical about people protecting their melons."

Shelby winced. David had died from massive internal injuries, but she knew the blood she'd seen on Tucker's shirt that awful night had come from a wound on David's head.

"Take it," Tucker said, offering the helmet again. "Just stay out of my store unless you're looking for a job."

"Yeah, right. Like you'd hire me."

"I absolutely would," Tucker said with a gravity that stopped Shelby's breath.

"Why?" The boy sounded more curious than insolent now.

"So you could work off your debt. Maybe we could turn you into a responsible citizen and save the community some grief." Tucker shrugged. "Of course, I'd have to watch the merchandise while you're around, and I'd be insane to let you operate the cash register. But you might earn my trust, eventually."

The boy's face twisted into a defiant smirk. "You're crazy." He pivoted on his heel and walked away.

"Hey!" Tucker barked after him, making Shelby jump.

The kid turned in the doorway, blue eyes bulging, every line of his slender body communicating disgust. *"What?"*

"When you were riding up Riverside Drive yesterday, did a guy in a red jersey pass you like you were standing still?"

The boy's defiant expression dissolved in an instant. "That was *you?*" he asked, forgetting his swagger.

Tucker's head dipped in calm acknowledgement.

"Dude, you were *flying.*" The kid's light-blue eyes had widened, and his tone was frankly admiring now as he shoved his straggly hair away from his face. "How fast were you —"

"Maybe you noticed I was wearing a helmet," Tucker interrupted. "All serious riders do. It's part of the look." He flung the helmet at the boy, who caught it against his chest.

The kid stared for a moment, then tucked the helmet under his left arm before turning abruptly and banging out the door.

When the taut lines of Tucker's body relaxed, Shelby thought it safe to approach him. "Why did you do that?"

He smiled wearily. "He reminded me of somebody."

They stood together, watching as the boy stopped on the sidewalk and fished something from a pocket of his baggy cargo shorts. When he placed a cigarette between his lips, Tucker sighed. "David was just like that."

"David?" Shelby repeated, shocked.

Tucker nodded. "When he first came to us. He talked tough, but he was scared to death."

No, that was impossible. David had been a carefree charmer, always laughing. Shelby just couldn't picture him as an angry teenager. Not like this boy.

"He'll stand there for a minute," Tucker predicted, still watching the boy. "Right where he knows I can see him, because he wants to show me that he doesn't care." Tucker's voice vibrated with compassion. "But he does care. Just look at him."

The boy tucked the helmet more securely under his arm, then cupped his hands around his cigarette and lit up. He took a deep drag and tilted his head back for a dramatic exhale.

As if the twisting cloud of white smoke had somehow affected Tucker, his voice turned husky. "Nobody wanted him, Shelby. He was resentful and rebellious, but my parents saw through that. On the inside, he was just a skinny, helpless kid who was terrified because nobody had ever wanted him."

As Tucker's gaze swung back and caught Shelby's, she glimpsed a naked pain that echoed her own. Her vision blurred suddenly, and her thoughts spun like the wreath of smoke that swirled around the boy's pale curls.

"Don't worry," Tucker said. "It won't be like that for your baby." With his dark eyes still locked on hers, he spoke with an intensity that made it impossible to doubt him. "Your baby wasn't planned, but that doesn't mean it isn't wanted."

Realization slammed into Shelby so hard she lost her breath. This man didn't even like her, but he was going to marry her in order to protect his brother's child. *Her* child.

"Thank you," she choked out, knowing it wasn't enough, just saying the words. But right now, with her heart swelling into her throat and tears ready to cascade over her lower eyelashes, that was all she had to give.

Tucker pressed his lips together as two tears rolled down her cheeks, and both he and Shelby pretended to be unaware of them. "You're welcome" didn't seem like an appropriate response. But then, neither did, "I owe you this," even though that was the truth. So he said nothing at all, and she turned, and he watched her walk away.

The front of the store was empty, so Tucker relieved some tension by shouting for Denny, who had drifted back to the workroom. "The redhead that was just here?" Tucker began as the high-school senior ambled toward him. "Which part of last week's stop-hitting-on-the-female-customers lecture didn't you get?"

Denny grinned, unrepentant. "Old habits die hard, boss."

Tucker set his face like granite. "You'd better kill that old habit right now if you want to keep working here."

"I'm trying. But you know a guy can't help looking."

"Well, stop looking at the redhead," Tucker

snapped. "I just got engaged to her."

Ignoring Denny's low whistle, he headed back to the workroom, where part-timers Marcus and Ted were assembling bikes from a new shipment. He dropped to sit cross-legged on the tile floor in front of the upturned bike he'd been working on, which happened to be one of his own. "Who took my Allen wrench?" he demanded, looking for the tool he'd laid down an hour earlier.

Marcus tossed it to him. "You look weird," he commented.

This from a twenty-two-year-old psych major with a shaved head and more earrings than Tucker had ever seen on a single individual. Tucker gave him a speaking glance, but Marcus failed to hear it. "I'm fine," he grunted, then as he turned the hexagonal wrench to loosen a brake cable, he tossed out a question. "Either of you guys ever been in love?"

"Sure, man."

Tucker looked up from his work and watched Ted skim his long blond hair back into a ponytail and twist a rubber band around it. "And . . . ?" he prompted.

Ted shrugged. "And I came real close to getting myself engaged." Leaning back against a scarred wood workbench, he grabbed a lidded paper cup and slurped down some coffee.

"Why didn't you?" Tucker asked.

Ted flashed a look at Marcus and snorted. "Just in time, I remembered that engagements often lead to marriage."

Tucker rolled his eyes as the college guys laughed. "How about you?" he asked Marcus. "Ever been in love?"

The future psychologist tugged thoughtfully on one of his earrings. "What exactly do you mean by 'in love'?"

"Never mind." He ought to have known better than to introduce this subject in the workroom, where the guys pretty much stuck to two topics of conversation. One of them was bikes, and although the other had something to do with women, it wasn't marriage. Tucker sighed. At twenty-nine he felt like an old man.

Turning his attention back to his brake job, he reminded himself that he'd always been a self-starter, an avid do-it-yourselfer. Why should marriage be any different from all the other goals he'd set and then attained? He'd study this. He'd study *her.* And he'd make sure they got it right.

Awakened in the night by sirens screaming through her open bedroom window, Shelby couldn't go back to sleep. After a considerable amount of pillow-punching and flopping from one side of the bed to the other, she was about to give up the fight and console herself with a glass of milk and a Hershey's bar when in the moonlight her restless gaze landed on the set of Russian nesting dolls that stood on her night table.

She wasn't sure why, but she'd dug it out of an old storage box the day she had discovered she was pregnant. As she reached for it now, thoughts of her father flashed through her mind and she experienced the familiar pang of grief mixed with anger.

He had gone to Moscow on business and missed Shelby's eleventh birthday. On his return he had apologized profusely, told her how much he loved her and presented her with the *matryoshka,* or little mother doll. And while it was entirely possible that memory lied, that night was the last time Shelby could recall ever seeing her father sober. For that reason, she both loved and despised this relic from her childhood.

She hadn't opened the gaily painted wooden figure in a long time, but now she pulled the oversize head off the hollow doll to expose the smaller doll inside it. She took that one out and pulled it apart, too, revealing another doll. She kept going until she reached the fifth doll, the solid wood baby, then she closed her fist around it, feeling oddly comforted.

She knew generations of Russian children had used these colorful folk art toys to learn concepts like small-smaller-smallest as well as counting. But the nesting dolls taught a larger lesson, Shelby realized now, one about family. From the great-great-grandmother on down to the new mother, each wooden doll surrounded and protected its baby.

As the first pink fingers of dawn poked into her room, Shelby remembered what Tucker had said about her baby being unplanned but not unwanted. She pressed her hands against her lower abdomen. There was no swelling there, not yet, but she could almost feel the tiny spark of life growing inside her.

"You're *wanted*," she whispered fiercely. "Don't you ever, ever doubt that you're wanted."

# CHAPTER FOUR

*"Your column is where?"* Even when he wasn't yelling, Bill Dietzel had a voice like a jet plane powering up for takeoff.

"It's still in my head," Tucker repeated. Thinking his right ear might as well be abused equally, he shifted the phone to that side.

"Well, get it out of your head and onto my desk!"

If only it were that easy. Tucker stared at the blinking cursor on his blank computer screen and sighed.

As a journalism student at Ohio State, he had interned with Bill at a major daily newspaper. One day, Bill had joked that he'd like to see someone write a column that explained women to men. "You're good with women," he'd said, pointing a finger at Tucker. "Tell the rest of us how their brains work."

Tucker wasn't really good with women. It

impressed his friends that he could score a woman's phone number just by smiling — women were really into dimples, and Tucker had two of them — but surely a guy who went through three or four almost-serious girlfriends a year was doing something horribly wrong.

Tucker adored women — thought they were one of God's best ideas ever — but he didn't begin to understand how their brains worked. That didn't stop him from writing an "explanation" of women, purely as a gag for his mentor. Bill loved it, asked for three more essays just like it, and launched "The Guy's Guide to Women," by Steve Tucker, one month later.

Although purporting to explain women to men, the humorous rants accomplished just the opposite, offering women a glimpse inside an average guy's head. The column was an overnight success and had been a Saturday staple for the past two years.

"This isn't like you." Bill's voice had dropped back to its normal decibel range, still plenty loud. "You're always a month ahead."

Tucker was terrified that his sense of humor had died with David. He hadn't written a decent paragraph in weeks. But today his father's back was a little better, so

Stephen had opened the bike shop and Tucker had taken the morning off, determined to write garbage for as long as it took, until the logjam in his head gave way and he was brilliant again.

So far this morning he'd written and deleted three pages, which was why he was staring at a blank screen right now.

"Son," Bill said in the low roar that was his version of gentle, "You know I'm sorry about your brother. But life goes on, and this is business. You fall behind, you're history."

"I know." Tucker pulled off his reading glasses and rubbed his eyes. "Maybe I could write something if you'd hang up."

"Okay, let's try that," Bill said, and hung up.

Tucker shoved his glasses back on and stared at his empty screen. "Write what you know," his creative writing instructors had always insisted, but Tucker had blithely disregarded that advice and written about women. And succeeded spectacularly. Now his agile mind was climbing all over marriage, another subject he didn't know beans about, and it occurred to him that he might parlay his cluelessness into a couple of good essays.

Bingo. Just after lunch he e-mailed two

columns and won back his editor's love. Then he headed to the bike shop.

It was an hour before closing when he glanced out one of the front windows and saw Shelby's car pull up. She climbed out, looking soft and pretty in a flowery sundress, but there was something jerky about her movements and her mouth looked tight. Tucker had about two seconds to wonder about that before the passenger door opened and he saw what she was looking so tense about.

That Diana Dearborn, a woman with zero people skills, had managed to become a successful real estate agent was a continual source of amazement to Tucker. What did she do, *intimidate* people into buying houses? He'd met the blond steamroller just twice, but that had been plenty. While Tucker honestly tried to get along with everyone, he just couldn't like Diana because she treated her perfectly lovely twenty-four-year-old daughter like a naughty child.

And Diana wasn't likely to endear herself to him today, not if she had dragged Shelby over here to call off the wedding. Giving the front door a hard push that set off a mad clanging of cowbells, Tucker went out to disabuse her of any notion she might have about making Shelby give up the baby.

Shelby was reaching for something in her backseat when Tucker called a greeting. She jumped, banging her head on the door frame as she spun around to face him.

"Ouch," he said, hurting for her.

"I'm fine," she said quickly, rubbing her head with a fierce concentration that suggested otherwise. As Tucker came to a stop in front of her, she darted a nervous glance across the car's roof at her mother.

Diana pulled her Audrey Hepburn sunglasses down an inch and peered over them. "Hello, Tucker," she said in a bored tone.

He wasn't thrilled to see *her,* either, especially when he knew why she'd come, but he nodded politely and waited.

"We're going next door," Shelby said, pushing a bright mass of curls away from her face. "To the bridal shop."

The bridal shop? Tucker relaxed. Women didn't go to bridal shops unless they meant to get married.

"Mom thinks they'll take my wedding dress on consignment," Shelby added.

So he'd been right the first time. Tucker shot an accusing look at Diana, but she was looking past him. She said something to Shelby about needing to speak with a client she'd just spotted going into the bakery a couple of doors down, then she muttered an "excuse me" in Tucker's direction and charged off.

As Shelby closed the car door, Tucker edged closer and peered inside the vehicle. He saw a plastic-encased cloud of gleaming white fabric and lace covering the entire back seat and was conscious of an odd tightening in his chest. "So you've changed your mind," he observed quietly.

"Changed my mind?"

He turned back to look at her. "About getting married."

Her bow-shaped mouth fell open and her slender auburn eyebrows drew together. "What makes you think that?"

He gestured to the lacy confection in the backseat, but in the next instant it occurred to him that marrying him in the dress she'd bought for David might violate some venerated wedding tradition. Women were funny about things like that.

"Oh." Understanding widened her eyes. "No, I haven't changed my mind. But I don't need a wedding gown, do I? Because we're not having a *real* wedding."

"Excuse me?" Tucker felt his forehead wrinkle. "We're going to say 'I do' and we're going to shove rings onto each other's fingers, right? What's not real about that?"

She gave him one of those purely feminine

looks that suggested his being born male precluded him from ever comprehending, but she'd try to explain this, anyway. "We're not having flowers and cake and all that." She pushed back a corkscrew curl that had strayed too close to one of her amazing violet eyes. "So I don't need a special dress."

Was that what she was looking so upset about? Flowers and cake? "Those things really matter to women, don't they?" Tucker guessed. "Those little things."

"They're not little things," she fired back.

*Score.* So this stuff was tricky, but not impossible for someone with a Y chromosome to figure out.

"They're the kind of things a girl dreams about." The little quaver in her voice hinted she was on the verge of waterworks. "How come it was okay for David to be crazy about his motorcycle and for you to be fanatical about your bikes, but it's silly for me to pine for a wedding gown and a few flowers?"

She had a point, and Tucker had just opened his mouth to acknowledge that when she stamped her foot. "*Why?* Why can't I at least have a pretty wedding? Is that so very much to ask?"

"Okay." Tucker raised his hands, desperate to stem her outrage or her tears or whatever other awful things she was about to unleash on him. She *wasn't* asking for much. Simmering with indignation at Diana's lack of support, he stepped up to the plate. "Just give me a minute," he said. "I can do this." He nodded firmly, convincing himself if not her.

She turned her head and looked at him sideways. "Do what?"

"I can be a sensitive guy." He nodded like one of those bobble-head dogs people put in their cars. "Really. I can."

And he would. Shelby Franklin needed a sensitive guy, and Tucker was determined to see that she had one.

*Sensitive?* Amazed beyond words, Shelby just stared. Tucker was so big and rugged looking, but there he was, insisting that he could be a sensitive guy. Yeah, right. What was he going to do, just reach inside his brain and flip a switch from the Neanderthal setting to Sensitive?

"Okay." He shoved his big hands into the pockets of his jeans and started pacing in front of Shelby. When he made a sudden lunge to the left, she looked down and saw he'd just avoided an enormous puddle of melted pink bubble gum. "We're keeping the dress," he decided. "Unless you want a different one. And I know we need to do this as soon as possible, because of the baby, but let's do it right."

*Do it right?* Was he serious?

"I'm serious," he said, stopping in front of her, closer that she liked, close enough for her to see the bright gold flecks in his brown eyes. "How quickly can everything be done?"

"How quickly can *what* be done?" Shelby's mother asked from behind her, making her jump. "What's going on?" she pressed when her question was not immediately answered.

"I have no idea," Shelby said, frowning hard at her deranged fiancé.

"We're planning our wedding," Tucker said.

"What's to plan?" Diana removed her sunglasses and carefully parked them on top of her exquisitely coiffed hair. "Get the license, then go see your pastor."

Tucker shook his head and turned back to Shelby. "Where do we sign up for flowers and cake?"

"Flowers and . . . *what?*" Diana emitted a deprecating little chuckle.

Tucker ignored her. "Couldn't you just call the people you already had lined up and tell them to dust off the original game plan?" he asked Shelby. "I'll pay for everything."

"That's ridiculous," Diana said before Shelby could open her mouth. "You're not having a real wedding."

"Yes, we are." There was an unmistakable challenge in the glance Tucker flicked at Diana. "We're having all of the usual wedding stuff. Caterers, photographers, uncomfortable clothes." He gestured expansively. "All of it."

*"Why?"*

"Because," he replied slowly and distinctly, "those things are important to your daughter."

Shelby sucked her bottom lip into her mouth and dropped her gaze to the hot asphalt. Nobody — not even David — had ever defended her to her mother. She stared at the pink circle of liquid gum Tucker had neatly sidestepped a minute ago and tried to determine whether she ought to feel humiliated or grateful.

"This situation is a little different," Diana said haughtily. "There's no reason to bother with —"

"Excuse me." Tucker's tone was positively arctic. "Could I please have a minute with my fiancée?"

"Fine." Shelby's mother shot her a thunderous look. "I'll wait here in the car." She took two steps and halted. She looked down, lifted her right foot experimentally, then made an angry noise in the back of her throat.

Tucker was suddenly gripped by a paroxysm of coughing. When Shelby looked at him and lifted a censuring eyebrow, he leaned down and whispered in her ear. "And people say there's no justice in the world."

Leaving Diana to scuff the sticky mess off the sole of her expensive Italian sandals, Tucker gestured to Shelby and she preceded him to the windowless side of the bike shop where a small, empty parking area was sandwiched between two brick buildings. "It's a little more private here," he explained.

Shelby hugged herself, shivering under the blazing late-afternoon sun. "She's not a mean person, Tucker. She's just ashamed because of the baby, and she thinks if we're determined to get married, we should just hurry up and get it over with."

"That's not her call to make."

Shelby closed her eyes. "It doesn't matter."

He folded her into his arms. She immediately panicked and pushed at the brick wall that was his chest, but he didn't let go. "It does too matter," he said.

His calm insistence shattered her control. "Okay, it matters!" she cried, grabbing a fistful of his T-shirt in each hand as her eyes overflowed with tears. "It *does!*" she said, pushing her face against his chest until she could barely breathe.

He groaned sympathetically and cupped a hand around the back of her head, holding her tightly against him. "I know it does," he soothed. "I know."

"I hate this," she squeaked a minute later as she moved her face in search of a dry spot on his T-shirt. "I'm not a crier. I don't know what's wrong with me."

"Don't you?" He leaned back and looked down at her. "Your fiancé died three weeks before your wedding. You just found out you're pregnant and now you're about to marry a man you don't love. Honey, I'd cry, too. I'd probably scream and throw things. I think you're showing admirable restraint here."

She chuckled wetly and pushed against his chest. "Stop trying to make me laugh." She sniffled, then looked up into his face. "This whole idea is crazy. It won't work, Tucker."

"It'll work. We just have to make an honest effort."

What dream world did this man live in? Weren't the divorce courts full of people who had made honest efforts? And most of those couples had probably been in love to begin with.

"I've given this a lot of thought," Tucker said. "If we stick together in troubled times and celebrate each other's joys, we won't be able to help falling in love." He nodded encouragingly. "Doesn't that make sense?"

Shelby sighed. "Nothing makes sense to me. And I can't even pray. I've tried, but I just don't feel like God's there."

"You know better than that," Tucker said gently. "He's there, whether we feel it or not. He's always there."

"But I *need* to feel it." Didn't God know that? Didn't He see how close she was to giving up? Her mother had given up, years ago, and wouldn't even go to church now. "I feel like I'm falling, but there's nothing to hold on to, and I —"

"Tell you what." Tucker's deep voice rumbled soothingly as his hands cupped her shoulders. "You just hold on to me for now. And I'll hold on to God. We'll get you through this, I promise."

They weren't in love. She wasn't even sure they were friends. She hadn't forgotten the way his eyes used to rest on her, radiating disapproval. But in all fairness, he'd changed since learning about the baby. Now he was offering her something to hold on to, and she was desperate enough to grab it.

"Come see me when you're ready to make wedding plans," he said. "And don't let your mother talk you out of anything. You need flowers and cake, and you're going to have them."

It amazed her that he had latched on to the idea that she needed this. But she *did* need it. If she couldn't have the marriage and the future she'd dreamed of, was a pretty wedding too much to ask?

"Let me go," she said, flattening her palms against his chest. As he loosed his hold, she sniffled again and wondered what her mother was thinking about this embarrassing display. She was guaranteed to get an earful when she got back to the car. "I'm sorry," she said. "I never fall apart like this."

"Maybe falling apart once in a while isn't such a terrible thing," Tucker suggested.

She denied that with a shake of her head. "I want to apologize for my mother, too. She's in a crabby mood today."

Tucker's dimples flashed as his mouth curved into an impudent grin. "I loved her face when she stepped in that gum."

Shelby couldn't help chuckling at that. "You're a beast."

"Am not," he contradicted, lifting his chin like a stubborn six-year-old and looking down his long, straight nose at her. "I happen to be a very sensitive guy."

Shelby allowed herself one last chuckle before turning away from him and schooling her expression for the benefit of her mother, who was scowling at her from behind a buggy windshield. Shelby mentally added Wash Car to her growing to-do list and then wondered why her mother hadn't already mentioned it.

Probably because she was too busy being ashamed of her unwed pregnant daughter.

Shelby stumbled, then instinctively turned around. But she fought the childish urge to run back to the man who now seemed to understand and accept her, even with this enormous blot on her character. As she quivered uncertainly on the sidewalk, Tucker slid his hands into his pockets, holding her eyes with his as he tipped his head forward. Go on. You can do this.

His calm, quiet strength infused her with the confidence she needed to face her mother. She nodded to show that she was okay, and then she turned to go.

Diana's car was in the shop for repairs, so

Shelby had agreed to drive her mother on several errands. As they backed out of the space in front of Shamrock Bike Shop, Shelby was perfectly aware that she was being punished with silence. But she couldn't prevent a smile from tugging at her mouth as she recalled the way Tucker had made her laugh.

Ninety minutes later, Diana's errands were complete. She continued her wordless disapproval as Shelby turned the car into a driveway in an upscale subdivision. Coward that she was, Shelby kept her foot on the brake and left the car in gear, ready to slam into Reverse and peel out as soon as Diana's door closed. But her mother issued a terse invitation, more of a command, really, so Shelby followed her into the house, aware that the simmering silence was about to boil over.

In the high-ceilinged living room, Shelby braced her backside against one arm of the sofa, hoping this wouldn't take long. "Don't perch," Diana said irritably, and Shelby sat down. She slipped out of her sandals and pulled her legs up, hugging them with her arms. She realized that her posture was a defensive one, but anyone who didn't watch her toes around Diana Dearborn was likely to get them stepped on.

"I still think this plan of yours is foolish," Diana began, drumming her perfect pink nails on the wooden arm of her chair. "But if you're determined to have a big wedding, you'd better —"

"Not a big wedding," Shelby interrupted. "A very small one. But I want all of the traditions."

Diana's mouth tightened as she lifted a thin eyebrow, signaling displeasure at being cut off. "As I was saying, you should hire a coordinator. Otherwise, you'll make a mess of —"

"And who's going to pay for that?" Jack Dearborn asked as he strode into the room pushing his arms into a navy sport coat. He reeked of spicy cologne, and it was all Shelby could do not to grimace at the sickening scent.

She looked into his remote hazel eyes and spoke with careful politeness. "I'm not asking you for anything, Jack. It was more than generous of you to buy my wedding dress." Would she be able to keep it now, or would her mother still expect her to take it back?

Diana's eyes had narrowed on her husband. "Aren't you a little spiffed up for a meeting with your business partners?"

Shelby wondered, too. Jack was freshly shaven and his dark, still-damp hair was carefully slicked back. He looked like a man leaving for a date, not a business meeting.

"Darling, I just cut the grass," he said with a smarmy grin. "I had to take a shower, didn't I?" He bent down to kiss his wife's cheek. "Don't wait up. We'll probably be half the night again. This audit's going to be the death of us."

Something in his breezy tone made Shelby uncomfortable. Could Jack be . . . ?

No, of course not. Diana wasn't a stupid woman, and she'd never turn a blind eye to that sort of thing.

"I still don't see why you need a real wedding," Shelby's mother said as Jack left them. "But if Tucker is serious about paying, take my advice, for once, and hire someone before you mess it up."

As harsh as that sounded, her mother had a point. Shelby had had six months to plan her wedding to David, but things were different now. A wedding coordinator would know how to pull the event together on short notice.

Shelby checked her watch. The bike shop had been closed for an hour. "I'm going to see Tucker," she announced. She might as well find out right now if he'd meant what he'd said earlier about her having "all those little things."

She'd never been to his house, but she knew it was one of the old stone cottages on the river. She checked her mother's phone book to verify the address, and ten minutes later she pulled into his driveway.

His native limestone house was snuggled in the middle of a verdant, tree-sprinkled lot that sloped down to the river. Bordering one long side of the property was one of the low dry-stone walls that had once been ubiquitous in this area and that still lined many of the roadsides.

Just thirty years ago Dublin had been a sleepy village surrounded by farms. It had since become a mecca for golfers, which had encouraged upscale housing developments and a thriving business community. But the bucolic spirit of the old village hadn't merely been preserved, it had been enhanced, so that anyone who now viewed the restored limestone buildings of the Historic District and admired the shops with their gaily painted shutters and masses of colorful flowers tucked in window boxes might easily think they'd been transported to old Ireland.

It had always amused Shelby, a California import, that Dublin's Irish heritage lay only in its name; two hundred years ago a surveyor had christened it after his birthplace because of the geographical resemblance. But now Dublin was all Irish all the time, a place where little red-haired girls were called Caitlin or Kathleen, and even the police officers wore shamrocks on their uniforms. The small city might be just twenty minutes from downtown Columbus, but it stubbornly retained its own unique personality, and Shelby loved it.

Tucker's property was a fine example of the local flavor. Even though the stone walls were crumbling, they lent his place an old-world appeal and framed a charming river view. Shelby slowed her car and allowed her admiring gaze to roll past the house and past an enormous weeping willow tree to where the slanting sunlight twinkled on the water.

She followed the curving asphalt driveway to the back of the house, where it ended in front of a detached one-car garage, also built of limestone. Its wide door was up, and from inside the structure rock music blared almost loud enough to rattle Shelby's car windows.

Tucker didn't react to the slam of Shelby's car door. He was absorbed in playing a riff on an imaginary electric guitar with all the energy and enthusiasm of a real-life rock star. He looked the part, too, in his faded jeans and an open Hawaiian shirt that flapped in the breeze his manic movements created.

Shelby went ahead and laughed out loud, knowing he'd never hear. When he stopped playing the air guitar and stepped over to his workbench, his head bobbing like a walking pigeon's in time to the music, she laughed again. Then she drew a little closer and waited for him to notice her.

He snatched up a faded red rag and wiped off a small, shiny piece of metal. When he turned and held the object up to the light to inspect it, he spotted his visitor.

"Could we talk?" she shouted.

He turned back to his workbench and leaned over a pile of tools to switch off the radio. Shelby's ears rang in the sudden silence, and her amusement faded as she reminded herself what she'd come for. "About the wedding," she began. "Mom thinks we should —"

"No." Looking oddly disgruntled, he held up two dirty hands to silence her. "I don't care what your mother thinks."

"I know, Tucker, but —"

"We are not going to let her call the shots on this."

Shelby's temper flared. "Do you think you could let me get a complete sentence out, you big —" She stopped, appalled. She wasn't a hothead. She wasn't *like* this.

As Tucker wiped his hands on the rag, one corner of his mouth jerked a little, as though he was holding back a smile. "Big what?"

"Nothing," Shelby muttered, wondering if an incomplete insult required a full apology.

"No, really." He tossed the rag aside and inspected his hands. Apparently unsatisfied, he wiped them on the seat of his jeans. "Big what?"

Annoyed that he appeared to be enjoying her discomfort, Shelby skipped the apology and moved on. "If you're still planning to marry me, I have a question for you."

He leaned back against his bench and folded his arms over his chest. "Still planning to." His voice was as deep as midnight in summertime. "Let's hear the question."

"I don't suppose you know what a wedding coordinator is?"

He gave her a lazy grin. "I've seen *Father of the Bride.*"

Shelby nodded. "Well, Mom isn't going to be any help, and I hate to ask Rachel for anything because she's already done so much. She's the one who made all the calls to cancel everything. But I'm a little rattled these days, and since we want to do this quickly, I just thought —"

"Do it," he said, cutting to the chase in that maddening way of his. "I'll pay for everything."

"Thank you." Now that she'd arrived at the big question, she felt herself blush. "But I'll need some guidance from you."

He arched his back, leaning away from her as though he were afraid of catching something. "Honey, I am not remotely interested in what color your bridesmaids wear."

"It isn't that . . ." If he was such a great mind reader, why wasn't he getting this? Was she going to have to spell it out?

"Oh," he said. "You want to know how much you can spend."

"Well . . . yes."

Looking almost comically relieved, Tucker whipped a checkbook from the back pocket of his jeans and opened it under Shelby's nose. "There it is. If that's not enough, we'll break out the credit cards. Don't worry about it."

It was more than plenty. "I won't spend that much," she promised, amazed that this had turned out to be so easy.

He shrugged and replaced the checkbook. "Just do what it takes." He gathered up a couple of tools and dumped them into an open box on his workbench. "Why don't you stay for dinner? We could discuss dates and the guest list."

Shelby was getting a headache and she needed to plan lessons for the violin students she'd be seeing tomorrow, but she owed Tucker something for this amazing generosity, so she accepted his invitation.

"And we need to go see Pastor Dean," he added.

*No.* Shelby cringed at the thought of looking her pastor in the eye and telling him she was pregnant.

"What's wrong?" Tucker asked, watching her with an intent look that further unraveled her wits.

"Would you mind speaking to him by yourself?" She fought to keep her voice at a normal pitch, but her nerves nudged it up. "I've already asked God to forgive me and I know I'll be showing soon and the whole church will know. But I'm not ready to face Pastor Dean yet. I just need a little more time."

As she spoke, his confused expression had hardened into the stony, protective look he'd worn earlier, when he'd faced down her mother. "Don't worry," he said. "I'll handle everything."

Equally embarrassed and comforted, Shelby just nodded her thanks.

Tucker escorted her back up the driveway to the front of the house, where they followed a curving flagstone walk that led to three wide stone steps. The charming little stoop was presided over by a great door constructed of dark, glossy wood and featuring a small shamrock-shaped stained glass window in vibrant shades of green and gold.

"Beautiful," Shelby breathed.

Tucker nodded. "David helped me hang the door a couple of months ago. He thought the shamrock was a bit much."

"I love it," Shelby said honestly. "It's very Dublin."

"My grandparents lived here all their married life," Tucker said. "They died within a few months of each other, when I was fifteen. Left me the house."

He hadn't reached for the door, and when Shelby shot him an inquiring look, he bit his bottom lip and looked away from her, obviously uncomfortable. "What's wrong?" she asked. "Is it a mess inside?"

"No, it isn't that." He looked back at her, his dark eyes clouded with worry. "There's something I haven't told you."

That sounded ominous. Shelby held her breath and waited.

Tucker shoved his hands into his pockets and shifted his weight from one foot to the other. He looked at his shoes, and then at the sky and then he closed his eyes.

"I'm afraid I come with a dog," he said.

# CHAPTER FIVE

A dog? Well, of course a guy like Tucker would have a dog. No doubt it was one of those huge, slobbery, obnoxious beasts that would stink up the house and leave giant rawhide bones between the sofa cushions. But considering the sacrifices Tucker was making, as long as the big brute could be kept far away from the baby, Shelby would accept Tucker's awful dog.

"I'm not allergic or anything," she assured him. She pasted an interested smile on her face. "What kind is it?"

"Just a little one," he said, holding up his hands as though cradling a soccer ball between them.

So it was still a puppy. "What kind?" Shelby asked again.

Tucker hung his head and pushed at a corner of his sisal doormat with the toe of his shoe. "Well, it's not a *real* dog. It's more of a poodle."

A *poodle?* Man's man Tucker Sharpe had a *poodle?* Shelby covered her mouth with her hand, but was half a second too late to stifle a very impolite snort.

"He's not purebred," Tucker said defensively. "He's a mutt-poodle." Appearing to gather up his dignity, he shook a warning finger in Shelby's face. "And we do not paint his toenails and shave him in weird patterns, do you understand?"

With a tremendous effort she wiped off her smile. "Word of honor," she agreed. "What's the mutt-poodle's name?"

"Roadkill."

Shelby blinked. "What kind of lunatic buys a poodle and names it Roadkill?"

Tucker's backbone snapped to attention so fast Shelby could almost hear it crack. "I did not buy a poodle. And he *was* Roadkill, or almost. I was driving home on a foggy night when the car in front of me hit him and kept going."

"And you stopped."

Tucker's eyes bulged in exasperation. "Well, of course I stopped. The vet kept him for two weeks, but we never found the owner, and I couldn't let him go to the pound. He's ugly, so nobody would have wanted him and he'd have been put down."

Admiration edged aside Shelby's amusement. "I'm sure he's a very nice dog," she said staunchly. She tried not to smile as she added, "And he can't help being a poodle, you know."

Tucker shot her a quelling look and opened the door.

Except for the glowing stained-glass shamrock on the door, the slate-floored entry hall was windowless and dim. Tucker flipped a switch and the small space flooded with soft light from a crystal lamp that sat on a narrow table against the wall.

"Beautiful," Shelby whispered, mesmerized by the sparkling facets of glass.

"My grandfather gave it to my grandmother on their fiftieth anniversary," Tucker said. "They never had much money, but she'd wanted a Waterford lamp for years." His voice softened. "He died just a week later."

"I'm sorry."

Tucker lifted a shoulder. "They had fifty good years together."

Shelby stared at the dazzling lamp base and tried to imagine where she'd be fifty years from now. Still married to Tucker? Unwilling to contemplate that, she gave herself a mental shake. "So, where's the poodle?"

"That's what I'm wondering."

She followed Tucker into a compact, maple-floored living room where pretty French doors flanked a cozy stone fireplace. One of the doors, Shelby noticed, was slightly ajar.

Tucker strode to it and flung it open. "Kill!" he bellowed, making Shelby flinch. Seconds later a small, reddish-brown animal rocketed past him, went stiff legged and skated across the polished wood floor, then made a wide arc and scrambled back to Tucker. The dog didn't leap at him, but quivered with obvious delight as Tucker calmly lifted one foot and gave him a friendly nudge with the toe of his shoe.

"This is your idea of an ugly dog?" Shelby dropped to her knees, incredulous. Just the color of cocoa powder, Tucker's poodle was a sweet little puffball with bulgy, soulful eyes and a long, delicate nose. "He's adorable," she insisted, patting the springy curls on top of his head. "Aren't you, baby?"

"He's a poodle," Tucker pointed out, his tone suggesting that being born a poodle was about the worst fate that could befall a dog. He folded his arms across his wide chest and stood there looking like an immovable mountain.

"Poor baby," Shelby crooned as the little dog licked her hands. "You have to put up with that big, awful bear."

"What?" Tucker's arms came uncrossed.

*Whoops.* Shelby tilted her head back and looked up at him. "I just said, 'Poor baby. You've had an awful lot to bear.' " She shrugged. "His accident, and everything." She returned her attention to the poodle. "I've always wanted a dog."

"Good. He's all yours."

She looked up again. "Why do you pretend not to like this great dog?"

"That is not a dog. It's a poodle."

"You should give him a real name," Shelby said.

"Like what?" Tucker made a derisive sound in the back of his throat. 'Snuggles'?"

"I can't call this sweet little dog Roadkill. It's mean."

"Yet you had no compunction about calling me a big, awful bear," Tucker shot back. "Wasn't *that* mean?"

Shelby tensed at his words, but when she looked up, his brown eyes were dancing. "Will steak and salad be okay for dinner?" he asked.

"That would be nice, bear," she said, testing his sense of humor as gingerly as she might have eased her weight onto the bottom rung of a rickety wooden ladder.

He grinned and Shelby relaxed. She

pushed up to her feet and walked over to the fireplace. Admiring the beautiful grain of the glossy, dark wood of the mantelpiece, she turned, a question on her lips, and saw Tucker straighten guiltily.

Right. So much for Mr. I-don't-care-a-thing-about-this-poodle. Roadkill's stubby little tail wagged hard as he tipped his head back and gazed adoringly at the big man.

Shelby narrowed her eyes. "Were you petting my dog?"

Tucker thrust out his bottom lip and slid his hands into his pockets, his expression one of flat denial. "It's mahogany."

"What?"

He nodded toward the fireplace. "The mantelpiece. It's a solid piece of mahogany."

"How did you know I was going to ask that?"

He just looked at her for a moment, then jerked his head to indicate the tour was moving on. Shelby followed him into a bright kitchen, which featured windows on two walls as well as above the sink. Like the rest of the house, the room was charming if not particularly spacious, and Shelby mentally hung her flea-market collection of blue-and-white dishes on one sunny yellow wall, saving a few to grace the small, rectangular oak table that stood in the corner beneath two windows.

Tucker jingled the keys in his pocket. "This house is old and quirky. There's only one bathroom, and you reach it by going through the master bedroom. The smaller bedroom would be best for privacy, because if you take the big one, you'll have me tramping in at odd hours to use the shower. But with your morning sickness, maybe you should be next to the bathroom."

She thanked him for that consideration and opted for the big bedroom. "And I hate to ask," she added, "but is there an out-of-the-way corner I could use for a teaching studio?"

"The dining room would be good for that. I've always eaten here in the kitchen, anyway." He backed up against the counter and crossed his ankles. "Why did you hate to ask?"

"It's your house," she said simply.

"From now on, it's *our* house. I really like it here on the river, and this place has some history. But if you'd rather live somewhere else, we could talk about that."

"No, I love it," she said truthfully. She liked his furniture, too. It was old and sturdy looking, probably inherited along with the house. The only modern pieces Shelby had noticed were a recliner and sofa in cappuccino-colored leather and a big-screen TV. It was typical guy stuff, but she could always throw an inexpensive quilt over the back of the sofa to cozy it up. Apart from that, the place needed only a few candles. And maybe she could install flower boxes under the two green-shuttered windows on either side of the front door. She'd plant them with bright red petunias.

Tucker's shoulders dropped a little, suggesting relief. "It's small, but there's room to build on. We could add a real studio for you. And another bathroom." He shrugged. "Whatever you want, Shel. Be thinking about —"

"Nobody calls me that."

A slow smile spread on his face, awakening his dimples.

Shelby shrugged, not caring all that much. Considering what this man had named his poodle, she was probably getting off easy. And at least "Shel" was better than "baby," which was what David had called her. She'd hated that, but she'd never asked him to stop because she hadn't wanted to explain about the *other* man who had called her that: her father.

"Make sure I know when you're expecting students," Tucker said. "I don't want to burst in with a couple of noisy friends when you're in the middle of a lesson."

"I'll post my schedule on the refrigerator," she promised. "Although this isn't a busy time for me. During the school year I have students every afternoon, but most of them drop their lessons for the summer. That's why David and I were planning to marry at the beginning of June."

Saying his name was like dousing herself with a cold bucket of reality. It wasn't David she'd be living with in this storybook cottage, but his brother.

"It's going to be okay," Tucker said quietly, reading her mind again. "You can have anything you want."

"That sounds very nice for me." She strove for a light tone. "But what do *you* expect to get out of this marriage?"

"The satisfaction of knowing I did the right thing. That's enough for now."

"And later?" Embarrassing as it was, the question had to be asked. She needed to hear him agree never to push for any kind of physical relationship.

His eyes were steady on hers. "I'll leave that up to you."

Her cheeks burned, but she couldn't allow him to believe she'd ever change her mind. "Tucker, I will never —"

"Here's the thing," he said calmly. "As we

learn to love each other, the rest will sort itself out. I'm not afraid to wait for God's timing on that."

Well, fine. If he was too stubborn to believe what she was trying to tell him, that was his problem. But there wasn't going to be a physical relationship, and no amount of time was going to change her mind about that.

Tucker concluded the tour, then lit his charcoal grill and went to take a shower. He had urged Shelby to make herself at home, so she assembled a salad and steeped some iced tea. She set the kitchen table, then propped her hands on her hips and surveyed her work, wishing for a pretty tablecloth or some candles.

Pregnancy had sharpened her sense of smell, so when she caught a warm whiff of something like a tangy ocean breeze, she knew Tucker stood behind her. She turned and almost lost her breath. There was something uncomfortably attractive about the way tiny beads of water clung to the loose waves of his short hair. And about the way the rich, coffee-brown color of his eyes was accentuated by his pale yellow shirt, the sleeves of which he'd rolled up, exposing his deeply tanned forearms.

A zing of awareness shot through Shelby,

causing her brain to stumble. Yes, he was a good-looking man, but he was still just Tucker. She ripped her fascinated gaze off him. "I couldn't find any candles," she said. "For the table."

"Don't have any." One side of his mouth hitched up, piercing his cheek with a deep dimple. "*Candles,* Shel? Are you going all romantic on me?"

She gave him a level stare that fully answered the question and warned him never to ask it again. "I like candles, okay?"

He grilled two perfect rare steaks. Then as he and Shelby ate, he talked about the bike shop. "I own twenty percent of the business," he said. "Dad's brother owns twenty, and the rest is Dad's."

He went on to disclose his financial details, what he made in a year and how he spent it. He told Shelby he'd already named her as the beneficiary of his life insurance policy, made an appointment to have his will drawn up and started a college fund for the baby. Then he asked if she had any questions.

Dazed, she shook her head. He'd really thought this thing through. "I suppose you'll want to draw up a prenuptial agreement," she murmured.

"No," he said, looking surprised.

"You have a lot to lose," she pointed out.

He tipped his head forward and looked at her from under raised eyebrows, the way teachers did when their students gave wrong answers. "That's defeatist thinking, Shelby."

"But divorce happens. And we're not even in love, so —"

"Honey. Take it from an athlete. You win by keeping your eyes on the finish line, not by looking back at where you started. I am not a quitter," he said, reaching for his iced tea. "And I am not going to fail at marriage."

"But some marriages just don't work out."

"This one will." Ice cubes tinkled against the sides of his glass as he lifted it and drank deeply.

Realizing that he wasn't going to budge, Shelby sighed. "Fine. If you're so determined to pool our resources, you can have half of everything I own. Which happens to be nothing. My car isn't paid for and I owe the credit-card company two grand."

Chuckling, Tucker picked up his steak knife. "I'll take my chances," he said as he sawed off a bite of rare sirloin. "Maybe you'll inherit a million bucks from a long-lost relative."

Shelby tried to laugh with him, but there was nothing funny about the fact that she had once been very close to someone who had actually had that kind of money.

Why was she doing this? She hadn't thought about her father in a long time, and now she couldn't keep her mind from wandering in that direction, thanks to her mother, who had awakened painful memories by comparing Tucker to him.

Tucker's fork stopped halfway to his mouth. "What is it?"

Shelby shook her head, flinging the black thoughts away like a dog shaking off water. "Nothing."

"Something's wrong." He put down his fork. "Tell me."

"I don't owe you an explanation for every thought that passes through my mind," she said testily.

"No," he agreed. "But if you want to talk about —"

"I don't." She stabbed her fork into a cucumber slice. Her father had absolutely *nothing* to do with her life now. He was out of it forever. She jammed the cucumber into her mouth and chewed viciously.

"Okay," Tucker said in a soothing tone. "I just couldn't help noticing that you seem a little agitated."

"I'm *pregnant,*" she flung at him. "I'm a whole *lot* agitated." She sprang up and began collecting the dishes.

Tucker stood, too. "Leave this," he said, taking the plates from her and replacing them on the table. He bent down and scooped up Roadkill. "You have to bond with your new dog," he said, pushing the poodle into her arms. "Let's go outside."

Two minutes later her mood had shifted again and she was comfortably ensconced in a chaise lounge on Tucker's pea-gravel patio, Roadkill in her lap. "I'm changing his name," she said, fondling one of the poodle's floppy ears.

"Don't. You'll trigger an identity crisis. Right, Kill?"

At the sound of his name, Roadkill twitched and wagged his abbreviated tail. He would have scrambled out of Shelby's arms and leaped into Tucker's if she hadn't tightened her hold.

"You're my dog now," Shelby cooed into the sweet little brown eyes. "Aren't you, baby?"

"Baby," Tucker echoed in exaggerated disgust.

Shelby giggled as Roadkill's long tongue snaked out and lashed her chin. "This is a great dog."

"That is not a dog." Tucker adjusted his chaise and settled himself. "It's just a poodle," he added, closing his eyes.

"And you're just a big, awful bear." Shelby waited for his eyes to pop back open, but they didn't. He merely folded his hands behind his head and smiled.

"It could be fun, Shel."

"What could be fun?"

"Marriage." He rolled to his side and propped himself up on an elbow to look at her. "We could make it fun."

"Without love?"

He studied her face. "Why are you so worried about that?"

"You don't believe in love?" she challenged.

"I believe in it. But you're talking about romance."

She frowned. "It's the same thing."

"Not at all. My dad says love is more than just a whipped-up emotion. It's an act of the will. And I think that must be true, because all through the Bible, we're *commanded* to love. We're even told to love our enemies. So love must be something we can control. Something we can *choose* to do, whether we feel anything or not."

Maybe. But Shelby's head had begun to pound and she couldn't think that deeply right now. She reached behind her neck and squeezed the tense muscles there.

"Headache?" Tucker sat up. "Turn around. I'll do your neck and shoulders."

"It's not that bad," she lied. He was *not* going to put those big paws on her. Yes, he'd held her in his arms earlier today, but she'd been hysterical then. She wasn't now, and she didn't like being touched. She lowered Roadkill to the ground, then fished for her sandals. "I have to go."

"Stay," he urged gently. "I won't touch you."

Shelby swallowed. So he had picked up on that.

"Lie down," he said. "I'll get you something."

Embarrassed, she sank back onto the chaise. "Thank you, but I can't take anything because of the baby."

"No drugs," he promised. He went into the house and returned a minute later with a thin white blanket draped over one shoulder, togalike. Handing Shelby a large bag of frozen peas, he directed her to place it behind her head. "My mom's version of an ice pack," he explained.

The peas shifted and conformed to the shape of her head, making a surprisingly comfortable pillow. Soothed by the cold, Shelby vented some of her tension in a long sigh.

"Having that behind your neck will lower your body temperature," Tucker said as he gave the blanket a light shake and allowed it to float down over Shelby. "I'll go do the dishes while you relax. In twenty minutes your headache will be history and maybe we'll take a short walk along the river."

She felt guilty about being revolted by the idea of his touch, so when he started to turn away, she impulsively caught his wrist. He glanced down at her hand, then looked into her face. She made herself smile as her hand clasped his. "Thank you, bear."

He peered into her face, past her too-bright smile, and it was clear he knew her heart wasn't in it. "Relax," he said, pulling his hand out of her grasp. "You're going to be okay, Shelby. Just try to trust me a little."

For the first time since losing David, Tucker was feeling hopeful about something. No, he wasn't in love, but he fully expected to be one day soon. Because even if a man couldn't *will* himself to feel that emotion for his wife, surely God would reward him for trying. And then at exactly the right time, it would happen.

It was just after nine on Saturday morning, and Tucker was seated in Pastor Dean Cansella's cramped, book-cluttered office saying all of that and spilling the rest of his guts for good measure. The pastor's head was tipped to one side, his gray eyes owlish behind thick glasses as he listened without interrupting.

"So we'd like you to marry us," Tucker concluded. "As soon as possible."

He felt he'd presented his case well, but Pastor Dean's solemn expression wasn't encouraging. "The marriage covenant is a very serious business, Tucker."

"We realize that." Resting his elbows on the chair arms, Tucker extended his legs, affecting a casual sprawl to hide his nervousness. "We understand it's for the rest of our lives."

"I'm sorry." Pastor Dean slowly wagged his head. "But I'm afraid I can't do what you're asking."

Tucker snapped his heels together and sat up straight.

"You're not in love with her," Pastor Dean said flatly.

Well, *no.* And he wasn't pretending to be. Hadn't he just explained all that? "Was Boaz in love with Ruth?" he challenged. "No. But she needed protection, and he was her dead husband's nearest relative, so he did the right thing and married her." Tucker silently congratulated himself on citing one of the biblical accounts of a marriage entered into purely for socioeconomic reasons. That union had been approved by God; why wouldn't *this* one be?

Pastor Dean sighed. "Tucker, you're both grieving. I'm advising you to take some time and consider —"

"What difference will *time* make?"

The pastor glanced at the ceiling as though soliciting divine help. "Before I marry couples, I require them to undergo premarital counseling."

"David and Shelby didn't," Tucker pointed out. He couldn't believe he was sitting here arguing with his pastor, but he was *right* about this.

"I advised them to," Pastor Dean said. "I told them I wouldn't marry them unless they went through the program. They agreed, but then we ran into some scheduling problems. So they decided to get married at the Park of Roses over in Columbus, with Ben Lawson officiating. Ben's not of our denomination, but he's a good man. I imagine he spent some time in conversation with David and Shelby, but I don't believe he's a stickler for intensive premarital counseling."

Tucker waved the difficulty away with one hand. "We'll do the counseling," he said, certain Shelby would agree. "But I hope there's an accelerated program, because we —"

"I don't do quickie weddings, Tucker, not even when a couple is expecting." Pastor Dean paused. "In fact, when a couple is under that kind of pressure, I generally advise them to spend a few months in serious discussions about —"

"A few *months?*" Tucker repeated, incredulous. In a few months, the baby would soon be here. "Okay, yeah, we could definitely use some counseling," he conceded. "But why couldn't we just start that now and continue after we're married? I'd have no problem with that."

"But I would," his pastor said firmly. "You're asking me to marry two people whose judgment is clouded by grief and worry about the future. And you're making an incorrect assumption about the counseling, anyway. I don't automatically marry everyone who completes our ten-week program. Sometimes I just don't believe a couple is ready for marriage."

Tucker's head had begun to throb. "So you're refusing to marry us no matter what we do," he stated. "But for the sake of argument, what if you're wrong about us? What if this is *right?*"

"What if it *isn't* right?" the pastor fired back.

Of course it was right. How could it not be right? The baby had to have David's name and be brought up by the people who had known and loved him. Shelby had to be supported emotionally and financially, and Tucker knew her pride would never allow her to accept his help unless they were married. This was a question of duty. Shouldn't Pastor Dean, of all people, understand that?

He didn't appear to. Angry and bewildered, Tucker pushed up to his feet. "I'm sorry, Pastor, but this *is* right. So if you won't marry us, I'll just have to find someone who will."

# CHAPTER SIX

Rachel was back from her week in Paris and needed a special dress for dinner with Greg's parents. "I still think you're out of your mind," she confided to Shelby on Saturday afternoon as they strolled through the doorway of a chic dress shop and waved off an eager saleswoman.

"I told you, I don't know what else to do." Shelby stifled a yawn and wished she'd taken a nap instead of coming here to look at clothes she could neither afford nor fit into.

Rachel pulled a tiny black dress off a rack and glanced over her shoulder, then leaned close to Shelby. "It's just that I can't see you marrying a man you don't love," she murmured in a discreet tone. "And please don't take this the wrong way, but what's in it for Tucker?"

"Nothing," Shelby took the black dress from her. "He just wants to take care of David's baby."

Rachel arched a pale eyebrow. "Not buying it, girlfriend."

"He has a poodle," Shelby submitted.

Rachel shrugged that off. "Most guys like dogs. Although I wouldn't have pegged Tucker as the poodle type."

"That's my point. Tucker *despises* poodles. But he saved a poodle's life and then adopted it, because he thought it was ugly and nobody else would want it. Doesn't that say something about his character?"

"Maybe." Rachel turned back to the dresses. "But stop kidding yourself that he's going to be satisfied with separate bedrooms."

"He's the one who brought it up."

Her friend stopped sliding hangers along the rack and turned to stare at her. "Okay, that's just plain weird."

Shelby sighed. Her mother had expressed a similar opinion. Repeatedly.

Rachel rested her hands on her narrow hips. "He's hiding something," she decided.

"You barely know him," Shelby reminded her.

"And *you* know him so *well*," Rachel retorted. "Come on, Shelby. The man is up to something."

"Right. Well, let's consider my attractions." Shelby folded the black dress over one arm and counted on her fingers. "One, I'm not beautiful. Two, I come with a bossy mother. Three, I'm never more than a hundred dollars away from being overdrawn at the bank. And . . ." She screwed up her face and pretended to think. "Oh, yeah. Four, I'm pregnant."

Rachel tilted her head to one side and thrust out her bottom lip, frankly appraising her friend. "I wish you'd stop complaining about your looks. A lot of women would kill for curls like yours, and your eyes are the kind guys want to get lost in. And maybe you could stand to lose a few pounds, but you're nicely proportioned. Men love that."

"Ha. You may recall that before David, my phone wasn't exactly ringing off the hook." Not for the first time, Shelby wondered exactly what David had seen in her. She'd never had the guts to ask.

"I just hate to see you rush into this marriage," Rachel said. "What if there's another Mr. Right out there for you? If you marry Tucker you'll be throwing away your chance of finding him. I mean, Tucker's great, but you're not in love with him."

Shelby sighed heavily. "I told you, I'm finished with fairy tales. All I care about now is my baby. Tucker understands that, so we're going to be just fine." Shelby pushed the dress she held into Rachel's arms. "Let's see how this looks on you."

Rachel's pretty face was troubled, but she nodded and took the dress. As she watched her friend walk away, Shelby struggled to make herself believe what she'd just said, that she and Tucker were going to be "just fine" together.

*Please,* she begged, moving her lips in a silent prayer. *Just this once, Lord, let something turn out okay for me.*

On Sunday morning Tucker drove Shelby to church. She was silent the whole way, staring out her window. Tucker stole as many glances as he dared, thinking how pretty she looked in her floaty, flowery summer dress, liking the way her coppery curls spilled over her shoulders and captured glints of sunlight in their little hills and valleys. But under the golden freckles sprinkled across her nose and cheeks, her face was pale.

"I saw Pastor Dean yesterday," Tucker said as he pulled into the church's parking lot. Better to get this out now, in case they ran into the guy before or after the church service.

Shelby turned to look at him. "Is he available on either of the dates we picked?"

Tucker ran a finger between his neck and the suddenly too-tight collar of his dress shirt. "Not exactly."

"When did he say he could do it?"

When it snows in Miami. Tucker cleared his throat. "I'm afraid we've hit a snag," he said, careful not to allow resentment to color his tone.

She nodded as though she'd been expecting that. "It's high wedding season. I was afraid he and the church might be booked."

"That's not the problem," Tucker said as he nosed into an empty parking space. "I mean, we didn't actually get as far as discussing dates."

"Did he insist on the counseling?" she asked softly. "I had forgotten about that."

"We talked about counseling, but that wasn't the snag. Well, not exactly."

Shelby gave him a wide-eyed look that squeezed his heart. "D-does he . . ." Her voice faded away. "Does he think I shouldn't wear a white —"

"No," Tucker said quickly. "He didn't mention anything like that. He just thinks we're too torn up by grief to be thinking clearly right now. He doesn't think we should get married."

"Oh." The single word was barely audible,

but it conveyed a world of bewilderment and pain, kindling in Tucker an overpowering urge to stand between Shelby Franklin and anything that could put that haunted look in her beautiful eyes.

"Even the best pastor can sometimes make a bad call," Tucker insisted. "I know he's wrong about this." He waited until Shelby turned to look at him, then added, "My uncle can marry us. He's a Christian and he happens to be federal judge."

Shelby frowned, obviously trying to remember. "Your mom's brother," she said slowly. "Ryan?"

"Reagan," Tucker corrected. "Reagan McCall." Tucker hoped she wouldn't ask him to contact the minister who had promised to marry her and David. There was no sense in risking another refusal from someone who didn't understand. "Uncle Reagan will marry us," he said, certain of that. "And I don't know if we can book the Park of Roses this late in the game, but we'll find someplace nice."

"Tucker, if Pastor Dean thinks it's such a bad idea, maybe we shouldn't —"

"Yes, we should," he said firmly. "And we're going to." Somewhere deep inside him, doubt stirred, but Tucker slapped it down. It wasn't as though he was pursuing any selfish agenda here. This marriage was for Shelby's good and the baby's. This was *right,* and if Shelby was a little uncertain, he'd talk her through it. "Don't worry," he said as he twisted his key out of the ignition. "I'll handle everything."

Having endured another sleepless night, Shelby was too drowsy to pay much attention to Pastor Dean's sermon or to the vague answers she gave well-meaning friends who wanted to know how she was holding up since losing David. Grateful when the service was over, she walked with Tucker back out to the parking lot, where she was revived somewhat by the brisk breeze that pushed her hair into her face and whipped the skirt of her long cotton dress against her legs.

As he handed Shelby into his SUV, Tucker glanced up at the heavy, darkening sky. "I want to show you something." When Shelby didn't object, he drove a little way up the east side of the river, where he pulled into a small picnic area and parked facing the water. "After I got my first car, I used to bring David here," he said. "It's a fantastic place to watch a storm."

Shelby could see why. This part of the Scioto River was actually a reservoir, and the broad expanse of water allowed a wide-angle view of the western sky and the roiling black thunderclouds that were rapidly approaching.

"Have you found a wedding coordinator?" Tucker asked as the trees surrounding the picnic area began to writhe and powerful gusts of wind rocked the SUV.

Transfixed by the awesome power of the storm, Shelby merely nodded. "I'm meeting someone tomorrow," she said after a moment, then remembered something and turned to look at Tucker. "I need your full name. For the invitations."

"Thought you knew that," he said as he stared through the windshield. "I'm Stephen Tucker Sharpe."

So he had been named for his father. And didn't it just figure that he shared a name with that Neanderthal columnist? Watching a gyrating tree, Shelby tossed out an idle question. "Have you ever read that newspaper column by Steve Tucker?"

His head swiveled toward her. "You honestly don't know?"

She opened her mouth to ask what he meant, but something clicked in her brain and she remembered Tucker had studied journalism in college. "You're Steve Tucker," she accused. "You're 'The Guy's

Guide to Women.' "

"Yep." He didn't look at all ashamed of it.

Shelby blinked at him. "You're the man every woman in central Ohio despises."

"Yep," he repeated in the same cheerful tone.

The rain came, stirring the water first, then pounding the grass on the bank before reaching the SUV. Lightning flickered, but the rumbling thunder was slow to follow and was barely audible over the rain that splatted so hard all around them.

Shelby drummed her fingers on her armrest and pitched her voice to be heard over the roaring rain. "Why didn't David tell me about you being the infamous Steve Tucker?"

Tucker hunched forward and folded his arms over the steering wheel. "The column's just something I do for fun and to make extra money." He looked over his shoulder at her. "I'm surprised David didn't mention it. He probably meant to, but kept getting lost in those incredible violet eyes of yours."

"They're just blue," she said, surprised and a little unnerved by his blatant appreciation.

He shook his head. "The ocean is blue. The sky is blue. Your eyes are not blue." He sat back in his seat and gave her a lopsided grin that employed only one of his dimples. "Why do you read Steve Tucker if you find him so annoying?"

Because he was also hilarious. Not that she was in any mood to confess that. So when Tucker made a soft sound of amusement and gave her a knowing look, she turned her head and studied the raindrop patterns on her window.

"Let's talk about you," he said. "I know you're an only child and a California girl. What's the rest?"

"We moved here when I was fifteen, so I'm not really a California girl." That was true. She barely remembered Los Angeles now. And it was better that way.

"Does your dad still live there? What does he do?"

She hid her clenched fists by folding her arms. "My father is dead. And I don't like talking about him."

Tucker was silent for a moment, then reached for the ignition. "You're exhausted. Let's get you home."

The rain had stopped by the time they reached Shelby's apartment. Tucker accompanied her to her door and waited in silence while she found her key and fitted it into the lock. When she turned the knob and glanced up at him, he smiled and reached out to touch her face. Instinctively, she jerked away.

"Hey." His tone held surprise and a gentle reproach.

"Sorry," Shelby mumbled to the knot of his tie. "It's just that I startle easily."

"Look at me, Shel." Issued in a deep voice as thick and sweet as honey, the command was impossible to ignore. When Shelby raised her eyes, he lifted his hand again, slowly this time. He curled it into a loose fist and stroked her jaw with the backs of his fingers. "What are you so afraid of?"

"Nothing," she said, aching to lean away from his hand but forcing herself to remain still. She was so tired she could almost feel her bones softening. Was he ever going to leave?

"You don't like being touched," he murmured. "Why is that?"

Her discomfort flashed into annoyance. "I'm not in love with you, Tucker."

He dropped his hand and gave his head a slow, stubborn shake. "It isn't just me. You don't like anyone touching you. You don't even hug the other women at church."

Resenting his knack for making her feel like a bug under a microscope, she pushed open her door. "I'm just not a touchy-feely person," she said with asperity.

No, she wasn't a hugger. Not usually. But she'd hugged David. And kissed him, even though it wasn't her favorite thing to do. So there was nothing wrong with her, she was perfectly normal, and Tucker had no business —

She stopped in the middle of her silent rant, horrified. Was that why she had disobeyed God with David? To prove she was *normal*?

"It's okay," Tucker said. "Don't upset yourself."

She turned on him. "Are you suggesting that I have some kind of problem?"

"Honey, I'm suggesting that you have all kinds of problems. But I am absolutely on your side."

She tossed her head. "There's nothing wrong with me."

"I know," he said in the soothing tone people in the movies used just before they slipped a straitjacket around the raving lunatic. "You're just worn out."

"More like *flipping* out," she muttered, addressing his tie again. Maybe she *was* crazy.

"No." Tucker patted her shoulder. "You just need a nap."

The wedding coordinator Shelby hired turned out to be a woman Tucker had dated in high school. Janni Barkhurst had traded her long blond ponytail for a sleek, stylish cut, but other than that, the former cheerleader was exactly as Tucker remembered. She still talked incessantly, words tumbling out of her mouth like corn from a hot-air popper, but her enthusiasm for the wedding was a comfort to Shelby, so Tucker was grateful.

A little of Janni's effervescence went a long way, however, and since Tucker had no interest in discussing frilly wedding details, he had surrendered his credit card and left the women to their planning. So on Friday afternoon when he saw Janni stroll into the bike shop with her sister, an avid mountain biker, he hightailed it to the workroom before Janni could buttonhole him and start chattering about flowers and cake.

An hour later he was filling out an order form for bike parts when one of his guys popped in to say he was needed out front. Approaching the cash register, Tucker groaned softly as he spotted two teenage boys, each holding a box of the top-of-the-line cycling shoes that had been on sale two weeks ago, when Stephen had scored a serious price break from the wholesaler. That discounted supply had quickly sold out, so if Tucker gave these kids the sale price today, he'd be ringing up a loss for the store.

The teenagers looked at him, happily expectant, and why shouldn't they be? Everyone knew Tucker Sharpe was the softest touch in central Ohio. He sighed and instructed Marcus, who was trying not to grin at Tucker's unconcealed exasperation, to give them the sale price.

At the sound of a sweetly feminine chuckle, Tucker's heart gave a strange, glad little leap. "Now I know why David called you everyone's best friend," Shelby said as he turned around.

In a slim black skirt and a sleeveless yellow blouse, with tendrils of that wild hair escaping her ponytail to cavort around the edges of her heart-shaped face, she was well worth looking at. But her smile didn't hide the worry in her pretty eyes, so Tucker reached for her arm, intending to steer her to a quiet corner and find out what was wrong. She jerked away, sending a wave of unease tumbling through Tucker's gut as an ugly realization crystallized in his mind.

Her smile had vanished and a pink stain was spreading under her freckles. "I'm sorry. You know I startle easily."

Oh, he knew. And now he knew *why*. He didn't risk touching her again, but gestured, and they moved to an unpopulated area of the store.

"I have to move out of my apartment." As if watching a lively honeybee, her eyes darted back and forth, looking everywhere but into Tucker's. "By tomorrow."

"What's happened?"

She licked her lips. "You know I expected to move to David's place. Well, when I told my landlady I'd be staying, after all, she upped the rent. I tried to tell her I couldn't afford it, but she wouldn't back down, so I didn't sign a new lease. And I —" She interrupted herself to take a deep breath. "Well. With everything that's been going on, I just forgot about it. And now she's rented the apartment. She told me to be out by five o'clock tomorrow because the painters are coming."

Relief sent a tingle of weakness to Tucker's knees. This was something he could fix. "Okay, just let me think a minute." He nibbled his bottom lip, mentally reviewing tomorrow's schedule and making a couple of adjustments.

Shelby hugged herself. "I know you're busy, and I hate to bother you with this, but I didn't know where else to go. Maybe I could sleep on Rachel's sofa. My furniture's rented, but I still need a place to put my things. I haven't thought it through yet. And

I don't even know about the legal part of this. Are they *allowed* to kick me out? I know I don't have a lease anymore, but —"

"Hey," Tucker said gently, hoping to stem the waterfall of words that tumbled from her. "Stop worrying. Do you think I'd let you sleep in a refrigerator box under the river bridge?"

"I'm sorry." She closed her eyes. "I know how crazy I sound, but I'm just . . . over-whelmed."

Tucker nodded. It was difficult to under-stand women under the best of circum-stances, and this one was not only grieving, but also pregnant. And unless he'd guessed wrong, she had at some point been smacked around by a man. An old boyfriend, prob-ably, because her stepfather didn't seem like the type. Not that you could always tell. Tucker just figured that a guy with a wife like Hurricane Diana would tend to follow the rules.

Later, he would encourage Shelby to talk about her past. Right now he needed to ad-dress the *crise du jour.* "I'll take tomorrow off and we'll move you into my house," he offered. "I can stay at Dad's until the wed-ding."

She exhaled heavily and looked so re-lieved, Tucker was afraid she might collapse.

Checking an impulse to put his hands out and steady her, he offered an encouraging smile instead.

"Thank you." Her voice had come out gravelly, so she cleared her throat. "I'll call you early in the morning, okay? I have a gig tonight, so I —"

"You have a what?"

"I have a gig," she repeated.

Somehow, Tucker had imagined violinists would have a classier way to say that. "You're playing tonight?"

She nodded. "At a wedding. One of the violinists in my friend's quartet is down with a migraine, so I'm filling in." She lifted a freckle-dusted arm and consulted her watch. "I'd better get moving. I have to leave in less than ninety minutes."

That worried Tucker because she was clearly exhausted. "Honey, are you sure you're up for this tonight?"

"Why wouldn't I be?"

Uh, because you're pregnant and you've been acting like a nutcase lately? Tucker schooled his expression and offered something a bit more diplomatic. "I just thought you needed some extra rest, being pregnant and all."

"I need the money, Tucker. My teaching job doesn't pay that well, and I'm still whit-

131

tling away at my college loans. The private lessons take up the slack during the school year, but like I told you, they drop off in the summer. I *need* this gig."

He wanted to kick himself. Why hadn't he guessed she needed money? Why had he assumed she'd ask for whatever she needed?

She wouldn't. Not Shelby Franklin. She'd starve to death rather than drop a hint that she could use some grocery money.

Well, he knew better now, and he'd be sure to keep an eye on her. He could do that. After thirteen years of looking after David, how much trouble could one little redheaded woman be?

"Boss man?" Over at the register, Marcus waved the telephone at Tucker. "Something about a lost parts shipment. Want to take it in back?"

Tucker raised a hand, palm out, and shook his head vigorously, indicating that he wasn't to be interrupted now. Business could wait. He needed to keep this conversation rolling until he assured himself that Shelby was okay. "So where's this gig?" he asked.

"Athens."

Not good. The southern Ohio town was two hours away. Was her old rattletrap car up to that? Was *she* up to it? "That's a long drive," he suggested.

She twitched a shoulder. "I need the money."

Tucker worked the problem in his head. Marcus could close the shop today. Stephen was home nursing his bad back again, but he could be reached by phone if a problem arose. "They don't need me here," Tucker said, stretching the truth a bit, but all in a good cause. "Why don't I just drive you to Athens?"

"No," she replied firmly. "Thank you, but no."

"Please, Shel. Or I'll worry all night long."

"Why would you —" She stopped, her auburn eyelashes fluttering as she lowered her gaze. "Oh. The baby."

"I'd worry about *both* of you," he said, wondering what had made her think she was nothing more to him than a baby carrier. No, he didn't love her, but he'd made her some promises, and he was going to keep them or die trying. Why didn't she get that?

"We're playing at the reception, too, so we won't be finished until late," she said. "You'd have nothing to do all night. But it was nice of you to offer."

He couldn't bear the thought of her driving home at midnight, alone and pregnant, in that old beater of hers, so he risked scaring her. "You don't want to drive all that way *alone,* Shel. Wouldn't it be terrible if you got sick?"

Her shoulders slumped. "I'm sick all the time," she admitted in a pathetic little voice. "Why do they call it morning sickness when it lasts all day long?"

He'd wondered about that, too. And she was looking a little green right now, as a matter of fact. "What does your doctor say about that?"

"I haven't seen the doctor yet. She's been —"

"You haven't seen a doctor?" Tucker's heart slammed into overdrive. Did this woman have a brain behind those incredible violet eyes, or not?

She shook her head. "The obstetrician I want has been on vacation. But she makes Saturday appointments, so I'll be seeing her tomorrow."

"Well, how do you know —" He broke off and glanced around to make sure nobody was within earshot. Leaning closer to Shelby, he pitched his voice to a confidential tone. "If you haven't seen a doctor, how do you know you're pregnant?"

In the space of two seconds her expressive eyes rounded in disbelief and hardened in anger. It was clear Tucker had said something wrong, but what? When he opened his mouth to ask, she held up both hands, palms out, in that universal feminine gesture that said he'd be a dead man if he uttered another syllable. "Just forget it," she said coldly. "Forget *everything.* If I'm pregnant, it's no business of yours. So just stay away from me!" She turned abruptly and charged the front door.

Slack-jawed, Tucker stared after her, waiting for a spark of comprehension to ignite his stalled brain. It wasn't until the bells on the door jangled violently that he realized his question must have sounded to her like an accusation.

Well. Didn't he just have an amazing knack with women?

In the parking area on the windowless side of the building, Shelby paced beside her car. What had she done? Why had she allowed her outraged pride to endanger her baby's future? She needed Tucker, and she'd just cut him loose.

"Oh, God," she whispered, rubbing frustrated tears from her eyes. "How many more times do I have to ask You to forgive me? You know how sorry I am. Why don't You answer when I cry out to You?" She folded her arms, hugging herself hard. What was she supposed to do now?

She needed to pick up some new violin strings. And she had to press the black silk skirt she was planning to wear tonight. She'd have to leave early because she'd never driven to Athens before, and who knew how many of those awful, traffic-snarling orange barrels she would encounter on the way? And what if she got sick while she was driving?

And where was she going to sleep tomorrow night?

She squeezed her dizzy head between her palms. Yes, she was flipping out again. Didn't she have enough troubles without her hormones playing these awful games with her emotions?

She marched over to her car and flung herself into it. She owed Tucker an apology, but that would have to wait until tomorrow. She already had more than she could handle today.

# CHAPTER SEVEN

Showtime. Tucker straightened his tie, then he straightened his backbone and pressed his thumb against Shelby's doorbell. Deciding to conceal his peace offering until he was ready to present it, he thrust his left hand behind his back.

It bothered him that she opened the door without even looking through the peephole or asking who was there. Dublin wasn't exactly a hotbed of violent crime, but still. She was a woman alone. A *pregnant* woman alone. A grieving pregnant woman who scared him half to death because sometimes he got the distinct impression she was just a hairbreadth from ceasing to care what happened to her.

Her heart-shaped face was the most expressive he'd ever seen, so he could usually look at her and know just what she was feeling. But at the moment he was too rattled to interpret the slight lift of her slender eyebrows and the delicate pursing of her strawberry-red lips. Also, he was more than a little distracted by the way she looked — *amazing* — in that long black skirt and some kind of black, sparkly, long-sleeved tunic thing. Her coppery hair was caught up in an elegant gold clasp, and she looked so sweet and vulnerable that Tucker's tongue swelled up.

The swollen tongue worried him, so it was a considerable relief when he opened his mouth and four intelligible words fell out, "I'm an insensitive jerk."

She raised her eyebrows in emphatic assent.

"I suppose all jerks are insensitive," he mumbled.

She granted him that with a curt nod.

He had actually prepared a speech and tried it out on Roadkill, but he couldn't remember a word of it now. Shelby looked beautiful, even though her eyelids were a little puffy, and knowing that he'd made her cry made him want to beat his stupid head against the brick wall beside her door.

She tilted her head to one side, waiting, and Tucker could almost see the little clock ticking away in her brain as her patience ran out.

"I just . . ." he began, then pushed his free

hand through his hair. "Look, I'm stumbling in the dark, here. What do you need me to say? That I'm sorry? Well, I *am. Profoundly sorry.*"

Her mouth twitched, and Tucker allowed himself a shallow breath. "I never meant to imply that you weren't pregnant," he said, picking up a little speed. "I *know* you're pregnant. I mean, you *must* be pregnant. Why else would you be acting the way you —" He stopped abruptly, not needing her sharply elevated eyebrows to tell him he'd just messed up again. In a last-ditch effort to salvage something from this disgustingly inept apology, he drew his hand from behind his back.

"Oh!" Shelby accepted the perfect red rose and held it up to her face for a delicate sniff.

"I'm an insensitive jerk," Tucker repeated, hoping they could just agree on that and move forward.

"No." She pressed the scarlet bloom against her mouth, hiding what might have been a smile. "You're a very sensitive jerk." She closed her eyes and sniffed the rose again. And yes, she was smiling. Tucker exhaled.

Finally, he'd got something right. He had charmed Shelby out of being mad. David himself couldn't have done it any better. But Tucker still needed to clear something up, so he stuck his neck out again. "About what I said earlier, I —"

"No, don't," she said quickly. "I over-reacted. I'm sorry for storming away from you like that. You asked me an honest question, and I —"

He lifted a hand and waved off her apology. "I don't know anything about pregnancy, but you've been awfully sick, so I just thought, what if it's something else? What if there's something seriously wrong with you?"

She looked stunned. "You were *worried* about me?"

He opened his mouth to reply, then thought better of that and nodded, instead. Considering the stupid things that had been coming out of his mouth lately, it seemed prudent to avoid unnecessary conversation.

She opened the door wider and stepped back. Tucker accepted the silent invitation and crossed the threshold. "I did a home pregnancy test," she explained as she closed the door behind him. "They're very accurate."

"But what about the sickness? That can't be normal."

"Mom says she was sick a lot, too. Not

everyone has it this rough, but it's not abnormal. And Mom says it's common to be sleepy all the time and to cry for no reason."

"But you have reasons to cry." Losing David three weeks before their wedding had wrecked Shelby's world. And with an unplanned pregnancy on top of that . . .

"I know. But I've been acting crazy. Maybe I can't help the mood swings, but there's no excuse for —"

"It's okay," he interrupted. "Please, let's forget it."

"All right." As she looked down at the scarlet bloom she held, something in her grave expression perturbed the normal rhythm of Tucker's heart. "I like roses," she said in a wistful tone that made him wonder if David had ever given her any.

He shifted on his feet, nervous as a high-school kid asking for his first date. "Do you think you could learn to like *me?*"

She smiled at the rose. "I think I could, bear."

Becoming aware of soft, flickering light and the faint aroma of vanilla, Tucker glanced around the barren living room. It had been stripped of whatever personality it had once possessed; Shelby's belongings were now stowed in the cardboard boxes stacked neatly in one corner. But three milky-white pillar candles glowed on the otherwise bare coffee table.

It wasn't anywhere near sundown, but the day had been overcast, and although there were two lamps in the room, neither was lit. "Is your electricity off?" Tucker asked.

"No. I just like candles. Partly for their scents, but mostly because —" She stopped, and her face turned pink.

"Because . . ." Tucker prompted.

"Well, there's just something hopeful about a candle flame, isn't there?" She lifted one shoulder and dropped it again. "Or maybe it's just me. I love the part in *David Copperfield* where the old man puts a candle in the window every night so his niece can find her way home in the dark."

"I don't remember that," Tucker said. "But I haven't read Dickens since high school."

Shelby's gaze shifted to the glowing trio of candles. "One day the girl made a terrible mistake and ran away. But even though she had disgraced her family, the old man prayed that she would come home. And every night the candle stood in the window, just like always, because he refused to give up on her. He loved her that much. Even after everything she had done."

Mesmerized by the undulating flames, Shelby stroked her chin with the rose. "I know it's just a story, but I need to believe it's possible for people to love that deeply. That unselfishly." She was silent for a moment, and then there was something defensive, almost defiant in her expression as she looked up at Tucker. "No matter what."

"Unconditional love," he murmured, watching the reflected lights in her solemn eyes. Didn't she realize that God loved her that way? "My mother called it 'love beyond reason.'"

Shelby bowed her head, and although Tucker could no longer see her eyes, he felt heartache radiating off her in powerful waves. Of course God loved her that way, but hadn't anyone else? With a half-formed notion of kissing some comfort into her, he dipped his head and swayed toward her. She dodged him, and at the same instant, her telephone rang.

She excused herself and picked up the cordless phone that lay on a small table beside the sofa. There was no answer, apparently, because she said hello a second time and then after a short pause said, "I know you can hear me, and this is getting annoying. Don't call here again."

Tucker tensed. "Problem?"

"No," she said, replacing the phone.

"How many times has that person called?"

"Just twice. The first time was right before you came. They didn't say anything, but I knew the line wasn't dead because I heard a car horn in the background."

"Do you know who it was?" Tucker reached the table in two strides and snatched up the phone. "Because you can hit star-six-nine and —"

"Tucker, it doesn't matter, because I'm moving tomorrow and this line will be shut off." She took the phone from him. "Besides, I have too much on my mind to waste time worrying about a couple of hang-up phone calls."

She *was* worried; he could see it in her eyes. But he opted not to risk stirring up her temper by arguing. She was right; everyone got hang-up calls. But he'd keep an extra-close eye on her, just to be safe. That was his job now.

She blew out the candles and retrieved her violin case from a chair. Still clutching the rose, she looked at Tucker. "Are you sure you want to drive me all that way?"

"Positive," he said, ridiculously pleased that she liked his small gift. "Let's go."

They were heading back home to Dublin

when Shelby heard the metallic click of a seat belt and looked over at Tucker. "You're cold," he explained as he wriggled out of his suit coat.

She thanked him and pulled the coat over herself like a blanket, savoring the silky warmth of its lining as she inhaled the soothing ocean-breeze scent that clung to its collar. She stole another glance at Tucker, strong and silent behind the wheel, then leaned back against the seat and closed her eyes.

Awakened some time later by the sensation of warm fingers lightly stroking her cheek, she reluctantly swam up from a deep, sweet dream where she'd been holding her baby in her arms. "You're home," Tucker said.

When he opened her car door, she returned his coat. He shrugged into it as they walked to her apartment. They were perhaps twenty feet from her door when Shelby noticed it was ajar. She grabbed Tucker's arm to make him stop.

"I see it." His deep voice was grim. He caught her by the shoulders and steered her to safety behind the trunk of a maple tree. "Stay here," he commanded.

He approached the door, nudged it open a little wider and appeared to listen for a moment. When he disappeared inside, Shelby hugged her violin case, her thundering heart making even more noise than the night song of the cicadas.

It seemed like hours before Tucker reappeared in the doorway and beckoned to her. She hurried inside, made a quick inventory and was relieved to discover that nothing had been disturbed. Belatedly she remembered her landlady had said she'd have to enter the apartment and give instructions to the painters. Feeling very foolish, Shelby explained that to Tucker.

"Okay." Pacing in the living room, he shoved a hand through his hair. "She left the door unlocked, and the wind pushed it open. I'm sure it's nothing to worry about, but just to be on the safe side, you'd better stay at my place tonight." Lifting his chin, he loosened his tie and unbuttoned his shirt collar with one hand. "I'll sleep at Dad's."

"No, just go home," Shelby said, automatically reaching for the tiny box on her coffee table. Striking one of the matches, she wrinkled her nose at the scent of sulfur. "I'll be fine," she added as she lit the trio of candles and shook out the match.

"I don't like the idea of you staying here," Tucker said. "Not after those phone calls and this. There's no telling who might have a key to this place now."

"I'll be fine," she repeated. "I'm not afraid."

That was mostly true. The phone calls didn't matter because she was moving tomorrow and would have a new number. And what Tucker had suggested about the apartment manager neglecting to lock the door made perfect sense because none of Shelby's things had been disturbed. So it was silly to get all worked up over "phone stalkers" who made no threats and "burglars" who stole nothing when there were plenty of *real* things to terrify her.

Marriage and childbirth and motherhood, for starters.

She finally got rid of Tucker, blew out the candles, changed into a pair of whisper-soft cotton pajamas and crawled into bed without even bothering to remove her makeup. Then in the darkness, she tried once again to connect with God.

"I talk to You, but I just don't feel like You're listening," she said aloud. "And I'm so alone right now and so horribly confused. I'm going to marry Tucker because I don't see any other choice. So if that isn't right, please stop it somehow, because I just don't know what else to do."

She slept fitfully and awoke early, even

before the rising sun pushed its yellow light through the narrow parting between her curtains. She was sick right on schedule, then showered and dressed and headed for the kitchen and some restorative coffee.

While the coffeemaker gurgled and hissed, filling her apartment with an invigorating aroma, Shelby padded to the front door for her newspaper. Disengaging the dead bolt with a deft flick of her wrist, she turned the doorknob with her other hand and was startled to feel a heavy weight pressing against the door. Giving a little shriek of surprise, she let go and leaped back. The door swung open and banged against the wall.

And the body of a man in a dark suit fell at her feet.

# CHAPTER EIGHT

Yanked out of a beautiful dream about leading his American cycling team into Paris for a stunning Tour de France victory, Tucker rubbed his eyes and fought to understand why he had been awakened so violently and why he was sprawled across the threshold of Shelby's front door and why she was staring down at him as if he was about as welcome there as a cockroach.

"G'morning," he mumbled, still waiting for his brain to come back online.

Shelby's horrified expression morphed to disgusted amazement as she rested her hands on her hips. "Why were you sleeping against my door?"

Groaning, he hoisted himself up. "Because you wouldn't let me take you to my house." He squeezed the back of his neck with one hand. "And I hope you feel terrible about that. I have a pain in my neck."

"So do I," she retorted, giving him a look

charged with meaning. "But get in here before the neighbors see you."

"Heads up!" piped a small, cheerful voice, and Tucker turned in time to catch the rolled-up newspaper a young girl pitched at him.

A few minutes later he was sipping an excellent cup of coffee as he watched his fiancée slick cream cheese on toasted raisin bagels. She looked unreasonably beautiful in jeans and a short-sleeved, sky-colored sweater that perfectly demonstrated how not-blue her eyes were. Her bright hair was fascinating in its damp disarray, half of it in a high ponytail and the rest bouncing in exuberant ringlets around her face.

Despite the faint purple smudges under her eyes she looked relaxed, and Tucker's ego urged him to take credit for that.

Yes, he was a hero. Without even meaning to do it, he'd scored some major points by sleeping against her door like a guard dog. She'd die before admitting it, but he knew she was impressed. And that was worth the ten zillion mosquito bites he'd endured, not to mention the sore back, the stiff neck and the ruined suit pants he'd snagged on the rough concrete.

He'd tried to talk himself into going home, but he was haunted by the thought of a stranger being in her apartment. And what about those mysterious telephone calls? True, hang-up phone calls weren't wildly unusual. But he just hadn't been able to shake his feelings of unease. And wasn't it his job to look after Shelby?

He'd walked to the parking lot only to return to her doorstep and argue with himself some more. In the end he hadn't rung the bell, but had sat down in front of her door, just to reason with himself and pray a little. And the next thing he'd known, it was morning and he was blinking up into Shelby's startled face.

The really odd thing was that he wasn't that heavy a sleeper. And yet somehow he'd passed several hours in a very uncomfortable position without waking up. So now he wondered: Had the Lord orchestrated this whole thing in order to make an impression on Shelby?

She set a plate of scrambled eggs and sliced ham in front of him. "This is all the cooking I do," she said, sliding two cheese-slathered bagel halves onto the edge of his plate. "I usually make a good breakfast, but the rest of the meals kind of fizzle out."

"You won't starve with me," Tucker assured her. "I cook." Thanks to Nichole, the chef he'd dated for almost a year. That relationship had stalled out, but she'd left him with a set of beautifully balanced German knives.

Shelby looked interested. "*You* cook?"

Pride straightened his backbone. "Most of the world's great chefs are men, you know. What do you like to eat?"

"Chocolate."

"For dinner," he clarified.

She flung him a mutinous look. "What's wrong with chocolate?"

So she was one of *those* women. Tucker curled his upper lip, pretending disgust at her addiction, but his devious mind was already working on a plan to exploit her weakness and worm his way into her heart. "I'll make dinner for you tonight," he offered. "We'll have chocolate mousse for dessert. That'll give you a good mainline hit that should last for days."

Her smile was a little tentative as she reached out one hand and gingerly explored the stubble on his cheek with her fingertips. "You're not really so bad, are you, bear?"

Unbelievable. She was actually touching him. But the tender moment didn't last, because the second bagel popped up from the toaster, startling her, and she turned away. Tucker sighed quietly and scratched a mosquito bite. It was probably just as well that she didn't get too close, with him so desperately in need of some private moments with a loaded toothbrush.

He reached for the newspaper that lay on the table and pulled out the section containing his column. He found his page and folded it back, then hooked a finger through the handle of his cup and sipped coffee as he glanced over the column he'd written more than a month ago.

When he put his cup down, Shelby moved beside him to freshen his coffee. She remained there, peering over his shoulder. "What's Steve ranting about this morning?"

Tucker leaned back in his chair and looked up at her. "Sending flowers."

"Flowers?" She edged closer to scan the article. Tucker sat very still, afraid that she'd forget about the half-full carafe she held in front of him.

" 'Having flowers delivered to a woman's home is a waste of money,' " she read aloud. " 'Flowers should always be sent to her place of employment so she can be envied by her coworkers for having received them.' " Shelby directed a cold stare at Tucker.

"I stand by my research," he said. It had certainly been extensive. Just a few months ago, a saucy florist had teased that after all the orders Tucker had phoned in she knew his credit-card number by heart.

He angled the paper so Shelby could see it better, and she continued to read. " 'Sending flowers to her office will also show her coworkers that the insensitive clod she's been complaining about is actually quite a thoughtful guy.' " Shelby turned a scathing look on Tucker. "Is this supposed to be funny, or do men actually think this way?"

Keeping one eye on the carafe, he gave his answer careful consideration. "Both," he said finally, even though that choice hadn't been on the menu.

She shook her head and continued to read. Tucker closed his eyes, wishing she'd get that coffee out from under his nose so he could concentrate on the scent of her damp hair, which smelled like crisp, sweet apples.

"Oh, come on, Steve," she grumbled. "This is *so* not true."

Tucker inhaled deeply, imagining a drenched apple orchard after a summer rain.

She looked at him again. "You can't honestly believe —"

"Honey," he interrupted. "I'm hardly in a position to debate anything. A moody pregnant woman is holding a pot of hot coffee directly over my lap and I have no idea when she had her last chocolate fix."

For an instant she looked surprised, then she swiftly turned away. As she replaced the carafe on its warming plate, her shoulders jerked and Tucker was almost positive he heard a snicker. He smiled to himself and tossed the paper aside.

He was determined to make this work. If Shelby would make just a small effort, he was willing to do all the rest and never complain about giving more than he got. They would be okay. And if she made half the effort he was planning to put into their marriage, they might even be good together.

Shelby saw the obstetrician late that morning and was reassured by the middle-aged woman's no-nonsense evaluation.

"Physically, you're fine." Dr. Gruesman leaned back against a cluttered counter in the tiny examination room and slid her hands into the pockets of her white lab coat. "But I'm a little concerned about the turmoil in your emotional life." She pushed an errant lock of gray hair behind one ear. "I'd like you to talk to a professional about what you've been through these past few weeks. I'll give you a couple of names."

"No, I'll be okay now," Shelby insisted. "I

just needed to hear you say I'm not crazy."

The doctor's round hazel eyes softened. "Not crazy, just pregnant. Some women breeze through this while others have it rough. But your being in that second group doesn't mean there's anything wrong with you or the baby."

With that worry off her mind, Shelby went home to finish packing. Tucker showed up with some boxes, which he filled with books and sheet music while peppering Shelby with questions about her doctor visit. When she lifted a heavy box, intending to haul it out to the SUV, he emitted a strangled cry and lunged at her.

"What are you *doing?*" he demanded, his eyebrows slanting in fierce consternation as he wrested the box from her.

Shelby braced her hands on her hips and stared back at him, unsure whether to be amused or annoyed by his assumption that a young, healthy, just barely pregnant woman was that fragile. "I am perfectly able to carry that, Tucker."

"I know you can carry it." Tall, dark and intractable, he hugged the box against his chest as though afraid she'd try to snatch it back. "I just don't think you *should.*"

Shelby hadn't yet glanced at the literature she'd picked up at the doctor's office, so she couldn't say he was wrong. And if she was honest, it was kind of nice to know he was so determined to protect her and the baby. Yes, he was a little neurotic about it — she still couldn't believe he'd slept against her door last night — but he made her feel safe.

When he carried the last load of boxes out the door, Shelby did a final walk-through of her apartment and then plopped down on the sofa, thinking hard. Their pastor believed this marriage was unwise, but Tucker was adamant that it was the right thing to do. *Was* it?

He appeared in the doorway. "Ready?"

Fear squeezed Shelby's heart. No, she wasn't ready. She was out of her mind to have thought she could go through with this. "I need a minute," she said, hugging herself.

Tucker crossed the room and sat beside her. "I've been giving this thing a lot of thought, Shel."

She turned to look at him, unsure whether to ratchet up her panic a couple of notches or feel relieved that he, too, was having second thoughts.

"I don't want to deceive anyone," he said. "But I don't want to cripple our partnership, either, and sharing the details of our arrangement with our friends and family could do that."

Shelby blinked. It didn't sound as though he was trying to back out. But what *was* he saying?

"I guess what I'm saying is that our sleeping arrangements are nobody's business but ours. So let's close the circle. This is going to be *our* marriage. Let's not let anyone else inside."

She finally saw what he was getting at. He was concerned that if well-meaning friends and relatives saw their marriage as an oddity, they would be tempted to interfere. But if Shelby and Tucker were going to live together and parent a child, they would need to forge a strong partnership. "We should present a united front," she murmured, testing the words.

"That's right. So from now on, it's just the two of us and God." He folded his hand around hers. "There's no need to rush anything. First we'll learn to be good friends. And more will come if we're honest and patient."

She had to get married. He didn't. And it was a heavy burden, knowing that by marrying Tucker she would prevent him from ever finding the happiness he deserved. When he finally awoke to reality, would he resent Shelby for trapping him? Her eyes had begun to sting, so she turned her head away.

"Shelby." Tucker's deep voice was almost unbearably tender, yet it held a note of reproach. "I know you're scared."

No, he had no idea. And he couldn't know how this awful guilt was squashing the life out of her. One tear lost its tenuous hold on her lower eyelash and tumbled down her cheek. When its descent was arrested by a large, warm thumb, Shelby wanted to jerk her head away but she closed her eyes instead.

Tucker made a sympathetic noise and squeezed her hand. "They prosecuted David's foster father, you know."

Startled by his abrupt shift to a new topic, Shelby opened her eyes and looked at him.

"He got off because David wouldn't testify against him. The authorities thought he was afraid, but that wasn't it. David couldn't testify because he'd been calling the man Dad for five years." Tucker paused. "And he figured a bad father was better than no father at all."

"Because he'd never —" Shelby's husky voice was barely audible, so she cleared her throat. "He'd never known anything different."

"That's right. And you understand that, don't you, honey?"

She shifted on the sofa and would have risen, but Tucker squeezed her hand again, holding her where she was.

"He was safe with us," Tucker said. "But whenever my dad made a sudden move, David would throw up his hands to protect his head. It took him a long time to unlearn that response."

"Poor David," she whispered, wishing she didn't understand.

"Yes," Tucker agreed. "And poor Shelby."

So he had guessed her secret shame. None of her friends knew, and she'd never been able to tell David, either. Maybe she could tell Tucker just enough to make him drop the subject and never pick it up again. "My father was a violent drunk," she admitted. "He didn't hit me that often. He usually went after my mother. But I —" She stopped, swallowing hard as the guilt washed over her. "I saw." And she had done nothing but cower in her room.

"Oh, honey."

The naked pity that rumbled in Tucker's voice made her want to scream. She didn't deserve it. She might have told a school counselor. She might have run to the neighbors or called the police. But she had never done anything. She made herself meet Tucker's troubled eyes. "I was fifteen when he . . . died. And Mom married Jack right after."

"I'm sorry," Tucker said. "Is Jack good to your mom?"

"Oh, yes. He's never hit her." Realizing what she had just said, Shelby emitted a short, bitter laugh. "Listen to me. If a man's not drunk and hitting, I think he must be a good husband. That's pretty sick, isn't it?"

A muscle in Tucker's lean face twitched, but Shelby kept going. "I know it's sick. I *know* that, but I can't —" She stopped, realizing that she was holding his hand in a death grip. She let it go and wrapped her arms around herself.

"I'm so sorry," Tucker breathed.

The compassion in his voice ignited her curiosity. "What was your childhood like?"

"Wonderful. I knew I was loved. So when David came, I was secure enough not to feel threatened by an instant brother."

Shelby thought of David's smile and tried to produce one of her own. "He was a sweet man, wasn't he?"

"Yeah. He got himself into a lot of trouble, but there was always something in him that people just couldn't resist."

"Charm," Shelby supplied. "And that

amazing zest for life." The first time she'd met David, she'd wondered how anyone could be so carefree. Later, she had agreed to become his wife because she'd hoped some of his happiness might rub off on her.

Tucker captured her hand again. "I'll make this work for us, Shel. Try not to worry so much."

She pulled her hand out of his. "You don't think a loveless marriage is something to worry about?"

"Not as long as we're honest with each other." He nudged her side with his elbow. "And you like me, Shel. Admit it."

The humor that danced in his dark eyes infected Shelby, curving her mouth into a reluctant smile. "With my rotten luck, you'll turn out to be as big a Neanderthal as Steve Tucker."

He pulled a comical scowl and got to his feet. "Come, woman," he said roughly, hunching his shoulders and swinging one arm in a dead-on imitation of a gorilla. "I'm taking you home now." He raised his other arm and pointed at the front door.

Chuckling, Shelby hopped up, before he could even think about dragging her by the hair.

# CHAPTER NINE

"Tucker, you may kiss your bride."

As Judge Reagan McCall beamed at his nephew, panic flashed in Shelby's chest like a nuclear explosion. In the three weeks since she'd moved into Tucker's house, she'd been so busy with Janni and all the wedding preparations, she hadn't given a thought to this awkward moment. But Tucker, looking as unperturbed as ever as they stood amid the lush greenery in the Victorian Palm House of Columbus's historic Franklin Park Conservatory, drew her into his arms and bent his head to press a brief kiss against one corner of her mouth. And it was actually quite nice.

Something in Shelby's expression must have communicated her surprise, because Tucker flashed a smug, dimply grin and came back for more. His second kiss landed squarely on her mouth, and for several seconds, Shelby forgot who and where she was.

"You look amazing," Tucker whispered as their family and friends applauded.

Ten minutes ago, it hadn't been at all difficult to walk down the steps into the brick-paved rotunda of the elegant Palm House. As dozens of white candles glowed and a string quartet played Bach's "Sheep May Safely Graze," Shelby had been lulled into a pleasant enchantment by the warm air and the earthy scent of plants. As though in a dream, she had glided toward Tucker in the fairy-tale gown she'd thought she'd never wear, so caught up in the beauty around her that she barely realized she was taking part in a life-changing ceremony. In that mental mist she had repeated the necessary words after Tucker's uncle without faltering. And now she was married.

She'd been dreading her friends' questions about this marriage. Apart from her parents, her pastor, Rachel and Stephen, nobody knew about the baby yet. But while people seemed surprised by Shelby's haste to marry David's brother, nobody had *asked* about it, so she'd put off the explanation.

She hadn't planned to deceive anyone that she and Tucker were deeply in love, but by kissing him — with an enthusiasm that had bordered on appalling — in front of their family and friends, she had just made everyone believe something that wasn't true.

"It's going to be okay," Tucker murmured, tracing the line of her jaw with his knuckles. "I promise."

She looked into his rich-brown eyes and managed a tremulous smile. She wanted to assure him that she could handle this, the reception if not the actual marriage, but a lump had formed in her throat and, to her horror, a tear slid down her cheek.

"Very appropriate," he whispered. "All brides cry, you know."

Another tear dropped as the quartet played the first notes of Beethoven's "Minuet in G" and Rachel handed back the bouquet of peach-colored roses and English ivy she'd been holding during the exchange of the rings. Suddenly it was all too much, and Shelby looked up at Tucker for a clue about what to do next.

Without a word he captured her free hand and tucked it under his arm and hustled her up the steps and away from the smiling, applauding guests. He dragged her around a couple of corners and then stopped, his head swinging left and right as though checking traffic before crossing a busy street.

Lacking a free hand to dab at her tears, Shelby opened her eyes wider, hoping to air-dry them. She executed an indelicate sniffle, then glanced up at Tucker. "What are you looking for?"

"Privacy."

Their wedding coordinator slipped an arm through Shelby's, tugging her in one direction while Tucker pulled the opposite way. "A wedding is not about privacy," Janni trilled. "That's what honeymoons are for." She beamed a dazzling white smile at Tucker. "We'll be doing photographs first, and then —"

"Photographs *next*," Tucker corrected, gently disengaging Shelby from Janni's grasp. "Right now, we need a minute alone." He pulled Shelby away, and since she was busy directing an apologetic, I-have-no-idea-what-he's-up-to look at Janni, she was only dimly aware of being gently but insistently pushed through a narrow doorway that tugged at the long, full skirt of her gown.

Tucker flipped a light switch, then closed the door and backed up against it. "Just a minute!" he barked over his shoulder when somebody rattled the knob. He let go of Shelby and folded his arms and gave her a self-satisfied smile.

She glared at him. "Are you out of your mind?"

"You need a minute to compose yourself," he replied in a maddeningly reasonable tone.

Her annoyance was overtaken by confusion as she looked around her. They were standing in a narrow space with a wall of metal shelving on one side and an industrial-size, stainless-steel sink on the other. "Where are we?" she asked as her gaze landed on an enormous bucket with a mop protruding from it.

"Utility closet," Tucker said. "Not intrinsically romantic, I'll grant you, but if you'll close your eyes, I'll make it —"

*Tucker.* This was not the time for games. "Everyone's going to wonder what —"

He laughed shortly. "No, they're not. They think I'm kissing you breathless right now."

Even as he said the words, someone pounded on the door. "Don't mess up her hair!" Rachel yelled, and Shelby heard a booming laugh, possibly Stephen's.

Tucker's eyebrows lifted in a silent I told you so.

As Shelby opened her mouth, two long fingers were laid over it. "Shh," Tucker said, shaking with suppressed laughter.

Her head snapped back in outraged dig-

167

nity and she shoved his hand away. "I am not going to pretend that —"

He stopped her protest with a kiss. After a moment his hand closed around her wrist and moved it aside, protecting her bouquet as his other hand pressed against the small of her back, drawing her closer.

She didn't know a lot about these things, but she suspected Tucker Sharpe was a world-class kisser. Only they shouldn't *be* kissing, because they weren't in love and this wasn't going to be the usual kind of marriage. Shelby was endeavoring to whip up some willpower to break their lip-lock and remind him of those facts when he ended the kiss.

"Don't do that," she said faintly, pulling her roses in front of her for protection. "I don't like it."

Okay, that hadn't come out right. She braced herself for Tucker's pert observation that, from where he stood, she'd appeared to like it just fine.

His smile widened, drilling deep dimples in his tanned cheeks. "I forgot myself." He let her go and reached inside his tuxedo jacket. "It's just that you're so beautiful tonight," he said, drawing out a handkerchief.

"Am I?" She'd been worried that she

looked just the way she felt — dizzy and terrified. She knew a moment's concern that he'd think she was fishing for compliments, but his expression had sobered, and for once, she was grateful he could read her mind.

"You look a little nervous, that's all." He dabbed at her damp cheeks with the hand-kerchief. Mentally, she gave him points for understanding the importance of blotting instead of rubbing. "People expect that of a bride," he continued. "But now that the ceremony's over, you should try to lighten up."

"I will," she said, wondering how she would manage it.

Janni had contrived to give her every one of the wedding traditions she'd dreamed of. But there had been nothing joyous about any of it, because Shelby wasn't in love, and what she wanted now more than anything was for all of this just to be over.

Tucker returned the handkerchief to his pocket. "Why shouldn't we have some fun?"

Shelby was just opening her mouth to tell him there wasn't going to be any more kiss-ing, there was no reason for it, they weren't going to have that kind of marriage, when he clarified his meaning. "Let's go have a nice dinner and enjoy our guests."

His left hand closed around Shelby's as he reached for the doorknob with his right. "You'll have to redo your lipstick," he added helpfully. "But the rest is perfect. Ready?"

The door swung open to reveal a dozen noisy wedding guests who elbowed each other and made teasing remarks about what they thought had been going on in the closet. Looking a little sheepish, Tucker turned to Janni. "We need some more lipstick."

The perky wedding coordinator studied his face. "No, you've got plenty on. But I'm not sure coral's your best shade."

The hall swelled with raucous laughter as Janni produced a lacy white handkerchief and dabbed at the bridegroom's mouth. Shelby knew she was blushing and looking every bit as uncomfortable as she felt, but when she met Tucker's twinkling eyes, she gave in. Then the tide of well-wishers surged and she allowed herself to be caught up on the wave of their exuberance, no longer caring where it took her.

Half an hour later, she and Tucker were filling their plates from the buffet when the candlelit reception hall began to ring with the insistent tinkling of spoons on glassware. "Kiss her!" someone called, and Shelby bit her lip and threw a worried glance at her new husband.

She couldn't kiss him again. That was dangerously thin ice she'd skated on earlier, and she wasn't going back there. So how was she supposed to handle this? She couldn't pretend to be in love with him, but neither could she explain their unusual arrangement to all of these people.

Perfectly composed, perhaps a little amused, Tucker put down his plate and raised his hand, asking for silence. When that was granted, he looked at Shelby. "When I kiss my wife," he said, speaking loudly enough for everyone to hear, "it will be for *her* entertainment, not anyone else's."

The room erupted with laughter, and one of Tucker's cousins thumped him on the back.

"I'll kiss her," a masculine voice boomed, and Shelby turned to face Stephen. Smiling as though she was some rare treasure, he cradled her face between his palms. "So you've become my daughter, after all." He pressed a reverent kiss against her forehead. "It's my great honor to welcome you to the family."

*Honor?* Shelby nearly choked. How could he use that word when he knew why she'd had to marry Tucker? She pressed her fingers to her mouth to stop it from trembling, but she couldn't do a thing about the tears that slid down her cheeks. As her world blurred, Tucker put an arm around her and whisked her to a dim corner of the room. He backed her against the wall, shielding her with his big body, and there, he again produced his handkerchief and proceeded to dry her tears.

Tucker looked over his shoulder and was relieved to see his dad handling things at the buffet table. One or two curious glances were flicked in the newlyweds' direction, but nobody appeared to think anything was amiss. They probably just assumed the couple had sneaked over here for some semiprivate kisses.

Just over two months ago, the people in this room had mourned together. But tonight they were laughing as if the world hadn't stopped spinning on that awful, rain-soaked May evening. It wasn't wrong of them, life did go on, but as Tucker folded his arms more tightly around his trembling wife, he wished he could cry with her.

Only a handful of people were aware of the reason for this hasty marriage. Everyone else appeared eager to believe that as Tucker and Shelby had comforted each other in the aftermath of David's death, they had fallen in love. Tucker had overheard two of his cousins talking about how "romantic" that was.

When he felt Shelby draw and release a deep breath, he eased back from her, catching one of her hands in his. "Better now?"

She nodded. "I'm a bundle of nerves tonight."

Yeah, he'd noticed. But he knew this wasn't just about her being pregnant. A little while ago she had promised herself "till death" to a man she didn't love. She was probably convinced she'd never be happy again.

But she would be. Tucker would see to that.

They filled their plates and sat down at the flower-strewn, candlelit bridal table. Shelby talked and laughed with their guests, but she didn't eat a thing. Although Tucker saw her lift her fork exactly three times, she put it down again without ever actually taking a bite. And nobody noticed.

An odd pain spiraled through Tucker's body. He was the only person in the world who understood what it had cost her to make those wedding vows. Yes, she'd clouded up and rained on him a couple of times, but she was fighting for her baby's future, and it just wasn't in her to give up.

173

He watched her profile, thinking about what she'd been through. Her father had abused her and her mother was emotionally unavailable. No wonder Shelby had trust issues, even with God. And it sure couldn't have boosted her faith any when she'd lost David and then found herself pregnant.

Tucker tried to imagine how alone she must feel, and how frightened. When she turned to him, smiling, he smiled right back at her, looking deep into her wild violet eyes and sending a silent message to her wounded heart.

Don't worry, honey. I've got your back now.

Tucker had brought it up several times, but Shelby had insisted that a honeymoon was not only unnecessary, but also ridiculous under the circumstances. So as soon as Janni decreed it was decent, the newlyweds headed home to Dublin.

"You didn't eat any dinner," Tucker remarked when he opened the door and Shelby bent down to greet Roadkill. "Would you like something now? I could make you a mushroom omelet."

"No, thanks. Too tired."

He pushed his hands into his pants pockets, spreading his tuxedo jacket and revealing the black silk cummerbund that cinched his lean waist. "You've had a stressful evening."

Hadn't they *both* had a stressful evening? Why did he look so relaxed, as though this was just another Saturday night? As though they hadn't just drastically altered the courses of their lives? Too tired to think about it now, Shelby started for her room, the full skirt of her gown rustling as she moved down the hall.

Tucker called to her and she turned. With his hands still in his pockets, he twitched a shoulder at her. "I meant it when I said you looked beautiful tonight."

"Thank you," she said softly, surprised at how quickly another of those awful lumps had risen in her throat. "And thank you for the wedding, Tucker."

"Was it what you wanted?"

She had no idea how to answer him. After she'd thrown that tantrum at the bike shop and he'd gone to so much trouble and expense to please her, how could she admit that from the moment they'd spoken their vows, she'd just wanted the whole thing to be *over?* "It was exactly the kind of wedding I used to dream about," she said finally. Except that in her dreams, she had always married for love.

She escaped to her room, where she changed into a modest pair of plaid pajamas, then opened the bedroom door and called to Tucker that the bathroom was free. She huddled under her log-cabin quilt, feeling a little awkward as Tucker walked past her in gray sweatpants and a white T-shirt. When he emerged from the bathroom a short while later, Shelby had turned her face into her pillow, feigning sleep.

Acutely aware of his soft footfalls on the carpet, she forced herself to take deep, even breaths. She heard him fumble with the bedside lamp, and then the room went dark. He lingered beside her for a minute, but although Shelby wondered what he was doing, she didn't open her eyes. When she heard his whispered "Amen," she realized he had been praying. Over *her.* Shame flooded her heart and she sat up. "Tucker?"

He paused in the doorway. "Hmm?"

"I'm sorry. I wasn't really asleep."

Silhouetted by the light from the hall, his face was dark and unreadable. "I wondered."

"It's just . . ." She drew her knees up to her chest and hugged them. "It's just so much to process. You know?"

"Yeah." He walked back over to her, switched the lamp on, and sat down on the edge of the bed. "I know."

She hung her head. "I don't even know where to start."

Very slowly, so as not to startle her, she guessed, he reached out, grasped her chin with gentle fingers and lifted, making her look at him. "We've already started." He shifted his hand to smooth a thatch of curls back from her face. "And I think we're doing just fine. Don't worry so much."

Her eyes closed as he continued to stroke her hair. When his thumb grazed her cheek, she leaned into his hand, mindlessly seeking more of the comforting warmth.

"You're exhausted," he said.

Her eyes popped open and she jerked her head away from him. She *was* exhausted, and that was the only reason she'd allowed him to touch her that way.

Tucker's gaze drifted past her and settled on the heap of beaded satin and lace Shelby had piled on a wingback chair. "I remember the day you bought that gown," he said softly. "I was standing by the front windows of the store when you and Rachel and your mom came out of the bridal shop." His voice deepened in what sounded almost like affectionate amusement. "You looked like you were walking on air."

She had been. But why had Tucker noticed? And why did he sound so nostalgic about it? He'd been against the engagement from the beginning, and that still hurt. "You didn't think I was good enough for David," she blurted like a bitter child.

Tucker's breath came out in a rush and he stared at her in apparent amazement. "Where did you get *that* idea?"

"I could see it every time you looked at me," she muttered, plucking at her quilt. "You were always so disapproving."

"Of the engagement, not you, Shel. You and David weren't right for each other."

She looked up. "Why not?"

Tucker traced one of the quilt's blue rectangles with his index finger. "I loved David." His voice deepened, resonating with pain. "But he could be reckless. He never meant to hurt anyone, but sometimes he just didn't think things through. I didn't believe he was ready for marriage."

It was true that David had lived for the moment. That was part of what had made him such a romantic figure. But as exciting as David had been, Shelby was beginning to believe she hadn't really loved him. Not in the serious, "forever" way she should have. Maybe she had just wanted to belong to someone. To believe that no matter what happened, someone would always keep a candle in the window for her.

"You cared for him," Tucker said, watching her face. "And I know he cared for you. But I was afraid that one day you two would hit a rocky patch and have trouble getting past it."

"What about you and me?" she challenged, finding it easier to be irritated with him than to admit he might have a point. "What makes our marriage any different?"

"It's worlds different," Tucker said calmly. "We don't have any romantic expectations to trip us up. We know this isn't going to be easy, but we're determined to make it work. And that's exactly why it's *going* to."

He reached for her hair again, and Shelby flinched. "Hey," he whispered, capturing one of the perfect ringlets her hairdresser had created and winding it around his finger. "I know it will take a little while for you to get used to me, but we're partners now. I want to be the safe place you run to when you feel like your world is caving in. After the Lord, of course." He released her curl and rose from the bed. "I'll do anything I can for you, Shel. Don't ever hesitate to ask."

Did he expect her to make a similar promise? She couldn't. She'd already made him more promises than she felt able to keep. Her throat closed up as she remembered her wedding vows. Did God expect her to keep those? She hadn't made them freely and joyfully. So did they still count?

Tucker reached for the lamp. "Sweet dreams, Shel."

He didn't close the door. Shelby watched him walk down the hall and make a right turn, switching off the hall light as he disappeared into his own room. He didn't close that door, either. Was that meant to be some kind of I'm-right-here-if-you-need-me message?

She didn't need him. She didn't need anyone. She lay back and closed her eyes, freeing a tear to roll down the side of her face, leaving a tickly trail before it dropped into her ear.

Why hadn't she asked?

Tucker sat on the edge of his bed and stared unseeingly at an autographed, framed poster of a sweat-soaked cycling team.

How could she have failed to pick up on it? He had just confessed that he had known David wasn't ready for marriage. Yet she hadn't asked why Tucker had kept silent, why he hadn't tried to warn her.

Blind loyalty. That was what his mother had called it. But she'd never known how

180

Tucker's sixteen-year-old heart had been seared by the sounds of his brother sobbing in his sleep on the other side of the bedroom they shared. Tucker's parents had never realized how bad it was, how often it happened. Night after night, for almost a year. And since they had no inkling of the horrors David alluded to only in his sleep, they'd never understood Tucker's need to bulldoze every obstacle to David's happiness.

He rubbed his eyes with the heels of his hands. Apart from ensuring that David's baby would have the happy childhood its father had been denied, there was nothing more Tucker could do for his brother. But he could do something for Shelby.

David had called his brother "everyone's best friend." But Tucker hadn't been Shelby's friend, had he? He hadn't stopped her engagement, so a child had been conceived. He hadn't stood his ground and refused to ride motorcycles on a rainy night, so her fiancé had died. It was all Tucker's fault that Shelby had been left alone and pregnant and afraid.

Whether she realized it or not, he owed her for that.

# CHAPTER TEN

In the sweatpants and T-shirt he'd slept in, Tucker padded barefoot and bleary-eyed into the hall, making his way to the shower. When he noticed that Shelby's bedroom door was closed, he reversed direction like a ping-pong ball bouncing off a paddle and headed for the kitchen, instead.

He ground and brewed some coffee, his heart clutching every time sunlight glinted off the unfamiliar gold ring on his left hand. He gnawed on the insides of his cheeks, wondering how he was ever going to make this marriage work. His track record with women didn't exactly engender confidence in the current situation.

He wasn't great with women, and that was a problem because there was one in his bathroom right now, probably throwing up her toenails, and she was wearing a ring just like Tucker's.

He lined up two oranges on a cutting

board and reached for his chef's knife. With a precision born of practice, he created four perfect halves with one mighty whack.

According to *Congratulations! You're Pregnant,* the book he'd stayed up half the night reading, some pregnant women wanted a light breakfast even after a bout with morning sickness. So Tucker whacked three more sets of oranges and juiced them all, then loaded his toaster with whole-grain bread, just in case.

As the last of the coffee dripped into the carafe, Tucker remembered something else he'd read in the book: Shelby should be cutting back on caffeine. He could hardly drink the coffee in front of her, so he poured the whole pot down the sink. Removing further temptation, he dropped the nearly full bag of his favorite beans into the trash.

He had just filled his grandmother's copper teakettle with fresh water when Shelby drooped into the kitchen. Her narrow shoulders slumped pathetically, and Tucker's heart twisted at the sight of the dark half-moons under her eyes.

He pulled out a chair and she sagged onto it. Then she propped her elbows on the table and rested her chin on her hands. "I smelled coffee," she moaned, squinting in obvious confusion at the empty carafe on the warming plate.

"Sorry. There isn't any." Hoping she'd conclude that her hormones were playing mean tricks on her olfactory nerve, Tucker didn't elaborate. "How about a cup of chamomile tea?" he asked, smiling encouragement at her.

Her nose twitched like a rabbit's, then her eyes narrowed dangerously. "You drank *all* of the coffee?"

"No. I poured it down the sink. It was bad." Realizing that his smile had slipped, he hoisted it back up. "Let's have apricot tea," he said brightly.

She sniffed the air again. "What was wrong with it?"

"Too much caffeine isn't good for us." Tucker pawed through a box of assorted herbal teas. "Apple Celebration?" he tempted.

"I need coffee," she said through clenched teeth.

"Perky Peppermint?" Hearing the edge of desperation in his voice, Tucker cleared his throat. "My mother always said peppermint was great for soothing an upset stom—"

*"I need coffee!"*

Whoa. Being screamed at by a caffeine-deprived pregnant woman was downright scary. "I'll go get some," Tucker volunteered, practically stumbling over his own feet in his eagerness to escape.

"Don't you dare buy decaf."

He halted in the kitchen doorway. "We'll get used to it, Shel," he said carefully, turning to face her again.

Her chair scraped on the quarry-tile floor as she stood up, all five feet and almost three inches of her, ready to take him on. Her violet eyes glinted like icebergs under a cloudless arctic sky as she stalked toward him. "You don't own me."

The air in the kitchen seemed to pulse with her anxiety, awakening every protective instinct Tucker possessed. Sending up a quick, silent prayer that God would settle her out-of-control hormones, he gently placed his hands on her shoulders. "No, I don't own you. But I worry about you and the baby. I just want to do everything right. And the book says you should cut down on caffeine."

She glared at him for several more seconds, then she suddenly deflated. "I know," she said, bowing her head. "I've been having just one cup in the mornings. I didn't think it would hurt anything, just one cup. But you're right."

He put his hand under her chin and raised her face. It took a moment, but then her eyelashes fluttered and she looked up at him. The hopelessness he read in her beautiful eyes twisted something in his gut, and he felt a spasm of anger directed at David. Yes, it took two people to make a baby, but how could David have allowed her to take such a risk?

"Why did you marry me?" she asked.

"To correct a mistake," he replied without thinking. Yes, that was true, but he regretted putting it so baldly.

Her eyes filled with tears. "It wasn't *your* mistake."

Yes, it was. More than she would ever understand. Ashamed, Tucker let her go and averted his face.

She appeared to take that for modesty. "Can you really be that unselfish?"

"I'm as selfish as the next guy. But I needed to do this. I couldn't have lived with myself, otherwise."

"What if you can't live with *me?*"

He looked at her then. "We'll be fine. You worry too much."

"What's wrong with me?" she moaned as two tears rolled down her cheeks. "I should be grateful. You've done so much."

He patted her shoulder. "Honey, just switch to decaf and we'll call it even."

He congratulated himself when that pulled

a faint smile from her. "I'm sorry, Tucker. Again."

"Don't worry about it. You're pregnant. And after everything I read last night, I'd say that considering how much the woman suffers in pregnancy and childbirth, it isn't too much to expect the guy to put up with a little weirdness." He held out his arms. "So this is me, being an understanding husband."

He was hoping to score another smile, but she gave her head a pathetic little shake. "I'm really trying to believe everything will work out, but —"

"Don't worry, Shel. Until you find your way there, I'll believe it for both of us. You just try to relax."

She expelled a ragged breath. "I need a Hershey's bar."

"I'll get you one," Tucker promised, thrilled to know there was something he could do to make her feel better.

She looked surprised. "Aren't you going to tell me there's caffeine in chocolate?"

"There's not that much. And I'm choosing my battles."

She lifted her chin. "Wise man." She didn't smile, but Tucker could have sworn those weary violet eyes twinkled at him in the instant before she turned away.

■ ■ ■ ■

"I haven't had this much alone-time with my violin since the conservatory," Shelby told Rachel on Friday when they met for lunch at a favorite Italian restaurant.

Rachel traced tiny circles on the tabletop with a perfect fingernail. "Well, with everything that's happened lately, I'm glad you're not in the middle of a school year and up to your ears in private students. You need this break."

Shelby nodded. "I've been immersing myself in Paganini. He's a real challenge, but my technique is definitely improving. And I think focusing on that is helping my nerves."

Rachel slanted her a knowing look. "It's not Paganini that's helping you relax. It's Tucker."

Before Shelby could respond to that surprising remark, their server arrived with two beautiful salads and a crusty loaf of cheese-stuffed garlic bread.

"But you really should have taken a honeymoon," Rachel said when the server left.

Shelby paused in the act of stirring fake sugar into her iced tea. "What for?"

Rachel rolled her eyes. "For the romance,

of course."

Shelby rapped her long-handled spoon against the rim of her glass, calling her friend to order. "There isn't any romance, Rachel. You know very well why we got married."

"I know why *you* did it," Rachel retorted. "And at the reception I figured out why *he* did it . . . Tucker's got it bad."

Frowning, Shelby picked up a fork and began to explore her salad. "You're out of your mind," she said calmly.

"Open your eyes," Rachel said as she sawed off a chunk of bread and put it on Shelby's plate. "Tucker's in love."

"No, he isn't. He's just —"

"Oh, please." Rachel's pale hair shimmered as she tossed her head. "It was so obvious. Every time you moved, Shelby, his eyes followed you."

That wasn't love, it was just Tucker being Tucker. Watching out for her and the baby. But as Shelby nudged aside an unwanted tomato and speared some lettuce with her fork, it occurred to her that maybe this wasn't something she ought to be arguing about. If Rachel and the rest of the world accepted her marriage as a normal one, things would be a whole lot simpler.

"He was so cute at the reception." Rachel's eyes danced as she lowered her voice in a comical imitation of Tucker's. "Are you okay, Shel? Need anything? Careful, honey, that coffee's hot. Here, let me blow on it for you."

Shelby couldn't help giggling at her friend's imitation. "He's not quite *that* bad."

Rachel put down her water glass with a thump. "Shelby, he's not *bad* at all. The man adores you, and I couldn't be happier. You've really landed on your feet."

Yes, she had. He didn't love her, but Tucker's commitment would never waver. It was simply who Tucker Sharpe was.

"So." Rachel folded her slender arms on the table's edge and leaned forward. "How's marriage?" she asked, waggling her perfect eyebrows.

Shelby had just filled her mouth with chewy, cheesy garlic bread, so she had a moment to consider her answer. She knew exactly what Rachel was asking, and Tucker's voice echoed in her head: *Close the circle.* Emotions crashed through her; gratitude mixed with admiration and perhaps even a dash of affection for her husband, and Shelby made a decision. "My marriage is fine," she said demurely. "And this bread is incredible."

After the lunch with Rachel, Shelby hurried straight home. Her roommate from her first year at the conservatory was in Columbus for an audition, and had promised that if she got away early, she'd try to swing by Dublin for some catching up.

Shelby's doorbell rang at three-thirty. Roadkill barked furiously, but Shelby laughed and shushed him and eagerly threw open the door.

She was immediately sorry. It wasn't her old friend on the step, but Tucker's juvenile delinquent. "Is Tucker Sharpe here?" the bike thief inquired. "He's not at the store, and I'd like to talk to him in private, anyway."

Shelby's mouth opened and closed like a guppy's as her mind spun over that question. The last thing she wanted to admit to this troubled teen was that she was home alone. But she *was,* unless she counted Roadkill, which she didn't, because at the moment he was cowering behind her ankles.

"I looked him up in the phone book," the boy explained. He tossed his head, swinging back longish blond curls that were eerily like David's. "I thought maybe we could work out a deal." His Adam's apple jerked as he swallowed. "I owe him for a bike."

So he was admitting it. Now Shelby was *really* speechless.

The boy cleared his throat. "My name's Bryan Arby."

"I'm . . . Shelby. Tucker's wife." Why was her voice shaking? How could she be afraid of a teenage boy? Judging by the way his blue eyes were darting back and forth, he was at least as nervous as she and Roadkill were. "Sorry," she said, then offered a feeble laugh. "I was expecting someone else, and you took me by surprise." She bent down and gathered the trembling poodle into her arms. "I'm afraid Tucker's not here."

Shelby had no experience with teenage criminals, but she was good with kids, and Roadkill helped break the ice. Inside of five minutes Shelby had a rudimentary grasp of Bryan's situation. His father had abandoned his family, so Bryan's harried mother was working two jobs, giving the unsupervised teen ample opportunity to act out his confusion and resentment. Bryan's language was a little rough, but the belligerence he had displayed when confronted at the bike shop was nowhere apparent.

Shelby's instincts warned her not to ask why Bryan had taken the bike. He probably didn't even know. But asking what had provoked this confession seemed reasonable, so she did that.

192

"He was, like, all in my face," Bryan said. "But he didn't call the police. And he gave me a helmet."

"I know." Shelby put Roadkill back on the floor. "I was there."

Bryan nodded as he watched the poodle trot away. "That kind of bothered me, because the helmet wasn't one of the cheap ones. It was like he was saying, 'Here, take it all. That's not what I care about.' "

"I think —" Shelby cleared her emotion-clogged throat. "Yes. I think that's what he was saying."

Bryan shifted his weight from one foot to the other, stubbing the rubber toes of his sneakers against the step. "And then yesterday I was riding some bike trails and got to talking to these two guys about equipment and stuff," he said, still rocking from side to side. "They said Shamrock had good prices and knowledgeable people, and they said Tucker Sharpe was some big-deal racing dude. Only they said he wasn't racing this summer because his brother was killed in a motorcycle wreck."

Shelby nodded and waited for him to go on.

Bryan stopped squirming and dropped his head. "That's how *my* brother was killed. Last year. And then my parents starting fighting all the time and stuff. And Dad left us."

Compassion hit Shelby hard. "Oh, Bryan, I'm so sorry."

"Yeah. My brother was older than me, seventeen, but we got along." Bryan reached into a pocket of his baggy, low-riding jeans and produced a pack of cigarettes.

"Would you please not smoke?" Shelby asked. "I'm pregnant."

He shrugged and replaced the cigarettes in his pocket. "So when I heard about this Tucker guy's brother, I felt bad about taking the bike. It's like I kicked him when he was down."

Shelby hugged herself and nodded her understanding.

"People say they know how you feel." Bryan flipped back his hair, defiant. "But they don't. Not if they haven't been through it. They *can't* know."

"You're right," Shelby said.

"I thought he was just some lucky jerk who had everything," Bryan continued. "Then I found out he lost a brother. And right now he's probably thinking nobody understands how he feels." The boy averted his face, surreptitiously dabbing at one eye. "But somebody does," he added, almost whispering now. "*I* do."

194

■ ■ ■ ■

Three hours later, Roadkill lay on the end of Shelby's bed, his bulgy brown eyes shifting back and forth as he watched her pace in front of him. When he abruptly jumped off the bed and shot past her, Shelby knew Tucker was home.

She stopped pacing and nibbled a thumbnail as she listened to his key scraping in the door lock. Then the door opened and she heard the low rumble of his voice and the jingling of the tags that hung from Roadkill's collar. She inhaled deeply, slowly let the breath go and went out to meet her husband.

She found him lounging against the kitchen counter, his long, denim-encased legs crossed at the ankles as he flipped through a stack of mail. He glanced up and smiled a greeting. "The yard looks good," he said as he used a key to slit open an envelope. "But I wish you had left it for me. It was too hot for you to be working outside."

She'd address that in a minute. First she told him, as casually as she could manage, that Bryan Arby had stopped by.

"He wanted to know if he could do anything," Shelby hurried on. "Like washing cars or cleaning the garage. He was very nice, not at all like he was at the bike shop. I let him cut the grass, and then I gave him lemonade and cookies."

Except for a muscle that twitched in his face, Tucker had gone dangerously still. "You let that kid into this house?"

"Why not?" she asked breezily. "After he finished mowing, we had a nice long —"

"He has a police record, Shelby." Tucker's voice vibrated with anger and his brown eyes glittered like topazes. "He's done a whole lot more than just stealing that bike."

"Wh-what?" Shelby pulled out a chair and sank onto it.

Tucker dumped the mail on the counter and drew up to his full height, rigid and immovable. "I talked to Ed, a cop friend of mine. Last year Bryan hit one of his teachers." Tucker paused, watching Shelby's face as horror coated her like freezing rain. "When she gave Bryan detention for swearing at her, he punched her in the stomach."

Shelby gasped.

"That's right," Tucker said harshly, his gaze dipping to Shelby's midsection before coming back to rest on her face. She looked down and discovered she'd unconsciously placed a protective hand over her abdomen.

But as shocked as she was, some instinct made her defend Bryan. "He's *hurting,* Tucker. His brother died and then his father left and his mom is working two jobs, so he's practically raising himself. He's sorry about the bike, and I'm sure he regrets hitting his teacher. I'm not excusing his behavior, but I think he's just acting out because —"

"I don't want him here," Tucker snapped. "I'll give him a job if he wants one. But he is *not* welcome in this house."

How could she make him understand that the kid had nearly melted her heart? "He's in *trouble,* Tucker, and he thinks nobody cares. He desperately needs a friend to —"

"I'll be his friend," Tucker growled. "*You* stay out of it."

His anger unnerved her, brought back awful memories of a man who raised his voice and used his fists, but something inside her had given way, flooding her heart with courage. "Pastor Dean says we should step outside of our comfort zone and reach out to people in trouble," she reminded Tucker. "Well, Bryan's in trouble. So I think we should risk something and —"

"Not *you,*" Tucker almost shouted. "I won't risk *you.*"

Shelby bit her lip and stared at him,

wondering how to crack his stubborn shell. "Will you give him a job?"

"I said I would. But he shouldn't have come here."

Shelby looked down at her lap and willed her fingers to stop strangling each other. "Tucker, you don't understand. He *talked* to me. We really connected. He just —" She stopped when Tucker slammed a fist against the counter.

"He hit that woman in the *stomach,* Shelby!" Tucker's face was contorted with fury. "So if he comes again, don't open the door. Just —"

Shelby watched him and waited, not daring to breathe.

"All right," he said in a subdued tone. He held up both hands like a beaten man trying to deflect a blow to his chest. "All right, I hear you."

His sudden surrender shocked her even more than the anger he had just displayed. "I didn't say anything," she squeaked.

"Not out loud," he said wearily, pushing a hand through his hair. "You said it with those eyes." He stepped over to the table and collapsed onto a chair beside her. "I know there's a line somewhere. But where is it, Shelby?" Shaking his head, he drew a ragged breath. "I can't see it. If I say that kid's never to set foot in this house, am I serving God by protecting you? Or am I interfering with your ministry to the boy? How am I supposed to know?"

The idea that rock-solid Tucker could be uncertain about anything made her head spin. "I don't know," she said slowly. "Now that I know he's been violent, I'm a little uneasy."

"Maybe he'd never dream of hurting you," Tucker said, his eyes asking for understanding. "But he did hit that woman."

"He's worth the risk, Tucker." The words were out before Shelby realized she'd made the decision. She took a careful breath and willed her racing heart to behave. "I want to be his friend. I want us both to be his friends. Please."

Tucker compressed his lips, but then he nodded.

"I think we should pray for him." Shelby's voice shook, but somehow she pushed out more words. "For opportunities to show him that he *matters*."

"Okay, let's do that." Tucker extended his hand.

Shelby stared. He didn't intend to pray right this minute, did he? Out loud?

"Come on," he urged, wiggling his fingers.

Shelby placed her trembling hand in his.

He gripped it, strong and sure now, and in a solemn voice that radiated confidence, he addressed their God.

# CHAPTER ELEVEN

Shelby was making a grocery list when her ballpoint pen quit on her. She rummaged through a kitchen drawer, but had found nothing more useful than a blue highlighting pen when Tucker's editor phoned.

"How's he treating you?" Bill Dietzel shouted.

Shelby held the phone away from her ear. She'd met Bill at the wedding, and she wanted to like him because Tucker thought so highly of him, but the man's loud voice made her nervous. "Better than I deserve," she said lightly.

"I seriously doubt that," Bill yelled. "My boy Steve would never have settled for less than the best woman out there."

"You're very kind," Shelby said. He was also dead wrong. His boy Steve wouldn't have married the likes of Shelby if he hadn't felt honor bound to do it.

"Would you mind jotting down my new

office phone number?"

Shelby snatched up the small notepad she'd been writing on a moment ago and carried the cordless phone into Tucker's room, where she pulled open his middle desk drawer and discovered a treasure trove of ballpoint pens. She wrote down the message, then cringed as Bill shouted pleasantries at her for another minute before thanking her and hanging up.

When she moved to close the desk drawer, her attention was arrested by a book, the cover of which pictured the clasped hands of a man and a woman, each wearing a gold wedding ring. Recognizing the name of a well-known Christian psychologist on the cover, Shelby put down the phone and opened the drawer wider. *"Lifetime Love,"* she read aloud, picking up the book to examine it.

This was so like Tucker. If he thought a book could teach him how to fall in love, he'd read it cover to cover. Shelby pictured him poring over these chapters, heroically struggling to make his heart feel something for the woman he'd married.

"Shel?"

She started. How had she missed hearing him come in? "I'm in your room," she called, quickly replacing the book.

He appeared in the doorway, looking pleased with himself and holding a rectangular basket of peaches by its wire handle. "Look what I found at the farmers' market."

"Mmm." Shelby leaned forward to admire the rosy fruit and breathe in its tangy-sweet aroma. "I love peaches."

"Things were dead at the store, and Dad's there, so I took off early," Tucker said.

"This is Bill's new number." Shelby tore the sheet off her notepad and handed it to him. "I apologize for getting into your desk, but I couldn't find a pen."

"No problem." He shot her a mischievous grin. "It's not like I'm hiding old love letters in there."

Shelby wondered if he had any old love letters. Was he the kind of man who would keep such things?

"No," he said.

She blinked. "What?"

"No, I don't have any old love letters."

He was doing it again. He knew it made her crazy, but he kept on doing it. Shelby's fingers curled tightly around the pen she still held. "Would you please stop —"

"Reading your mind?"

"Tucker," She shot him a quelling look. "You know it makes me crazy when you —"

"Finish your sentences?" he asked with an

innocent air that pushed every one of her buttons.

She made a frustrated sound in the back of her throat and snatched the basket from him. His low, wicked laugh chased her all the way to the kitchen, but as she deposited the peaches on the counter, a smile tugged at her mouth.

"He really knows how to get me going," she confided to Roadkill, who was basking on the tile floor in a late-afternoon sunbeam. Raising his head from his paws, the poodle regarded her with placid eyes. Then his mouth stretched open and his long tongue curled as he yawned.

Shelby propped her hands on her hips and sighed. "I should have known you'd be on *his* side."

She finished scribbling her grocery list and returned to Tucker's room. He was seated at his desk, tapping away on his computer. "What are you working on?" she asked companionably, already having forgiven him for tormenting her.

He glanced up without breaking the rhythm of the clacking keys. "A column about why women don't understand fishing."

Shelby watched his face, wondering if there was something different about him or if it was just the way the small oval lenses of the black-rimmed glasses he wore for computer work showcased his dark, almond-shaped eyes.

It wasn't the glasses, she decided. An inexplicable contentment appeared to have settled over Tucker. It was almost as if he enjoyed being married. But how could he, given their unconventional arrangement?

It was that silly book, it had to be. Tucker believed he had it all figured out. They'd follow the prescribed steps and then they'd fall madly in love and live happily ever after.

Right. He probably believed in the Tooth Fairy, too. But Shelby felt a niggling admiration for him, just the same. What must it be like to be so strong, so confident all of the time?

He stopped typing and leaned forward, propping his left elbow on the desk, one long finger stroking his upper lip as he studied the computer screen. "It can't be all that entertaining to watch me pound away on this keyboard," he said.

"I was waiting for you to get to a stopping place." Unnerved by the attractive way his curvy mouth tilted into a smile, Shelby filled the air with more words. "You look like a completely different guy in those glasses."

He leaned back and his graceful fingers

resumed their pattering. "Still *your* guy," he said amiably.

She let that one go. "I'm heading to the grocery store," she said, waving her shopping list to prove it. "Any requests?"

"Milk and yogurt." He swept her with a worried look. "I'm not sure you're getting enough calcium."

She took prenatal vitamins the size of a baby's fist. She was getting plenty of everything. "I get enough," she assured him.

"Maybe not. I read yesterday that eating chocolate might inhibit the body's ability to absorb calcium. So maybe we should pump a little extra dairy stuff into you."

She tapped her foot. "Anything else, doctor?"

"You might pick up some cocoa powder and pecans."

Her spirits soared. "Are you going to make brownies?"

He gave her an amused look. "If you're good." He turned back to his screen, frowned and deleted several keystrokes. "I won't be here when you get back. I just need to proofread this, and then I'll walk Kill. After that I'm going for a ride."

"Don't worry about my dog," Shelby said. "I'll walk him when I get back."

"No, I'll take him. It's ninety-six degrees

outside, and you'll be exhausted after the shopping."

Yes, she tired easily these days, but she wasn't *that* fragile. "It's not like I'm going to melt," she protested.

One side of his mouth kicked up. "Honey, with all that chocolate in you, you just might," he drawled, looking handsome and amused and a whole lot happier than a man who had not married for love had any reason to look.

Ten minutes later, Shelby was climbing out of her car in the grocery store parking lot when she recognized one of three teenagers loitering outside the video rental shop next door. Like his companions, Bryan Arby held a soda in one hand and a cigarette in the other.

Had he seen her? Would he welcome being greeted in front of his friends? Shelby sent up a quick, silent prayer as she walked across the sweltering parking lot toward the boys.

"Hey, Shelby." Bryan's expression was guarded as he dropped his cigarette on the sidewalk and ground it out under his shoe.

Shelby glanced at the other two boys, including them in the greeting she smiled at Bryan. "Tucker definitely wants to hire you, Bryan. He says you should fill out an application."

"Oh, Bryan's independently wealthy," one of his friends sneered as the other blew a puff of smoke in Shelby's face.

When Shelby coughed, Bryan slapped the back of the smoke-blower's head with his open hand. "Don't be a jerk, Blaine."

Shelby smiled again and forced a breezy tone. "I'd better go get my groceries. I'll see you later, Bryan."

"Right." Relief showed in his pale-blue eyes. "Later."

Shelby hustled away, praying again, this time that God would nudge the boy to think about the company he kept.

By the time she wheeled her cart out to her car, the boys had gone. Shelby paused to lift her hair away from her perspiring neck for a moment's relief. But she didn't stand still for long, because the heat radiating from the asphalt burned through the thin soles of her sandals, scorching her tired feet.

Tucker had been right, as usual. Today's heat coupled with the high humidity had sapped her energy.

Even though she'd been expecting it, the oven blast that assailed her when she opened her car door took her breath away. She slipped her key into the ignition to get the air conditioner going, then began loading groceries into the backseat. As she settled the last bag on the floor, a drop of sweat rolled down her spine and she shivered.

She quickly backed out of the car and looked around her. It was broad daylight in a town that didn't have much crime to speak of. So why was she having these horrible thoughts about being grabbed from behind and —

*Stop it.* No doubt she could blame some weird hormonal surge for the sudden chill she'd felt.

She reminded herself of that a couple of minutes later when she again experienced the creepy feeling. She had just glanced into her rearview mirror and noticed that a gleaming black Lexus had followed her through her last two turns. Of course it was just a coincidence; Dublin wasn't that big a place. But when she drove through the Historic District and turned onto the narrow street that led down to the river, the car was still behind her.

Uncertainty flashed into real fear. She passed the stone house and kept going, thinking that if the car continued to follow, she'd just head for the police station. Then she saw a bicycle whip around the corner at the top of the hill.

Recognizing Tucker's red jersey, she braked hard and steered to the side of the road, almost laughing her relief. She looked into her mirror and saw the black sedan pull into a driveway, back out fast and speed off in the opposite direction. "Wise move," she said as she hit the button to lower her window. "You really do *not* want to meet my bear."

Tucker coasted toward her, his powerful body showcased in black cycling shorts and the form-fitting jersey, and stopped beside her window. "I've got a mechanical problem," he said, pulling his helmet off. "Need to grease a bracket." He glanced back at the house. "Did you forget something at the store?"

"No." She looked over her shoulder. "Tucker, did you see that black Lexus?"

"Just somebody turning around." With the back of his arm, he wiped perspiration from his forehead. "Can't be a local, or he'd know better than to drive so fast in this neighborhood." He looked at her intently. "Are you feeling sick?"

She shook her head, then realized that unless she explained everything, Tucker would fix his bike and ride off again, leaving her alone when she was feeling all jittery. "W-would you mind coming into the house?"

she asked.

Suspicion flickered in his eyes. "Who was in that car?"

"I don't know. But it was following me." There. She waited for his face to relax, waited for him to laugh.

He didn't. "Let's get you inside," he said tightly.

She insisted on helping to carry the groceries in. By the time Tucker settled her at the kitchen table with a glass of vegetable juice, she had spilled the whole story. But he continued asking questions as he put the food away. "And you didn't get any part of the license number?" he asked for the third time.

"I just didn't think about it."

"Okay." He looked grim as he stowed a bag of carrots in the vegetable crisper. "You were scared."

She tapped her short fingernails against the side of her glass. "I suppose it's silly, but I was."

"Not silly," he said, closing the refrigerator too hard.

"Maybe he thought he recognized me from school or something," Shelby ventured. She could easily imagine that. Get a little closer, get a better look; nope, it's not her; drive on. That made a lot more sense than some evil-stalker scenario. This was *Dublin.* People didn't get murdered here. Yes, she'd been creeped out for a minute, but with all these crazy hormones bouncing around inside her these days, everything spooked her.

Tucker pushed a hand through his sweat-dampened hair. "We're reporting this."

Shelby sat up straighter. "To the police? What's there to report? I told you, I barely even saw the guy."

"Then I'll just mention it to Emilio and Kristin," he said, naming two of his bike-riding cop buddies. "Our quiet little street isn't patrolled very often, but they'll give it some extra attention if I ask."

"All right. Thank you." She was already feeling better.

Tucker gave her a long, serious look. "When you're home alone, I want you to keep the doors locked. Even in the daytime. If you're out in the back yard, make sure the front door is locked. And if you're in the front —"

"Okay, okay," she said, growing irritated. Reasonable precautions were one thing, but she wasn't going to be a prisoner in this house.

"And you know Kill's good about barking at strangers," Tucker continued. "But I still want you to check the peephole before you open the door to anyone."

She bristled. Next he'd tell her not to cross the street without holding somebody's hand. "I'm not a child, Tucker. I appreciate it that you're taking this seriously, but let's not blow it out of proportion. Yes, I was a little rattled just now, but if it hadn't been for that other time, I might not even —"

"*What* other time?" he barked, his brown eyes bulging with shock, worry and exasperation. "Have you been followed before?"

"I'm not sure," she said, squirming under his unwavering gaze. "A few weeks ago there was a red pickup truck that seemed to be everywhere I went. But I —"

"And there were the phone calls," he muttered, running his hand through his hair again. He pinned Shelby with a stern look. "Have you had any more of those?"

"No. But everybody gets calls like that, right? You can't tell me *you've* never had any."

"This is just too many coincidences," he said. "So we're going to be extra careful. The next time you feel the slightest bit uneasy about *anything,* Shelby, you're going to call me."

She was a little offended by his now-hear-this tone, but it was comforting to know he was so concerned about her safety. Memory rushed back and she heard again the words he had spoken on their wedding night: *I want to be the safe place you run to.*

Never in her life had Shelby had a safe place to run to. Even David hadn't offered her that. She watched the muscles in Tucker's sturdy right arm flex as he stowed a gallon of milk in the refrigerator. "I might have called you," she admitted finally. "But I don't have a cell phone."

He unzipped one of the back pockets of his jersey and produced a tiny blue phone, which he set on the table in front of her. "Use this until we get you one of your own. If I'm not here or at the store, just call 9-1-1."

As he folded the paper grocery sacks and stashed them in the pantry, Shelby watched his broad back and thought about how strong he was, not just physically, but emotionally and spiritually. She'd done the right thing in marrying him. Capable and fiercely protective, he'd be an excellent father.

Shelby picked up the phone and pressed it against her heart, so relieved that she nearly burst into tears.

The next evening Shelby and Roadkill

snuggled together on the leather sofa, watching a comforting array of candles flicker on the coffee table as they listened to a Beethoven symphony. As contentment rolled over Shelby like a warm, gentle wave, she petted Roadkill. But he stiffened, then leaped off the sofa and scrambled to the front door, barking shrilly.

Shelby was already on her way when the bell rang. Reaching the door, she didn't grasp the knob, but rose on tiptoe and peered through the little lens. And saw an answer to prayer.

"Quiet down," she commanded the yapping poodle. Like a barking, dancing toy dog whose switch had been turned off, he stilled immediately. Shelby chuckled and opened the door.

She greeted Bryan Arby with a warm smile and told him Tucker wasn't home yet. "But come in and wait," she urged, eager for an opportunity to talk to Bryan. "Let's have a cold drink."

He followed her to the kitchen, explaining that Tucker wasn't at the store and he wasn't comfortable talking to anyone else. Pointing to the refrigerator, Shelby urged him to help himself, then she ducked into the dining room — now her studio — to switch off the CD player. "Grab me a diet cola," she called over her shoulder.

"That was Beethoven's Fifth Symphony," Bryan said when she returned to the kitchen. "You didn't have to turn it off."

Shelby smiled her thanks as he handed her a canned soft drink. "Are you into classical music?"

"I like everything." His mouth tilted into a smile that made him look more like a sweet boy than the hard-edged kid he tried to be. "But late at night I listen to the classical station because Mom's room is next to mine, and she doesn't want to hear my other music when she's trying to sleep."

Shelby snapped the tab on her can and folded it back. "I'm a violinist," she said, hoping that would interest him.

He stopped gulping cola and said, "Hey. You any good?"

"Come and see." She led him into the studio, where she unsnapped the violin case that lay on one of the dining chairs lined up against the wall. When she lifted her instrument from its blue-velvet bed, Bryan's eyes shone with admiration.

He moved closer and with two careful fingers, lightly stroked the gleaming wood. "Is it worth much?"

Shelby felt a shiver of apprehension, but she forced a light tone as she tightened and lightly rosined her bow. "Actually, it was *this* thing that maxed out my credit card. A good bow costs a thousand dollars and up." She snuggled her instrument under her chin and without bothering to tune, played a snippet from a Bach sonata.

"Wow." The unabashed admiration in Bryan's light-blue eyes was one of the most satisfying compliments Shelby had ever received. "So what are you, like, in a group or something?"

"Sometimes I play in a string quartet," she said, returning the violin to its case. "But mostly, I teach kids how to play." She hesitated, then asked, "Would you like to learn?"

Interest flared in his face but was gone in an instant. Bryan looked down at his sneakers. "I don't have any money."

Excitement squeezed Shelby's heart. "But would you like to learn?" she asked again. *Lord, help me reach him.*

When Bryan looked up, his features were arranged in one of those stony, I-don't-care looks he excelled at. "Maybe."

"The violin's a difficult instrument to play well," Shelby cautioned. "You have to be intelligent, coordinated and have an ear for music. But most of all, you have to practice every single day." She swept him with what she hoped he would take as an assessing look. "Not many people can handle all that."

He flipped his hair back. "I'm real musical."

Concealing her eagerness, Shelby lifted a shoulder, giving I-don't-care right back to him. "I guess I could give you free lessons for a while. One hour a week."

Again his eyes blazed with interest, but he quickly doused the fire. "Problem." He spread his hands, demonstrating their emptiness, except for the soda can. "I don't have a violin."

But Mr. I-don't-care was hooked. "I know where you can rent one," Shelby said with studied casualness. "You can afford that now that you'll be working for Tucker."

Bryan shoved his free hand into a pocket of his baggy jeans. "I don't think he's going to pay me. I owe him money."

"You'll be making what I start all the other guys at," Tucker said from the doorway.

Strange. She hadn't heard him come in, and unexpected noises from behind her usually made Shelby's heart skip. But this time Tucker's rumbling voice had been a welcome sound.

She turned and found his alert, black-coffee gaze searching her face. I'm all right, she communicated with a smile.

The bunched muscles in his jaw instantly relaxed and his shoulders dropped as he released an audible breath. If a movie director had instructed him to look desperately relieved, he couldn't have done it any better, Shelby thought with amusement.

Tucker's gaze shifted to Bryan. "I'll keep half of your earnings until you've paid your debt. That'll leave you with some spending money. But when school starts I'm going to insist on seeing some good report cards or you'll be gone."

Bryan's studied coolness had deserted him. His mouth hung open and the entire room seemed to pulse with his amazement at Tucker's remarkable generosity. "That would be g-good," he stammered. "Thanks."

Shelby checked an impulse to hurl herself into Tucker's arms and just beamed at him, instead. Read my mind, she implored silently. Know how grateful I am.

He looked straight into her eyes and smiled.

# CHAPTER TWELVE

Shelby cleared several sheets of music off her wooden stand and replaced them with something thirteen-year-old Beth Hays had never seen. "Up for a little sight-reading?" she asked, pretending to be unaware of her student's wide-eyed concern.

As Beth shook her head at the new music, Shelby heard the front door open and close. Some odd-sounding bumps and thumps followed, accompanied by some incoherent groaning and grumbling that didn't sound like good-natured Tucker at all.

"It's just a nice little waltz," Shelby assured Beth. "Let's do it together." She picked up her violin, wincing at the sound of chair legs scraping across the kitchen's quarry-tile floor. Another muffled thump jarred loose memories of her father coming home late at night, staggering drunk. Tucker wasn't a drinking man, so Shelby quickly peeled her mind off that, but what was he *doing* in there?

She excused herself and hustled to the kitchen, where she found him in front of the sink with one foot on a chair as he turned on the tap, full blast. Shelby gasped when she saw that he was wringing blood from a yellow dish towel.

He glanced over his shoulder, his face pinched and pale. "I apologize for the noise," he said, almost grunting the words. "I've had a minor mishap."

*Minor?* It looked as if he'd been lucky to live through it. One of his muscular arms was badly skinned from elbow to wrist. And from the knee down, the front of his right leg was covered with blood. Her morning sickness aside, Shelby wasn't squeamish, so it wasn't seeing the blood that shook her. It was the idea that Tucker had been hurt, that he might have been *killed,* that made her clutch the edge of the counter for support.

Lightning-quick, he pulled his leg down and shoved the chair at her. "Sit," he commanded. "Head between your knees."

Shelby worked to swallow a bubble of hysterical laughter. Tucker looked as though he'd just had an unfriendly encounter with a meat grinder, and he was worried about *her* feeling woozy. But she sat. "You got hit by a car," she squeaked.

"No, I didn't." He limped over to the table, dragged another chair to the sink, and put his leg up again. "Just picked up a little road rash."

"Road rash?"

One corner of his mouth jerked in what Shelby took to be a combination of humor and pain. "I have sensitive skin," he said, squeezing water out of the towel. "Whenever it comes in contact with fast-moving asphalt, I get this odd reaction."

She let out the breath she'd been holding. He couldn't be seriously hurt if he was joking about it. "What happened?"

He dabbed the towel against his dirty, bloody leg. "I'm afraid I took out a squirrel. He darted in front of me and hit my wheel. And I went endo."

"You went what?"

"The bike stopped, but I kept going. 'Endo' is the classic involuntary maneuver in which a cyclist flips over his handlebars." He held up his free hand and made a rapid circular movement with his index finger.

Shelby attempted to translate. "End over end?"

"Yeah. It's real exciting on a downhill at thirty miles an hour. I took off like an Olympic gymnast. Wish I had it on tape."

Trust Tucker to be a comedian at a time

like this. "It's a wonder you didn't break anything," Shelby said faintly.

He grimaced. "Actually, I broke my collarbone. I've done it before, and it's a feeling you don't forget." Although his words were casual, his voice sounded strained. He turned the blood-soaked cloth, revealing a three-inch-long gash on the outside of his kneecap. "I need some stitches, but I can't drive like this. Would you take me to the urgent-care clinic after your lesson?"

He was carrying this tough-guy act entirely too far. "I'll take you right now," she said, rising from the chair.

"Honey." He dropped the sodden towel in the sink and caught Shelby by the arm. "This is not an emergency. We can go later."

"But you're *hurt*," she whimpered, close to tears. What if he had landed in front of a speeding car? What if he hadn't come home at all?

She pressed her lips together and told herself she was making a mistake by leaning so hard on Tucker. She had no business depending on him. God had taken David. How did she know He wasn't planning to take Tucker, too?

She was sorry about his accident, but glad for this reminder that it was dangerous to trust him too much. To *like* him too much.

Still, he needed medical attention. Shelby squared her shoulders. "We're leaving *now*," she said firmly, "Just as soon as I see Beth out."

The clinic was only a couple of miles away, but the strained silence inside Shelby's car made the drive interminable. Agitation had sealed her lips, and Tucker didn't say a word, either, until she stopped at a traffic light. Then he turned to look at her. "It must have been hard on you, seeing all that blood. I'm sorry, Shel."

"Just be careful," she said tiredly, keeping her eyes on the road, even though she was going nowhere. "*Please,* Tucker. Don't do that to me again."

He leaned back against the headrest. "We had no business riding that night," he said quietly. "Why didn't I stop it?"

For a moment Shelby didn't understand, then she realized he was talking about David. Because he thought *she* had been talking about David. "I never blamed you for his accident, Tucker."

"You should have. It was my fault."

She looked at him. "That's ridiculous."

He sighed. "I never could tell him no. Even when I knew it was wrong. He'd give me that piratical smile, and every single time, I just —" He closed his eyes. "Well.

You know how he was."

She did. David had been full of life and laughter, and whenever anyone tried to rein in his reckless exuberance, David would flash that irresistible, don't-spoil-my-fun grin.

Shelby hadn't been able to resist David any better than Tucker had. But now she felt a guilty tightening in her stomach. She had been unfair to David, playing at love when she hadn't really felt it. And there was no way, now, to make it up to him.

The light changed and Shelby eased her foot off the brake and onto the gas pedal.

"He joked about it," Tucker said. "That night. He said, 'Come with me, Tucker, and make sure I don't kill myself.' "

"It wasn't your fault," Shelby said.

Tucker shook his head like a dog who wouldn't let go of a bone. "If I hadn't agreed to go, he might have backed down."

"And he might have gone by himself and died in the street without his brother to hold him," she fired back. "It wasn't your fault, Tucker."

"Yes, it *was*," he said fiercely. When Shelby glanced over at him, his dark eyes met hers in a stormy challenge. "I made David the way he was. And *you*, of all people, should *blame* me for that."

His vehemence stunned her. "What are you talking about?"

"Turn left here," he instructed, ignoring the question.

They had a short wait after Tucker checked in at the clinic's reception desk, but he seemed reluctant to talk anymore. Was he in that much pain? And what was all that about being responsible for David's recklessness? When he was X-rayed, stitched up, bandaged and back in Shelby's car, she asked. "What did you mean when you said you made David the way he was?"

He bit his lip and readjusted his arm sling.

"Never mind," she said quickly, pitying him as he grunted softly and shifted in his seat. "We can talk later." But in her mind, she replayed his words: *I made David the way he was. And* you, *of all people, should* blame *me for that.*

No, she didn't blame Tucker for anything. On the contrary, she *owed* him. He'd done so much for her and the baby.

His accident must really have shaken him up. And he was missing David. That was more than enough to account for his strange confession, so Shelby dismissed it from her mind.

"You need some fresh air and exercise,"

226

Tucker said on Sunday morning as they drove home from church. "How about a bike ride in the woods? It's a beautiful day for that."

"In the woods?" Shelby echoed, shocked. "You want to take me *mountain* biking?"

"Honey. This is Ohio. Stop looking at me like I just suggested a sprint up Pike's Peak."

All right, so central Ohio wasn't known for its hills. But Shelby wasn't the most athletic person in the world, and Tucker's idea of a nice little ride would probably kill her.

He rolled his eyes at her hesitation. "We'll stick to the paved trails and the instant you break a sweat, we'll stop."

"Should you be riding?" she asked. How could he even think about it, with a broken collarbone and all those stitches?

"Oh, it'll be risky," he said in a tone that mocked her concern. "Poking along beside you, I could lose my balance and fall over sideways."

Shelby would have smacked his arm to punish him for the lame joke, but half the bones in his big, dumb body were probably already broken, so she stuck out her tongue, instead.

"Oh, that's mature," he teased.

They went home long enough to change

out of their church clothes and eat a quick lunch of soup and sandwiches, then they hopped back into the SUV. "How's Bryan working out?" Shelby asked as Tucker drove to the bike shop.

"He's punctual, and he doesn't appear to be a slacker. I promised to take him for a long ride, just the two of us. You should have seen his face."

Shelby smiled, imagining it. "You're a nice guy, Tucker."

He nodded amiably. "And a great kisser." Grinning, he looked over at her. "Doesn't it ever bother you that you're letting all this go to waste?"

Yes, it did. Tucker wanted a real marriage, but Shelby would never be able to give him one. She sighed and looked out her window, wondering how long it would take him to accept that.

"Hey." His chuckle sounded only half-hearted. "I was angling for a laugh, not your pity."

"I don't pity you," she lied as he pulled up to the back door of the bike shop. "You knew what you were signing up for."

He let that go and twisted his key out of the ignition.

Twenty minutes later Shelby was tricked out like a well-sponsored professional cyclist as she rolled her new titanium steed out to the mostly empty parking lot and mounted up. Tucker watched her first few experimental strokes on the pedals, then called to her to be careful while he locked up the store.

Her body remembered this. You *didn't* forget how to ride a bike, and Shelby's confidence doubled every time she pushed a foot down and felt the wheels spin faster. With the warm wind in her face, she zoomed to the farthest end of the parking lot and for a few moments she was eleven years old again, young and wild and free on a sunny summer day.

Tucker twirled his key ring around one finger, watching Shelby as faint misgivings stirred in his gut. She wasn't athletic, but what was he so worried about? A six-year-old child could handle the trail he had in mind for her today.

If only she didn't look so delicate. She had just the right amount of padding in all the most interesting places, but with those fine-boned arms and legs, she just didn't look all that sturdy. He shook his head and went to lock the store.

An hour later, his edgy mood hadn't evaporated. He'd expected to be bored stupid on this trail, but it was turning into quite a strenuous ride. He was wearing himself out protecting Shelby. Was she riding too fast? Did she see that exposed tree root in the trail, just ahead of her? Was she drinking enough water?

"Am I pushing you too hard?" Shelby teased when he asked for the third time if she was ready for a break.

She had no idea. Tucker rolled to a stop beside her, noting the slight flush of her cheeks and the way her violet eyes glowed with pleasure. It was good to see her having fun, but he couldn't help worrying. "You're doing great," he said as they dismounted, took off their helmets and pushed their bikes under the dense canopy of a sycamore tree.

"There you go again," Shelby teased as she sank into the lush, cool grass. "Humoring the cranky pregnant woman."

Tucker snorted his amusement. She punished him with a playful shove and he fell back on the grass, laughing, ignoring the silent bolt of lightning that zapped his broken clavicle.

She flopped down beside him and raised herself on one elbow. "You have great hair," she said, thrusting her fingers into it.

Tucker shut his eyes and tried not to think about kissing her. He failed utterly.

Her fingers skimmed his scalp and then lifted, catching tufts of his thick hair and tugging lightly before letting go. "How come guys always get the best hair?" she demanded.

Tucker opened his eyes and looked straight into hers, so close. Her hand stilled and Tucker could almost hear a faint crackle as a spark of undefined emotion leaped between them. "Kiss me, Shel." He was shocked when the words jumped out of his mouth, but Shelby's lips parted softly as she gazed back at him with those beautiful not-blue eyes. Would she actually do it? Tucker closed his eyes and waited.

Whatever he had expected, it wasn't this. She gave him a full, sweet, deliciously long kiss, the kind he hadn't even hoped to experience for another couple of decades, the way things had been going lately.

"Tucker?" Her voice trembled with uncertainty.

"Yeah," he whispered, wanting to assure her that he'd felt it, too. This wasn't recreational kissing, but something with solid emotion behind it. It was wonderful, terrifying and comforting, and he didn't want it to end. She tried to move away, but he pulled her head down again.

Seconds later, she ended it. "I'm sorry,"

she muttered, her face turning pink as she scrambled on her hands and knees to retrieve her helmet. "I shouldn't have done that," she added, pushing up to her feet. The back she presented to Tucker remained board straight as she pulled the helmet over her bright hair and fumbled to fasten the chin strap. Tucker watched in bemused silence as she picked up her bike, mounted it and rode away.

Like a man who'd just had the wind knocked out of him, Tucker lay still in the grass. Whatever she wanted to pretend to herself, those had not been one-sided kisses.

He'd noticed several days ago that she was no longer flinching when he touched her. In the beginning her fear had been almost a palpable thing. But Tucker had been as patient as a horse-whispering cowboy with a skittish mare, and she was finally beginning to trust him.

He grinned up at the cotton-ball clouds that peeked at him from between gently swaying treetops. She was fighting it, and considering what she'd been through, he couldn't blame her. But she was definitely beginning to feel something for him. Something a whole lot more exciting than gratitude.

He curled up to a sitting position, grateful

for the pain in his shoulder because it proved he wasn't dreaming any of this. He filled his lungs with the earth-scented air of the forest and marveled.

He and Shelby were teetering on the edge of love. What would it be like when they finally fell?

He could hardly wait to find out.

# CHAPTER THIRTEEN

Tucker and Roadkill were out for an after-dinner stroll on Monday evening when Shelby filled the copper teakettle and placed it over a flame on the gas range. Selecting a tea bag from the box she'd found in the pantry, she thought again about yesterday afternoon and gave herself another mental kick.

Why had she kissed Tucker? It hadn't meant anything, but judging by the way he'd been looking at her since that regrettable incident — as if he knew a delightful secret she didn't — he must believe she was starting to fall for him.

She wasn't. End of story. And even if she *wanted* to, love didn't work that way. You couldn't just order it like a pizza and expect it to be delivered when and where you asked.

All right, she liked and admired him. And she was grateful for what he was doing for her and the baby. But none of that was love, so it had been stupid, stupid, *stupid* to kiss him.

She sighed. She'd been feeling out of sorts all evening, and right now she had a vague, crampy feeling low in her belly. Maybe a toasty cup of Perky Peppermint tea would help.

At least she wasn't sick. Come to think of it, it had been two whole days since she'd driven the porcelain bus, as Tucker so inelegantly put it. Was her morning sickness finally subsiding? What a relief it would be when those awkward dashes to the bathroom were a thing of the past.

The teakettle whistled. Shelby switched off the burner and poured boiling water over the tea bag she'd dropped into a mug. As her tea steeped, she opened the newspaper that lay on the counter. "The Guy's Guide to Women" had just been switched to Mondays, so she located the column and folded the paper back.

Now that she knew what kind of man he really was, Steve's rants were more entertaining than ever. She was grinning even before she got to the second paragraph, where he'd written:

The challenge of buying presents for a

woman is compounded by the fact that she'll compare your gifts to those her friends receive from their husbands and boyfriends. "Did you hear what Jake gave Tiffany?" is the post-holiday question every man learns to dread.

A smart man realizes that if he gives too small a gift, his woman will make him suffer. But if he's too extravagant, he'll be ostracized by his male friends for raising the bar.

Since there is so little margin for error, men should always consult their buddies before buying any gift for a woman.

Shelby chuckled. Too bad she couldn't broadcast to all womankind what she now knew about Steve Tucker; that underneath his rugged exterior throbbed a heart of solid gold. He was no Neanderthal, but a sweet and remarkably sensitive man.

As she continued to read, Shelby pressed a hand against her abdomen to ease a mild cramp. Was this kind of discomfort normal? She tried to remember where she'd last seen the pregnancy book. The spasm hit again, harder, and Shelby dropped the newspaper and glanced wildly around the kitchen. Where had Tucker left that book?

She heard the front door open, heard the

faint jingling of the metal tags on Roadkill's collar as he bounded inside and tried to stand still while Tucker unfastened the leash. Tucker strolled into the kitchen, but his usual cheerful greeting died on his lips when he saw Shelby slumped against the counter, clutching her abdomen. "Honey?" His hoarse whisper told her he had correctly assessed the situation.

Shelby's mouth worked, but fear had stolen her voice. She jerked involuntarily as another cramp sliced through her middle, and she saw her own terror reflected in Tucker's dark eyes. Feeling an awful rush of warmth between her legs, she refused to look down. But Tucker looked, and it was his horrified expression that ripped from Shelby's throat an anguished cry that had nothing at all to do with physical pain.

He lunged forward and scooped her up into his arms. "No!" he groaned as he clutched her tightly against his chest and rocked her like a small child. "No, no, no, no!"

"Don't let this happen!" Shelby wailed. As she folded her arms around Tucker's sturdy neck, desperation made her plead for an assurance she knew he couldn't give. "Promise me!"

She tilted her head back and met his

frightened eyes, darker than ever in a face that had gone white, and waited for him to tell her everything would be all right. "Don't worry," he always said to her, and she waited for him to say it now.

He didn't. The generous man who had made her so many promises and faithfully kept them all wasn't making *this* one, and Shelby knew why.

# CHAPTER FOURTEEN

It was just one of those things, Dr. Gruesman told them. She didn't know exactly what had gone wrong, but she insisted it hadn't been Shelby's fault. Miscarriages were far more common than most people realized. Even Dr. Gruesman had lost a baby that way.

None of that comforted Shelby as she reclined in a hospital bed and stared with hot, dry eyes at a relentlessly cheerful expanse of floral wallpaper. She was getting a cramp in her neck, but she kept her head turned toward the wall because that was easier than looking at Tucker's tortured face. She just wasn't up to that, or to conversation, or even tears. She was floating alone on a vast, black ocean of grief, and she wanted to be left alone.

Why had God done this to her? She had tried so hard, done everything she could to give her baby a wonderful start in life. She had even married a man she didn't love.

All for nothing.

She ground her teeth as Tucker lifted her limp hand and pressed his face into her palm and told her for the hundredth time how desperately sorry he was.

Why had God allowed her to marry Tucker? She had asked Him for guidance, begged Him to prevent the marriage if it wasn't the right thing for her to do. Clearly, it *hadn't* been right, but God hadn't seen fit to clue her in. She turned her head and looked at Tucker. "We should talk about what we're going to do now."

"Do now?" he echoed, drawing her hand to his chest and pressing it against his heart.

"About our marriage."

He looked at her sideways. "Our marriage?"

"We got married for one reason." To her ears, her voice sounded as toneless as a robot's, but it was a perfect reflection of the way she felt inside. "And since that reason no longer exists, why should the marriage?"

Tucker's brown eyes widened like a startled deer's.

"I'm sorry we did it." Shelby pulled her hand away from him and twisted her mouth into a brief, bitter smile. "It seems my little problem wasn't worth all this trouble, after all."

For an instant he looked even more shocked, but then his eyebrows snapped together. "It wasn't a 'little problem,' Shelby." He kept his voice low, but it throbbed with outrage. "It was a *baby.*"

The rebuke barely registered. Shelby's heart was saturated with misery; there was just no room for any more guilt or grief. She sighed. "I wanted so much to be a mother."

"I know." Tucker recaptured her hand and kissed her knuckles. "But you heard Dr. Gruesman. There's no reason you can't get pregnant again."

She jerked her hand out of his and sat up suddenly, accidentally bumping the table next to her bed and knocking over a half-empty cup of water. *"No reason?"*

"We're married," he said steadily, righting the cup and snatching a handful of tissues from the box on the table. "So when you're ready, there's no reason we can't —"

"No *reason,*" she repeated testily, stabbing him with a look that told him exactly what she thought of his bold assumption. "I've been telling you from the beginning that I would never —"

"Honey, please." He finished mopping up

the water and disposed of the soggy wad of tissues. "Let's discuss this later, after you've had some rest."

"There's nothing to discuss," she said hotly. "You married me so David's baby would have a father. That was incredibly noble of you, and I was more grateful than you'll ever know. But if there isn't going to be a baby, why should there be a marriage? You can have your freedom back."

"I signed on for life," he said with quiet dignity. "There were no conditions attached to the vows I made."

Shelby flopped back down onto her pillow and folded her arms. "Well, *I* don't want to be married anymore."

"What *do* you want?" Tucker asked in a tired voice.

She wanted God to stop smacking her down every time she drew a breath. She closed her eyes. "I just want all of this to be over."

"What about the vows *you* made?"

Her eyes flew open. "You can't seriously expect me to —"

"Honor them," he finished, his voice flat. "No. I guess I can't seriously expect you to do that."

His hopeless expression reminded Shelby that she wasn't the only one devastated by this loss. He had wanted the baby, too, because it had been David's. "I'm sorry I lost it," she said.

"Honey, stop saying that," he implored. "You make it sound like you failed in some way."

She shook her head, denying his compassion. She had failed in *every* way. Suddenly chilled, she grasped the thin blanket that had slipped down to her waist and pulled it up over her shoulders. "I need to be alone," she said, turning back to the wall and those happy flowers.

"I'll be in the waiting room across the hall," Tucker said.

"No," Shelby said to the wallpaper. "Just go home. Please."

He moved to the doorway. "That pill the nurse gave you was to help you relax," he said quietly. "Please stop fighting it, honey. Just close your eyes."

She waited until he left the room, then she did that.

Scheduled to undergo a quick surgical procedure the next morning, Shelby slept fitfully. Two or three times during the night she sensed a comforting presence beside her in the darkness, imagined a deep, soothing voice, a gentle touch. She knew none of it was real, but this dream world was kinder than reality, so she clung to it.

"Daddy," she whimpered when a large, warm hand was laid against her cheek. In the way of dreams, she was suddenly very young, four or five, maybe, and she was riding on his shoulders. His stride was confident, not staggering, and his breath didn't smell funny, and her mother was there, and they were happy.

When she opened her eyes, the harsh light of morning had flooded the hospital room and Tucker was sitting in the chair beside her bed. Rumpled and unshaven, sober and silent, he met her eyes and waited for her to speak.

"I thought maybe it was all just a bad dream." Her voice was husky from emotion and lack of use, so she cleared her throat. "I thought maybe I'd wake up and find it wasn't true."

He looked away from her and shook his head. A moment later, a nurse came in to prep her for surgery.

Tucker was beside her when she awakened. "Everything looks normal, Dr. Gruesman says." His gaze wavered for an instant, and a muscle twitched in his jaw. "And she repeated there's no medical reason why you can't get pregnant again."

Shelby wasn't so woozy that she missed

his careful inclusion of the word *medical.* She'd been just awful to him last night, and the poor man probably thought talking to her now was like navigating a minefield; if he didn't step just right, she'd blow up in his face. She squelched a guilty sigh.

"Dr. Gruesman was called away after your surgery," Tucker said. "She'll be in to see you early this afternoon, and she'll release you then." He paused. "And I called your mother. *Twice.*"

"Thank you," Shelby murmured, wondering at his bitter tone.

He flung himself out of his chair. "What's *wrong* with her?" he thundered, pacing beside the bed. "Why isn't she here?"

So that was it. Tucker didn't have all the facts; it was only natural that he'd assume her mother just didn't care. "She's not very demonstrative," Shelby said mildly.

He shot her a disbelieving look. "And why is that?" he demanded. "You're the sweetest person in the world, and she —"

"Don't." Shelby put up a hand, stopping him. "Please, Tucker. I know she seems a little distant sometimes, but —"

"A little distant? A *little?*" He barked out an ugly laugh. "Shelby, that woman is so distant she's practically on the moon! What's wrong with her?" he demanded again, curling his hands into fists. "Why isn't she here?"

"She doesn't like hospitals."

"This isn't about what she likes. Your heart has just been broken, and your mother should be here!"

"It's because of my father," Shelby said, desperately wishing Tucker hadn't pushed her into explaining this. "Hospitals make her think about . . . when my father . . ."

Tucker had gone still. "When he used to hurt you both."

Shelby closed her eyes and nodded, remembering the handful of times Diana had been hurt seriously enough to require emergency treatment. Nobody who knew her history could blame her for avoiding hospitals, even after all these years.

Tucker dropped back into the chair and then with a soft groan of anguish, surged forward and slumped over Shelby's bed. He lay across her arm, the top of his head pressing against her side. His face was buried in the folds of the cotton blanket, so she barely heard his muffled, "I'm sorry, Shel."

She pulled her arm out from under him, but didn't push him away. Instead, she laid her hand against the back of his head, her fingertips absently caressing the short, silky hair on his nape as she stared up at the flat white ceiling. After a minute her hand wandered higher, allowing her restless fingers to delve into the luxurious softness where his hair was longer. "I probably wouldn't have been a good mother, anyway," she sighed.

He shook his head against her ribs. "You *were* a good mother." Even muffled by the blanket, Tucker's deep voice conveyed fierce loyalty. "Your every thought was for that baby."

"Thank you, bear." Her voice came out pinched because gratitude was swelling her heart and crowding her airway. "Thank you for believing in me."

"Oh, Shelby." His head pressed harder against her ribs. "Believing in you is the easiest thing I've ever done."

Neither of them moved for several minutes, but then Shelby remembered something. "Tucker." Guessing he'd fallen asleep, she lightly squeezed the back of his neck. "Hey, you forgot Bryan."

He lifted his head and blinked at her. "What?"

"You were supposed to ride with Bryan this morning."

"Yeah." He sat up and checked his watch. "In half an hour. I'd better call him right now."

"You could still make it." Shelby reached for the bed controls.

"I'll call him, Shel. He'll understand."

"He won't," she said with conviction. She pressed a button and the bed whirred and raised her to a sitting position. "All he'll know is that you made him a promise and didn't keep it. That's what his dad keeps doing, promising that they'll spend time together and then telling him something has come up at the office. I know this is different, Tucker, but you can't expect him to understand. He's just a kid, and he's been hurt."

Tucker's mouth tightened, but he didn't respond.

"*Please,* bear. Show him he's important to us."

"All right." He rubbed the black stubble on his jaw. "Dad's just down the hall. Will you let him sit with you for a while?"

*Stephen?* Shelby stared. No wonder Tucker had gone ballistic about her mother not coming. "Why is he here?" she asked, misery adding a brittle edge to her tone that she hadn't intended.

Tucker slanted her a look of reproach. "He's *concerned* about you. You're family."

Not for long, she wouldn't be, and that hurt. But she ought to have realized she could never have truly belonged to the Sharpe family, no matter how kind Stephen had been to her. Families were gifts from God, after all.

And God just wasn't in the habit of giving gifts to Shelby.

Tucker changed into his cycling clothes and was dragging his bike out the front door when Bryan pedaled down the drive.

"Sorry I'm late," the boy said as he dismounted and laid down his bike. "I was renting a violin," he announced proudly, then pointed toward the house. "Mind if I go tell Shelby?"

"She's not here," Tucker said. "She's in the hospital."

Bryan's slender body tensed visibly. "*What?* Is she okay?"

"Yes," Tucker replied, but then his innate honesty compelled him to shake his head. "No. Not really. Something bad happened last night, Bryan. Shelby had a miscarriage."

"You mean she lost her baby?" The boy looked stunned. "That's *terrible.*"

Tucker could manage only a bleak nod as a fresh onslaught of grief slammed into his gut.

"But Shelby's okay, right?" Bryan's blue eyes were wide with concern. "I mean, you're *here,* so she must be okay."

"She's very upset. But physically, she's all right." Tucker watched a young gray squirrel dart up the trunk of a black walnut tree. As his eyes were drawn upward, he frowned, resenting the cloudless blue sky. It was a sparkling clear morning, just as perfect as the one after David died, and there was just something about beautiful weather that made sorrow even harder to bear. "She'll come home later today," he told Bryan.

"But shouldn't you be with her? How can you even think about going for a bike ride now?"

"I promised you we'd ride today. I told her you'd understand, but she made me come. She didn't want you to be disappointed."

"But I don't think we should be having a good time right now," Bryan protested. "Isn't Shelby, like, upset and stuff?"

"Yeah," Tucker acknowledged in a choked voice. She was upset and stuff. But she wasn't crying, even though her heart had been pounded flat. Why wasn't she crying?

He had to get back to her. She could rail at him all she wanted, but he wasn't going to ride today. "Would you accept a rain check?" he asked Bryan.

"Dude. That's what I'm trying to *tell* you.

I can't believe you guys even thought about me." In his signature I-don't-care move, Bryan flipped his blond curls back from his face.

"Of course we thought about you." Tucker silently thanked God for giving Shelby this insight. This trip home *had* been necessary. The ride wasn't the important thing; Bryan had just needed Tucker to show up for it.

"It's not like I'm anybody special," the boy said gruffly.

Tucker's heart clenched as he recalled a long-ago night when David had used those exact words. "Don't talk stupid," he told Bryan, echoing the reprimand he'd given David back then. "God cares about you, and so do we."

Bryan's spine straightened and he seemed to grow five inches and age as many years. "I'm sorry about your baby," he said gravely, holding out his hand.

Tucker hesitated, then grasped it and squeezed hard. "Thank you. I'll tell her you said that."

"Will you tell her something else?"

"Sure."

"She's been pestering me to go to church with you guys." Bryan looked down and kicked at the grass with the toe of his shoe. "Tell her I'll go. Just one time, though." He looked up, an apology in his blue eyes. "I'm just not into all that God stuff, so I don't think I can promise any more than that."

"Then don't. A man who makes a promise and doesn't keep it isn't much of a man."

Bryan nodded solemnly. "You tell her I promise one Sunday."

When Bryan had gone, Tucker returned to the house. He opened one of the French doors in the living room so Roadkill could go out, then he slogged to the kitchen and filled the poodle's food and water dishes. That chore completed, he slumped against the counter, bracing a hand on either side of the sink.

He would never look into a little boy's or girl's face and see David. But what hurt even more than that was having to witness Shelby's horrible grief.

It was impossible to see God's wisdom in any of this. Shelby's faith had been foundering for some time now, and this latest heartbreak would surely drag her under.

*"Why?"* Tucker cried, slamming a fist on the countertop. "There has to be a *reason!*"

As the ghosts of his angry words floated in the air around him, Tucker fought to control his ragged breathing. Who was he to question the wisdom of God?

He was just a man. But he knew God

understood grief and frustration, so he didn't hesitate to ask, softly this time, "*Why, Lord?* You know she can't take any more."

# CHAPTER FIFTEEN

"Does it hurt?"

Tucker had stopped for a red light and was looking over at Shelby, his voice as tight and unnatural as his white-knuckled grip on the steering wheel. She didn't understand his question until she followed his anxious gaze and saw her palms resting against her abdomen in the unconscious, protective gesture that was universal among pregnant women. She moved them. "No. It doesn't hurt." Not in the way he meant.

"I hope you'll be able to sleep a little," he said.

Oh, yes. She craved sleep now. She ached for oblivion and was grateful for the lingering anesthetic that would help her achieve it.

"We'd better get some food in you," Tucker said a minute later as he pulled into their driveway.

"I don't want anything."

"I'll just make some coffee, then. Wouldn't that be good with a nice, fudgey brownie?"

"No," she said as he brought the SUV to a stop in front of the house. "Thank you."

"Hey." Tucker attempted a grin, but his eyes failed to light up. "You know you've never met a brownie you didn't like."

Couldn't he just leave her *alone?* "My baby's gone," Shelby said through clenched teeth. "You can't fix that, Tucker. You can't make it all better with chocolate."

She saw a spasm of pain cross his lean face and didn't care. There was no compassion in her now, just furious grief, and she loosed it on him. "You always tell me everything's going to be all right. I almost believed you could *make* everything all right." She hated the hysterical pitch of her voice, hated the ugly words she was hurling at him, but was helpless to stop because something inside her had broken. "But you can't make *this* all right, can you, Tucker?"

"No." He hung his head. "I can't make this all right."

Roadkill met them at the front door. Shelby sensed his eager quivering but didn't glance down. She wasn't going to risk her heart again, not even on a dog. She walked away, and when Tucker called her name, she only quickened her pace. Gaining the sanctuary of her bedroom, she closed the door, shutting out the whole world.

Tucker tipped his head against her bedroom door and listened for movement inside the room. Satisfied that she was asleep, he penned a note and left it on the kitchen table.

On his way out the front door, he met Diana coming up the walk. He explained that Shelby was asleep and that he had an appointment. "But please go on in," he added as her flawlessly madeup face darkened. Did she actually think he meant to bar her from seeing her daughter?

Although Tucker hadn't wanted to leave Shelby alone in the house, he wasn't wild about leaving her in the care of her cold-fish mother, either. But wasn't his presumption that he knew what was best for Shelby a large part of what was making her so miserable right now? Clearly, he *didn't* have all the answers.

Sliding behind the wheel of his SUV, he tortured himself by wondering what David would think of him now.

It wasn't like he'd *wanted* to marry Shelby, he told himself as he pulled out onto the road. And because it hadn't been an easy thing to do, not by any stretch, he'd thought it must be the *right* thing. So when Pastor Dean had advised against the marriage, Tucker had plowed ahead, dragging Shelby with him.

Now the baby was gone and Shelby had flung herself into a sea of despair. And she'd said it all, hadn't she, when she'd pierced Tucker with those anguished, dry eyes and yelled that he couldn't make any of this right?

Becoming aware that he was bearing down too hard on the gas pedal, he eased off. But the brilliant summer afternoon was just too perfect. Tucker slid his sunglasses on, mitigating some of the unbearable beauty. That's right, he thought bitterly, shut the world out. It's what *she* does.

Remorse followed on the heels of that ugly thought. If he had the slightest idea what God expected him to do now, he'd do it, whatever the cost. But God was silent, and Tucker had never felt more alone in his life. He signaled for a turn and pulled into the church parking lot. Maybe Pastor Dean could help him find some answers.

The secretary wasn't at her desk, but Tucker was expected and the pastor's office door stood wide open, so he approached it and rapped twice on the door frame.

"Tucker." Pastor Dean rose from behind

the mountain of books on his desk and hurried over to envelop Tucker in one of his signature embraces, which was part handshake and part bear hug. "I'm so sorry about your loss."

Tucker held his body taut, refusing to be comforted by the friendly touch, rejecting the man's sympathy because he couldn't possibly have deserved it any less.

Pastor Dean closed the door and indicated one of the vinyl chairs in front of the desk. It was the one Tucker had occupied the last time he'd been in this office, the day he'd thumbed his nose at this godly man's wisdom and gone his own stubborn way.

He would have preferred to hide behind his sunglasses, but good manners won out and Tucker removed them, hooking them on the neckband of his T-shirt. Then like a child who knew he deserved chastening, he sat down and bowed his head. "I thought it was the right thing to do," he began in a husky voice. "But now everything has fallen apart and, as sorry as I am, I can't fix it."

Resuming his seat behind the desk, Pastor Dean removed his glasses and polished them with a wrinkled handkerchief. "What is it that you're sorry about?" he asked, squinting at Tucker.

"Getting married." Tucker exhaled hard,

venting his self-disgust. "You were right. We shouldn't have done it. I told myself it was all about honor, but it was just stubborn pride." He shook his head. "You knew that, didn't you?"

"I can't read hearts," the pastor said quietly. He slid his glasses on and adjusted them on the wide bridge of his nose. "But you did seem rather desperate to get married."

"I pushed her into it." The honest, awful words burned Tucker's throat and made his voice raspy. "She was scared and confused, but I promised her I'd make everything all right."

"It was a difficult time." The pastor's voice vibrated with compassion as he rested his forearms on a stack of books and laced his fingers together. "Both of you were hurting."

"And now it's even worse," Tucker went on, barely hearing him. "We've just lost David all over again. And she says there's no point in staying married."

"I'm sorry to hear that."

"I should never have talked her into it." Tucker rubbed the back of his neck. "Pastor, how does a man carry a load like this?"

Pastor Dean's bushy gray eyebrows rose a fraction. "He shouldn't try. He should drop it at the foot of the cross. This is one of the sins our Savior died for, Tucker. If you have confessed it, lay it down. Thank God for His forgiveness. Then ask Him for strength and courage to face the hard times ahead."

Strength to continue watching Shelby fall apart? To just stand there, completely powerless, and *watch,* knowing that he had dragged her into this unwanted marriage? Could even God give a man *that* much strength?

His heart saturated with despair, Tucker stared at the faded carpet, shaking his head. "I've ruined her life."

"Oh, now, that's a little harsh," Pastor Dean said in tones of gentle deprecation. "Maybe you did run ahead of God, but I've been watching you, and frankly, I wish every man treated his wife with the respect and tenderness you've shown to yours."

Tucker's head jerked up at the unexpected affirmation.

"You and I may have disagreed about this marriage, Tucker, but it's now an accomplished fact. And the truth is, son, you've done an awful lot of things *right.*"

"But God took the baby," Tucker reminded him. "And now Shelby's trapped in a marriage she never wanted."

"Have you asked her to forgive you for

your part in that?"

Tucker let out a harsh breath. "If I can't forgive myself, what business do I have asking her to do it?"

"Ah. Fascinating question, that." Behind his glasses, Pastor Dean's big gray eyes snapped with interest. "I suppose you meant it to be a rhetorical one, but I'd like to attempt an answer, if you'll permit me."

Startled, Tucker just looked at him.

"The fact is, you *can't* forgive yourself. If you sin, God expects you to confess and repent and then seek *His* forgiveness. You confess, you repent, He forgives. That's the deal." He unclasped his hands and turned his palms upward in a gesture inviting Tucker's consideration. "If we could forgive *ourselves* for sinning, why would our Lord have died on the cross?"

Tucker nodded dumbly. Of course he knew that. Hadn't he learned 1 John 1:9 as a kid? *If we confess our sins, he is faithful and just to forgive us our sins and will cleanse us from all unrighteousness.* There was nothing complicated about that. God's forgiveness was complete.

"Now for the other part of your question," Pastor Dean continued. "You're implying that asking Shelby to forgive you is something you would do merely for your own benefit." He slid the stack of books forward, making a space to fold his arms on the desktop. "But holding on to resentment takes a lot out of a person. Wouldn't you rather see Shelby let go of that?"

"Yes," Tucker whispered, dumbfounded. Again, he *knew* this stuff. Where was his brain today?

Pastor Dean regarded him with fatherly concern. "Tucker, you're exhausted. I'll pray with you now, but then you'd better go home. Things will look a little clearer after you've had some rest. And we can talk more tomorrow or whenever you like."

Tucker wouldn't hear of her moving out. He insisted that if they couldn't live together, he would be the one to go.

That made no sense to Shelby because the house was his. But she was desperate to be alone, so she agreed, privately resolving not to stay long. Just a couple of weeks, maybe, until she could pull herself together and find an apartment.

It took only an hour for Tucker to pack his things and load the SUV. Shelby hid out in her studio, playing arpeggios on her violin, doing her best to concentrate on technical perfection and not notice Tucker's trips in and out the front door.

When he spoke from behind her, telling her he'd be leaving in a minute, Shelby lowered her violin, but didn't turn around.

Hearing a soft plop, she turned her head and saw he'd tossed his house key atop the stack of sheet music on the table beside her. She frowned at it. "What's that for?"

"You'll want to feel safe."

That was ridiculous. She laid her violin on a chair and turned to look at him. "I'm not afraid of you, Tucker."

"Yes, you are. You're terrified that you might begin to feel something for me."

She was too agitated to refute that, and he turned away. She stared at the empty doorway for a full minute before something snapped inside her and she stalked to his room. "I'm doing you a favor," she said to his broad back as he leaned over the bed, tucking his laptop computer into its carrying case. "You need to get on with your own life."

"Thanks for thinking of me," he said dryly.

She sagged against the door frame and watched as he zipped the case. They weren't really married, so what was this sense of loss that kept nipping at her heart? She shoved it away. "You'll meet somebody," she said. "You'll fall in love without even trying.

I want you to have that, Tucker. You deserve it."

"I made promises to you," he said, yanking his printer's cord from the electrical outlet. "And I'll keep them."

She let him see her exasperation. "Tucker, it's not like this was ever a real marriage."

"I have a piece of paper that says different."

"You know what I mean."

"Yes, I know what you mean." He folded the power cord into a bundle. "But marriage is a whole lot more than sleeping together, Shelby. Haven't you figured that out yet?"

"I don't care. I don't want it. I want my old life back."

"Honey," he began in a maddeningly patient, let's-be-reasonable tone. "You can't have your old life back."

"Yes, I can. And I will."

He tucked his printer under his good arm and picked up the computer case. "And one day you'll meet a wonderful man and fall in love and everything will be beautiful, right?" His expression turned stony. "No, I don't think so. Because you'll never forget David and the baby and your first husband, will you, Shelby?"

"Stop it," she cried, fighting a juvenile

urge to cover her ears.

He shook his head, relentless. "We're your baggage, honey. Wherever you run, you'll carry all three of us with you. You can hire a lawyer and make yourself single again, but you can't change history. This was real, Shelby. This *happened*."

"No," she squeaked. She *wouldn't* carry them with her. She'd forget, just like she had forgotten her father.

Tucker hung his head, and they were both silent for several moments, until Roadkill trotted into the room. Tucker glanced at the poodle and then looked at Shelby, his eyes full of apologies. "He's staying here."

"No," Shelby protested. "He's your dog. I couldn't —"

"You know I never wanted him," Tucker said gruffly. "He'll be good company for you, and he'll bark at strangers."

Shelby sighed. "Please stop worrying about me, Tucker."

"I will, honey. Just as soon as I forget how to breathe." He leaned down and kissed her cheek. "I'll be at Dad's. If you need me to come over and kill a spider or something, just call."

"I'll be fine." She would be fine if it killed her.

He squatted down beside Roadkill. "I

expect you to behave like a real dog," he said, ruffling the poodle's ears, then he straightened and walked past Shelby.

She squeezed her eyes shut, not wanting to see him leave. His footfalls sounded like bullets on the slate floor, then they stopped and Shelby heard the door open. After a breathless silence, it closed softly.

And Shelby was alone.

# CHAPTER SIXTEEN

Whether worn out by grief or because she was still feeling the effects of anesthesia, Shelby slept most of that evening and even made it through the night without any trouble. The next day was difficult, and the following night pure misery. At 2:00 a.m. she wandered into Tucker's room and pulled open the top drawer of his nightstand, hoping to find one of the spy novels he liked to read. But the drawer contained only one book, his copy of *Lifetime Love.*

Waves of regret rolled through Shelby as she sat on his bed and leafed through the book. Its pages were no longer crisp, but dog-eared. There was a stain from a coffee cup on one page, and a phone number penciled in the margin of another. On the inside of the front cover, he'd made several lists with a blue ballpoint pen. One summarized Shelby's likes and dislikes in books and movies. Another detailed her preferences in food. Her birth date was recorded, as was the date of their wedding.

Tears stung her eyes as she flipped through the book and read some of the passages he'd marked with a highlighter. How many hours had he pored over this book, determined to learn how to fall in love with his wife?

Overcome by a longing she didn't understand, Shelby picked up the phone. If Tucker was still up reading or writing, he might have his cell phone turned on. She entered that number and after just one ring, heard his deep, soothing voice: "I was hoping you'd call tonight."

She peeled her dry tongue off the roof of her mouth. "You weren't asleep?"

"No. I can't sleep."

"I can't, either," she confessed, trapping the phone between her ear and her shoulder as she pulled Tucker's pillow into her arms.

"Second thoughts about this?" he asked.

"No," she said quickly. "No. I was just —"

"Thinking about the baby. Do you want me to come over?"

It wasn't fair to ask him for anything. She shouldn't even have called him. "No," she said, squeezing the pillow tightly as she rocked back and forth in her agitation. "Thank you. It's just that I don't have anybody to talk to. Nobody understands."

She stopped and rolled her eyes, wondering if she could possibly sound any more pathetic.

"I'll be right there," Tucker said, and hung up.

Roadkill stood in the bedroom doorway, his ears pricked up, his bulgy brown eyes intent on Shelby's face. His short tail gave a couple of hopeful little wags, but he didn't leap at her until she tossed the pillow aside and held out her arms.

"I'm sorry," she said, gathering the wriggling poodle to her. She had ignored him for two days, but he licked her ear, holding no grudges, just happy to be wanted again.

She set him on the floor, then looked down at her gray Mozart sweatshirt and pink flannel pajama pants. Deciding she was modestly, if not fashionably attired, she tugged the scrunchie out of her hair and smoothed her wild curls, then wandered into the living room, where she lit some candles.

When she opened the front door a few minutes later, she smiled at Tucker and stepped back, giving him a subtle signal not to touch her. He read it perfectly and bent down to greet Roadkill, instead.

In silence they made their way to the living room, which was lit only by flickering candle flames. When Shelby sat on the sofa, Tucker moved behind it and rested his hands on her shoulders. An automatic protest rose in her throat but quickly died as he began to knead her tense muscles.

"Talk to me," he urged in a melting-chocolate voice she had no power to resist. "Tell me the stuff nobody understands."

Shelby closed her eyes. "Mom came to see me again. She says that although it hurts now, it will be better in the long run, not having the baby. Then Rachel called and said the same thing. They were both trying to comfort me, but they don't understand. They think I should be relieved. They think I can go back to being who I was before I met David." She opened her eyes and twisted her neck to look up at Tucker. "But I'm *not* relieved."

"I know." He palmed the top of her head and made her face forward again.

"And maybe I didn't love David the way I thought," she said as Tucker squeezed the back of her neck with a warm hand. "But he was a sweet man and I don't ever want to forget him."

"I know." Tucker's strong fingers began making small, circular movements on the ridges between her neck and shoulders.

"I can't go back," she said. "I can't be the

270

person I was. Too many things have happened, and I'm *different* now."

"I know, honey."

She closed her eyes, beginning to relax. "Nobody understands that."

"I do. And God does." Tucker continued his gentle ministrations until Shelby yawned, then he patted her shoulders. "Come on. I'll tuck you into bed."

"It's no use," she said miserably. "I won't sleep."

"You will tonight." He blew out the candles, then followed Shelby to her bedroom. When she lay down, he pulled the quilt up to her chin and kissed her forehead. He waited for Roadkill to settle at her feet, then he reached for the lamp.

"Tucker," she said urgently. She had to keep him talking. She didn't want to be alone, not yet.

"I'm not going anywhere." The room went dark, then the mattress dipped as he sat on the edge of the bed. "Scoot over a little," he urged, and she did. The bed jiggled and she heard a soft scuffling followed by two muted thumps as he dropped his shoes on the carpeted floor.

She tensed when he stretched out beside her.

"It's all right," he soothed, slipping his

arm under her head. "Just go to sleep."

This was a bad idea. Shelby knew that, but she was too upset and exhausted to remember why.

"Let it go, sweetheart." The rich timbre of Tucker's voice was as soothing as warm water. "You need to sleep."

She must have done that, because some time later she awoke to a sweet but unfamiliar warmth. Cocooned in her quilt and clasped in a pair of strong arms, she could barely move, but she didn't care because she didn't feel so alone now.

She had sent Tucker away, but when she'd needed him, he had come home. He hadn't asked for explanations or apologies, and he hadn't laid down any conditions. He was simply here, just as he had promised he would be, for better or worse.

Only he'd never known "better," had he? Again and again, he'd seen Shelby fall apart. Time after time, he'd calmly picked up the pieces and put her back together.

It had to stop. They would never have a real marriage, so even if he didn't realize it, she was doing him a favor by pushing him away.

Only she couldn't do it tonight. Maybe not tomorrow, either. The truth was that she didn't know how she'd ever get past this crippling grief without his help.

He sighed and shifted his head on the pillow, his mouth and chin grazing her forehead. Emboldened by the darkness and the knowledge that he was sound asleep, she reached up and lightly stroked his stubbly jaw with one finger. "Stay," she whispered. She closed her eyes, savoring his warmth. "Please stay, bear. It's so much better when you're here."

In the green glow of the light from Shelby's alarm clock, Tucker gazed down at his sleeping wife's form. Better to leave now than be thrown out when she awoke. She'd be ashamed of her weakness and she wouldn't thank him for staying with her.

But it had been so sweet, holding her, feeling her tense body relax in his arms and knowing that for a while, at least, she was at peace. He must have lain there watching her for a full hour before he, too, had drifted to sleep. Then when he had awakened just now and felt her silky curls tickling his chin, felt her small, soft hand resting against his neck, his heart had been stabbed with a hopeless longing.

She wasn't willing to give them a chance. And that was almost hilariously tragic because Tucker now knew beyond any doubt that he was deeply, irrevocably in love.

He turned away from her and sucked in a couple of deep breaths, working up the nerve to push himself through the bedroom doorway and out of her life.

"Tucker?" she called softly. "Are you leaving?"

His chin dropped to his chest. "Isn't that what you want?"

She didn't answer, so he turned around. She was propped up on an elbow petting Roadkill, who had been at the foot of the bed a minute ago but had now taken Tucker's place beside Shelby. "I'm not sure what I want," she said in a small, lost voice.

Tucker was glad for the semidarkness because it kept her from seeing what he had just discovered and didn't yet know how to hide. If she saw it she'd feel sorry for him and even worse than that, she'd feel guilty. "You two go back to sleep," he said, thrusting his hand into his pocket for his car keys.

*"Tucker?"*

He stopped in the doorway, hating the edge of panic he'd heard in her voice. "It's late, Shel. I have to go." Before he said something he'd never be able to take back.

"You don't have to go back to your dad's," she said. "Wouldn't you rather sleep in your own room?"

He smacked down the foolish hope that leaped in his chest. "You wanted me gone, remember?"

"What if I've changed my mind?" Her voice was steady, but pitched a little too high.

"Have you?" he made himself ask in an impatient tone that suggested he didn't care all that much.

"You're right," she said, hugging Roadkill to her chest. "It's very late."

He couldn't help himself. "Is it *too* late, Shelby?"

She wouldn't look at him. "Go on," she said in a choked voice that told him she was close to tears.

He meant to, but his feet were no longer taking orders from his brain. Anything you want, his heart drummed over and over. Anything. "I could stay," he said. "Is that what you want?"

"I don't know," she moaned, bowing her head over Roadkill. "Tucker, I don't *know* what I want."

He gave her several seconds to think about that, then he offered a gentle suggestion. "Maybe this isn't a good time for you to be making decisions."

She raised her head. "Would you stay if I

asked you to?"

With a tremendous effort he refrained from throwing a hopeless look at the ceiling. Why didn't she understand? Hadn't he shown her a thousand times? He dropped the keys back into his pocket, then walked over to the bed and sat beside her. "Whatever you want, Shel." Feel it, his heart begged. Feel it the way I do.

She leaned her head against his shoulder and sighed. "I'm not promising anything. Do you understand that?"

He did. And for now, it was enough. He kissed the top of her head and got to his feet again. "Go back to sleep," he said, forcing a light tone to reassure her. "You can dream about the chocolate-chip pancakes I'll be making for breakfast."

On Saturday evening Shelby was heading to her bedroom with a wicker basket full of freshly laundered towels when she nearly collided with Tucker in the hallway.

"Let me do that," he said, reaching for the basket.

"I think I'm capable of folding a few towels," she snapped.

He let go, biting his lip and nodding a silent apology as he faded back against the wall and allowed her to pass.

Grumbling inwardly, Shelby upended the basket of fluffy, sand-colored towels on her bed and began folding them. This just wasn't working. Tucker had been home for three days, but they hadn't fallen into their old, easy companionship. He was trying too hard, and that made Shelby feel even more on edge.

Roadkill trotted into the room and leaped onto the bed. "Get down," Shelby said roughly, pushing him away with an impatient hand. "I don't need dog hair on my clean towels."

"Shel?"

At the sound of Tucker's voice, low and tentative, Shelby's heart flooded with shame. "I'm sorry," she said, careful not to glance up as she plucked another towel from the pile and matched up its corners. "I don't know what's wrong with me tonight."

"You're grieving," he said from the doorway. "You've just suffered another devastating loss. Why are you always so hard on yourself? It's not wrong to *feel*, Shelby."

Yes, it was. For her, it was. Because if she gave in to her emotions just once, she'd never get them back under control. Once the monsters were out of the closet, there would be no stuffing them back inside.

"Let's get out of the house for a while,"

Tucker suggested. "We could go to the Irish Festival."

Shelby loved Celtic music, and the annual Dublin Irish Festival, which featured some of the biggest names in the genre, was a treat she gave herself every summer. But although she wasn't in the mood for lively fiddle tunes and step dancing demonstrations tonight, she owed Tucker an honest effort to pull herself together, so she assented.

She'd thought she was too keyed up to enjoy herself, but an hour later, she was smiling. Tucker captured her hand, and she was content to let him hold it as they browsed the booths and conversed with craftsmen. Shelby purchased an Irish linen handkerchief and a fragrant bar of heather-scented soap. Tucker made her laugh by buying himself a coffee mug that said, "I'm not Irish, but kiss me anyway."

They strolled the paths between several small stages where live music was being performed continuously, and when they heard something Shelby particularly liked, they stopped to listen for a while. As was usual when Tucker ventured out in public, he was greeted every ten paces or so by a friend. He was stopped by cops and firefighters, fellow business owners, a couple of cycling enthusiasts and — of course — three spectacularly beautiful women, including a raven-haired Irish singer who told Shelby this was only her second trip to the States.

So of course you know Tucker, Shelby groused silently. It wasn't possible that an attractive woman could have visited Dublin and missed the city's main attraction. Feeling an odd sizzle inside her chest when the singer dropped a coy reference to "the time we spent together last summer" in that annoyingly charming lilt of hers, Shelby tried to look politely interested but said little.

When the woman finally walked away, Tucker looked at Shelby. She knew she ought to say something, but the words, "She seems nice" simply refused to cross her lips.

Tucker studied her face for a moment, then chuckled. "I love it that you're jealous."

"I didn't say a thing," Shelby said airily.

He snorted. "Not out loud." He tucked her hand in the crook of his arm and started to stroll again. "It was hardly a romance, Shel. I took her to dinner and then I picked her up and drove her to the airport the next morning."

Shelby forced herself to yawn. "That was very nice of you."

"I'd love to meet her brother," Tucker said

with feeling. "He's a world-class cyclist. He had to drop out of this year's Tour, but he did great in the spring classics. He actually finished third in the Paris-Roubaix."

So where Shelby had seen a beautiful woman, Tucker had seen the sister of a world-class cyclist. That was a comforting thought, but it stirred up questions she didn't want to ask herself right now. Like why she'd never been jealous when beautiful women had spoken to David.

Darkness fell early, and a cool breeze stirred the air, bringing with it the musty smell of rain. Holding two brimming bowls of Irish stew, Tucker gestured with his elbow to indicate a large tent. Shelby preceded him inside, and they found places at one of the long tables in front of the stage. There they enjoyed their stew and Shelby nibbled a chunk of rustic Irish soda bread as Tucker regaled her with a hilarious story about the legendary temper of his half-Irish grandfather.

The early-August evening grew unseasonably cool as a thunderstorm threatened, then passed just north of them, leaving Shelby shivering in her T-shirt and khaki shorts. When she rubbed the goose bumps on her arms, Tucker gave her a thoughtful look and then excused himself, saying he'd be back in ten minutes.

He returned with two insulated cups of coffee and an armful of honey-colored Irish wool. "I saw this in one of the booths earlier," he explained as Shelby took the cups from him and set them on the table.

Her expressions of thanks were muffled as he piled the bulky fisherman's sweater on her head. When she found the neck opening and popped through, he grinned. "Thought I'd lost you."

"Why didn't you get one?" she asked, pushing her arms into the sleeves of the heavy garment.

"They didn't have any big enough."

When they sat down again, Shelby reached up to drape one arm across his broad shoulders in an attempt to share some her sweater's warmth.

He shook his head at her. "Thanks for the thought, but I've got a better idea." He scooted his chair until he sat directly behind her, his knees on either side of her hips. Then he handed her a steaming cup of coffee and leaned forward, folding his arms around her.

The crowd applauded wildly as a well-known Celtic group bounded onto the stage. Shelby rested her head against the curve of Tucker's shoulder and sipped her coffee as the band slid into a toe-tapping reel. Warm and comfortable now, she enjoyed the music and even the fresh, damp breeze that ruffled the curls on her forehead.

After a few minutes she put her cup on the table and settled back against Tucker. She felt a brief pressure on the top of her head, as if he had just kissed her there, but she didn't mind. Her eyelids drooped, and despite the loud music and the boisterous, hand-clapping crowd, she relaxed so completely that she might almost have fallen asleep.

As a catchy waltz drew to a close, Tucker brought his hands together to applaud. "This is nice," he said in Shelby's ear. When she nodded, he put his mouth even closer, sending a thrill up her spine as he added, "The music isn't bad, either."

Twenty minutes into the set, the tempo slowed and the lead singer began a sad, sweet ballad about a fisherman caught in a storm at sea. As his boat was dashed against a rocky coastline, the fisherman implored the wild wind to carry his loving farewells to his sweet young wife, who was heavy with a child the fisherman would never hold in his arms.

Shelby felt Tucker's arms tighten around her, but this time they didn't comfort. The song seemed to go on forever, its plaintive lyrics sharply underscoring the devastating losses Shelby had so recently endured. Maybe she hadn't really loved David, but she had built her dreams around him. Now he was gone, and the baby was gone, and while Shelby was confused about the feelings she was beginning to have for Tucker, she knew she would never risk dreaming again.

But the emotions she'd held back for so long were fighting to break free, and Shelby was on the edge of panic when she pushed herself out of Tucker's arms. "I need to go home," she said, springing up from her chair. She hurried out of the tent, picking up speed as she passed the stakes and ropes, heading sightless and mindless into the night.

Tucker caught her behind the stage and practically dragged her into a canvas-roofed area that was being used for storage. *"Cry,"* he ordered, pulling her roughly against him. When she tried to push him away, he tightened his grip. "Just *cry,*" he said harshly, like a man who'd been pushed past endurance. "Nobody will hear you."

"No." She made fists against his chest, holding herself away with rigid arms.

"Let it go, honey." His voice was pleading

now. "You can't keep this inside any longer."

She had to. Apart from all that blubbering she'd done when she was pregnant, she hadn't cried, hadn't *really* cried, in years. And she knew that if she started now, she'd never stop.

"All right," Tucker said after a moment. "Let's go home."

They didn't speak again, and when Tucker unlocked the front door of the house, Shelby slipped past him and fled to her room. She slammed the door and groped her way to the bed and then just sat there in the dark, miserable and dry-eyed.

After a few minutes she noticed that a slim moonbeam was spotlighting the set of Russian nesting dolls on her bedside table. Focusing her helpless rage on her father's gift, she snatched it up and hurled it against the wall, splitting the silence with a feral cry as the dolls broke open and their empty wooden shells rained down on the carpet.

She kicked off her sandals, ripped back her quilt and crawled into bed as the dam that had been holding back her grief finally gave way. She drew her knees to her chest and hugged them tightly, wishing she could make herself small enough just to disappear.

On the edge of his bed, Tucker sat hunched over, his elbows resting on his knees as he pressed his face into his hands. He'd been trying to pray, but the violent sobs coming from the other room were ripping through his chest, riddling his heart like bullets, breaking his concentration.

As far as he knew, she had never cried like this. Even the awful night he and his father told her about David, she'd just crumpled into a chair, shocked and silent. There had been something hideously unnatural about her grief, and as sharp and new as his own pain had been, Tucker had never pitied anyone more in his life.

When she was pregnant she had cried easily and often, but those short-lived tears had been an outlet for stress, not expressions of soul-searing grief. She had never cried like this. Not until tonight, when she had finally broken, giving way to the body-shattering sobs that had been building in her for weeks, perhaps even for years.

After an eternity she grew quiet and Tucker spoke softly to Roadkill. With the poodle at his heels, he walked to the closed bedroom door and tapped gently. There was no answer, so he carefully turned the knob and pushed the door open.

Light spilling in from the hall enabled him to see that Shelby's quilt was pulled over her head. Its steady rise and fall told him she'd finally drifted into an exhausted sleep.

"Go," he whispered to Roadkill. When the poodle trotted obediently past him and leaped onto the bed, Tucker felt a small measure of relief. When she awoke she'd find a warm little bundle of comfort curled up at her feet.

In the dim light Tucker noticed several small objects scattered across the floor. So that was the crash he'd heard. He wasn't quite sure what the funny little doll was, but he knew she kept it on her bedside table, and that had to mean it was important to her. He dropped to his hands and knees and crawled around on the carpet until he'd collected all the pieces — nothing was broken, it turned out — and figured out how to fit them together. Then he replaced the doll on the table.

He trudged back to his own room and collapsed on the bed, feeling drained. "Please, Lord," he whispered. He meant to go on, but no other words came. He felt Shelby's pain, and it was blinding, deafening. It numbed all of his senses and robbed his brain of every coherent thought. He clenched his fists and squeezed his eyes shut and again whispered his feeble, one-word prayer.

"*Please.*"

# CHAPTER SEVENTEEN

Dressed and ready for church, Shelby sat on the edge of her bed, chewing a fingernail as she rehearsed her apology. The phone rang, startling her, but Tucker caught it on the first ring. He was in the kitchen making Shelby a wonderful breakfast that she didn't deserve and wouldn't be able to swallow, not with this lump of shame stuck in her throat.

She thrust out her chin and exhaled hard, ruffling the curls that lay against her forehead. Then she stood, squared her shoulders and propelled herself out to the kitchen.

"Shelby." Tucker's voice was oddly pinched as he replaced the cordless phone in its charger. "Honey." He grasped her by the shoulders, steadying her for what had to be bad news. "Your stepfather had a heart attack this morning."

"Jack?" she asked stupidly.

Tucker squeezed her shoulders. "He's in

the hospital, and it doesn't look too bad, but they're not sure yet."

Shelby nodded, stunned. She didn't actually love Jack, but this was still a shock. Why did these awful things keep happening? "Where is he?" she asked.

Tucker named the hospital and relayed the information Diana had given him. Shelby knew her mother would be half out of her mind with worry, and being inside a hospital would push her to the edge of hysteria. "You go on to church," she said, not eager for Tucker to see that. "I'll call you later."

"No," he said, looking shocked. "I'm coming with you."

"You don't have to." She didn't want him there. If he thought he'd seen "crazy" last night, just wait until he saw Diana Dearborn trapped in a hospital waiting room.

"We're a family, Shelby. This is what families do."

"We're not a family, Tucker."

"We'll save that argument for later," he said tightly. "Right now, your mother needs you." He switched off the gas burner under a pan of oatmeal. "And you're too rattled to drive, so stop fighting me. I'll drop you at the hospital and you can call when you want me." He turned away, and as he pulled his car keys from his pocket, he muttered something that sounded like, "If you ever decide that you *do* want me."

They didn't speak all the way to the hospital, but when Tucker pulled up to the main entrance and Shelby reached for her door handle, he put out an arm to stop her. "Wait." His hand closed around hers. "I'm sorry. We should have done this before." He bowed his head and Shelby did the same.

When Tucker ended the prayer, Shelby again reached for the door handle, then hesitated. "Come in with me."

He shook his head. "It's okay. I'm sorry I lost my temper."

"Maybe you shouldn't listen to everything I say," she suggested. "Sometimes I'm a little confused about what I want."

He huffed out a breath and gave her a wry, weary smile. "No joke," he drawled with a tender sarcasm that made Shelby smile.

Minutes later, his hand pressed the small of her back and steered her off the elevator and toward a waiting room. A shockingly unkempt Diana spotted them and rose from a creaky vinyl sofa, clutching her handbag with the white-knuckled trepidation Shelby had expected.

"Mom." Knowing better than to touch her mother without an invitation, Shelby stuck to Tucker's side. "How is he?"

Diana shoved a messy lock of straight blond hair away from one eye. "Not dead, unfortunately."

Shelby gasped. Did her mother realize what she had just said? She exchanged a shocked glance with Tucker.

"I'd appreciate it if you would drive me home. I came in the ambulance, so I don't have my car," Diana snapped.

"Diana, what's going on?" Tucker asked gently.

Her eyes bulged and then she exploded. "His *girlfriend* is in there! She's one of the nurses here. He asked for her, and she's in there right now, plastered to his side." She stopped to draw a couple of quick, angry breaths. "Well, she can have him! He looked me right in the eye and said, calm as anything, 'I'm sorry, Diana.' Well, he's not half as sorry as he's *going* to be!"

Appalled, Shelby edged closer to Tucker's side. Their hands bumped, and his instantly folded around hers.

"I don't know why I'm surprised," Diana raged. "It's not like I didn't see this coming."

Shelby stared. "What do you mean?"

"I knew he was seeing her," Diana said. "I just wasn't expecting him to dump me like this." She shuddered. "In a *hospital.* When he knows how I —" She pressed her pale lips together and shook her head. "It's that horrible antiseptic smell."

"Come on." Tucker's dark eyes burned with compassion as they rested on Shelby's mother. "Let's get you out of here."

Twenty minutes later, Diana strode up her porch steps and unlocked the door. Hanging back, Tucker caught Shelby's arm. "What was that guy *thinking?*" he demanded in a fierce whisper.

Shelby lifted a shoulder. She'd made every effort to get along with Jack, but they'd never been close. And her mother would be okay. She watched Diana disappear into the house and felt a pang of sympathy quickly followed by one of admiration. Her mother was a survivor.

"What kind of man could *do* that?" Tucker persisted.

"She'll be all right," Shelby assured him. "She's had a shock, and she's mad. But she'll be all right."

Tucker looked stunned. "She doesn't *love* him?"

"She does, I think. But she was never really . . ." Shelby searched for the right word.

"Invested," Tucker supplied, bitterness in

his voice. "So he can make her mad, but he can't break her heart."

Unwilling to acknowledge that he'd nailed it, Shelby hugged herself and looked away from him.

"Because she never trusted him with her heart to begin with," he concluded.

"No," Shelby admitted. "I don't believe she did."

"Because she doesn't allow herself to feel. Keeps her emotions under lock and key. Even with you, her only child."

"Yes," Shelby whispered. But while Diana had never been demonstrative, Shelby had always known that deep down, her mother truly loved her. Whenever she needed reassurance of that, she could call up shadowy memories of being held and sung to as a young child. Shelby didn't think that kind of love could die, but she knew firsthand that it could be buried.

"And she's taught her daughter well," Tucker continued. "Because *you* don't get invested, either, do you, Shelby?"

Why was he turning this into an attack on her? "You're so wrong," she said, thinking of the baby. She'd been plenty invested there.

"The baby." He nodded. "You hate that you cared so much, and you're determined that you'll never care like that again. That's what last night was about."

"I don't know what you mean."

"Oh, yes, you do. You never cried like that before and you never will again. You're finished now, aren't you?"

"I'm not going to stand here arguing with you." Shelby pointed at the front door. "My mother is in there all alone."

"I know. But when you go in there, she'll still be alone. And so will you. Because you're doing the same thing she did all those years ago, aren't you? Shutting down your heart."

Unable to take any more, Shelby whirled away from him and bounded up the porch steps. She knew he wouldn't follow her into the house, not without an invitation, and she hadn't issued one.

She made some coffee and angrily sucked down two cups while her mother completed the morning grooming routine that had been interrupted by Jack's emergency. Twenty minutes later Diana strolled into the living room, neatly coiffed and outwardly composed. Shelby looked up from where she huddled in a corner of the uncomfortable sofa and waited for her mother to speak.

"So." Diana's tone was breezy and conversational as she sat down at the opposite end of the sofa. "You and Tucker looked very cozy, holding hands at the hospital."

Still fuming over that scene in the driveway, Shelby gave a carefully indifferent shrug. "I'm going to end the marriage."

"Don't be ridiculous," her mother said mildly. "I know I wasn't in favor of it, but Tucker is financially secure and he treats you well enough. So in a couple of years, when the timing's better, you should have a baby."

"I will never have a baby."

"Nonsense. You had a simple miscarriage. Lots of women have them. So there's no reason —"

"Tucker and I don't have a real marriage," Shelby said stonily. "There won't be another baby." And there would never be another *man,* either. She was finished with all of this. Love, marriage, babies — none of those things were for her.

Surprise flickered across her mother's face. "I knew it was that way in the beginning, but I naturally assumed . . ."

"You assumed wrong." Shelby folded her arms.

Diana leaned forward to center a decorative china bowl more perfectly on the coffee table. "Then he's seeing someone else."

*"No."* Shock had pulled the protest out of Shelby's mouth, and she was embarrassed by its vehemence. But even though she was angry with Tucker, she couldn't let anyone besmirch his honor. "Not Tucker," she said, more calmly. "He isn't like that."

"Some men can be very discreet. Just look at Jack. He's been seeing that girl for a year."

Shelby stared.

"Oh, I've known about her almost from the beginning," Diana said, waving a hand. "But he was a good husband, so —"

*"Jack?"* Shelby croaked out. "A good husband? Maybe he never got drunk and hit you, Mom, but he didn't treat you with tenderness and respect, either."

Diana's lips curled into a sarcastic smile. "I suppose you're going to tell me Tucker is a wonderful husband."

"He is." He *was*. And he deserved a real wife.

"When a woman gets to be my age," Diana said softly, "she worries about ending up alone. She'll . . . put up with things."

Shelby felt hot tears prick her eyes. It was beyond unbelievable that her proud, strong-willed mother had "put up with" infidelity. "But, Mom, it isn't *right*."

"I know. That's why I was so hard on you when you got pregnant. I wanted *you,* at least, to get everything right."

But Shelby couldn't get *anything* right. The world was spinning too fast, and she was losing her grip. "Daddy did this to us," she said, recalling Tucker's accusations, all of which were horribly true. "Mom, he *damaged* us."

"All that was a long time ago." Diana's voice was brisk as she examined her manicure.

"I need to talk about it," Shelby said. "I know it's been nine years, but lately, it's all I can think about. I'm trying to forget, Mom, just like you did. But it just isn't working."

Diana got up and walked over to the fireplace, where she rearranged some glass candlesticks on the mantel. "I never forgot," she said, very softly.

Equally stunned and encouraged by that revelation, Shelby swallowed hard. "Could we talk about it, then?"

Diana seemed to consider that for a moment, but then she shook her head. "Not today. Some other time."

"Just let me say one thing," Shelby pleaded. "Just let me say I'm sorry. For not telling. I could have told someone and made it stop, but I never did, Mom, and I'm *sorry.*"

"It wasn't your fault." Diana returned to the sofa and sat down heavily. "It was mine." She closed her eyes briefly. "I know I've always been hard on you. But I thought it was what you needed to stay strong." She pressed her fingertips against her temples. "I can't talk about this right now."

"It's okay," Shelby said quickly. "You've had a terrible morning. We don't have to talk at all if you don't want to."

After a few moments of silence Diana said, "Shelby, I'm sorry about the baby. I should have supported you in the beginning. I'm sorry you ended up marrying Tucker just because —"

"Don't, Mom." An apology from her proud, stubborn mother was more than Shelby could bear. "It doesn't matter anymore."

Staring at the cream-colored carpet, Diana smoothed a hand over her hair. "Why don't you stay here with me?"

Shelby hesitated. "Do you really want me to?"

"Yes." When Diana looked up, there was an unfamiliar light in her eyes. "I know I've never been there for you when you —"

"I've done okay," Shelby interrupted. Maybe that wasn't the truth, but it was what her mother needed to hear.

"Well, if you and Tucker don't have a real marriage, you might as well move in here. I don't want to rattle around in this house all alone."

"I'll stay with you," Shelby promised, looking down at the gold ring she was turning around on her finger. "There's nothing to keep me with Tucker now."

An hour later, arms folded close to her body, Shelby stared unseeing out her mother's living-room window. A flash of light, the midday sun glinting off metal, captured her attention and she saw Tucker's SUV roll into the driveway. Unwilling to have this conversation within her mother's earshot, Shelby hurried outside, reaching Tucker's door just as it opened.

The harsh sunlight emphasized the worry lines between his eyebrows as he shook his head at her. "Honey, about all those things I said earlier . . ." Instead of finishing the sentence, he gathered Shelby into his arms and hugged her hard. When he pressed his mouth against her forehead in a fierce kiss, she allowed herself two seconds to savor it before gently pushing against his chest.

"How's your mother?" he asked, letting her go.

"Better than I expected. But she needs me."

He nodded. "She's acting tough, but she's devastated. You should think about staying the night with her."

Shelby stared at the open collar of his yellow shirt. "As a matter of fact, I've just made a decision about that."

"Okay. I'll run you home to pick up your toothbrush and —"

"Tucker," she interrupted. "I'm moving in with her." Not daring to meet his eyes, she rushed on. "At least for a while. I wouldn't have wished this on Mom, but now that she's alone, I have an opportunity to repair our relationship."

Tucker remained silent, so she continued. "We talked about my father just now. About what he did to us."

"I'm glad the two of you are finally talking, Shel. But you don't have to move in here. I've yelled at you twice today, and I know that was wrong, but —"

She looked up and stopped him with a shake of her head. "Tucker, you've been great. Better than I ever deserved. But we have to stop pretending. It's just not going to work for us."

He closed his eyes. "Honey, don't do this."

"We tried, Tucker." Unable to bear looking at his wounded face, she again fastened her gaze on his shirt collar. "You've been amazing, and I'll always be grateful. But that's all I'm ever going to feel for you because it's true, what you said. I'm just like my mother. We *don't* get invested." Her eyes filled suddenly, but she managed to blink back the moisture. "And you deserve better, bear. You deserve so much more than I'll ever be able to give you."

He just shook his head.

She expelled a long breath. "But this isn't just about me leaving you. Mom has *asked* me to stay here. And since I never did anything to stop it when my father hurt her, I don't want to miss this chance to —"

"You were just a kid," Tucker broke in, almost irritably. "What could you have done to stop it?"

The old shame washed over her. "I never called the police. I never told anyone. I never did *anything.*"

"Honey, you were a victim, too. You were scared."

She briefly considered and then discarded that excuse. "I'm not sure I was scared. What I mostly felt was . . . blank."

"What do you mean?"

Having come this far, she went on to explain. "When somebody does that to you, you don't feel it." She spoke slowly, piecing the sentences together, wondering how to make him understand. "Your brain just kind of shuts down. You can feel the impact of his fist, but somehow it doesn't hurt because your mind refuses to believe it's really happening. One time, I remember thinking, 'Is this what being dead is like? Knowing but not feeling?' "

Tucker slumped against the door of the SUV, a sick look on his face, and Shelby realized she'd gone too far. There had been no need to share that ugliness with him. Why had she even allowed herself to remember? "But all that was years ago," she muttered, praying that he would drop the subject and go home.

Tucker clamped his teeth together to hold back a howl of anguish. Hearing her speak of it in this dispassionate way was even more horrible than the violence he had so vividly imagined.

"It wasn't that bad, really," she insisted. "It wasn't like what happened to David. Daddy was fine when he wasn't drinking. He came to school events and he taught me to fly a kite. He was a good father."

"He wasn't a good father!" Tucker almost shouted.

She looked stricken. "I didn't mean that he was anything like *your* father," she said in a tiny voice. "It's just that —" She sighed. "I'm bent, Tucker. Something's wrong with my heart. I didn't love David, I know that now. I did feel something for him, but I didn't love him. Even you, as wonderful as you are, couldn't make me fall in love."

"You haven't given us much time," he chided, reaching for one of her copper-colored curls.

She shook her head, breaking the contact. "It wouldn't make any difference. What's wrong with me can't be fixed."

"I don't believe that. And you shouldn't, either. Where's your faith?"

"I believe in God, honestly I do, and I try to be good. But I guess I don't really trust Him to take care of me."

"Because you think you don't deserve it," Tucker said softly. "Honey, that's so wrong."

"Don't you get it? He *hasn't* taken care of me. My father was an alcoholic and an abuser and my mother all but ignored me because she lived in her own world of pain. And then I grew up and thought I'd marry David and everything would finally be all right. But God wouldn't let me have that. Then I found out I was pregnant and —"

"You married a man you didn't love," Tucker contributed.

"And then I lost the baby," she said bitterly. "So where was God, Tucker? When all those awful things were happening to me, where *was* He?"

Somehow, Tucker managed to push a few words past the painful obstruction in his throat. "Come home, Shel. Let's talk about this."

She gave him a long, sad look. "Let me go, Tucker. *Please.*"

Words of love scalded his throat, but he pressed his lips together, holding them in. She wasn't ready to hear them.

"I've prayed and prayed," she said quietly. "But even when I try to be good, everything goes wrong. Like with you."

"Nothing's gone wrong with me," he argued, frustration sharpening his tone. "I'm still here." As he spread his arms, she backed up a step, so he dropped them again. He sent up a silent, desperate prayer for the miracle he needed. "I'm sorry we lost the baby, but we're still married."

Something in the liquid violet of her eyes extinguished Tucker's last hope. "Only on paper," she said in a low voice. "And even that won't be for much longer. I'm sorry."

# CHAPTER EIGHTEEN

Either Shelby had stopped going to church, Tucker decided as he opened the cash register and pulled out a stack of twenty-dollar bills, or she'd found a new one, a place where she wouldn't run into her husband. He hadn't seen her in twenty-three days.

With practiced fingers, Tucker flipped through the twenties, counting under his breath. It was killing him to stay away from Shelby, but what enabled him to do it was the memory of her eyes as she begged him to let her go. After what he had done to her, rushing her into a marriage that had turned out to be tragically unnecessary, how could he deny that request?

If she ever wanted him, he'd be there in a heartbeat. He never turned off his cell phone; he even took it into the bathroom when he showered so he'd never miss hearing it ring.

And he'd done something else. The day she'd moved out, he'd gone to his father's house and hunted up the electric candles his mother had always put in the windows at Christmastime. There were twelve of them, so Tucker had put six in each of the windows flanking his cottage's front door.

How pathetic was that? The things burned day and night, lighting the way for someone who meant never to come home. But like the man in her favorite story, Tucker just couldn't make himself give up. He sighed, restacked the pile of twenties he'd been counting before his mind wandered and started over.

Someday he'd get past this, he told himself as he totaled the figures on his bank deposit sheet. People didn't actually die of broken hearts. They merely wished they would.

As he stuffed the deposit sheet and money into the zippered bank pouch, the cowbells on the front door jangled and Tucker huffed out an annoyed breath. Apparently, he'd forgotten to lock the door when he'd flipped the sign over to Closed. But it was just a few minutes after five, so he shut the register and assumed a friendly, may-I-help-you smile. It went flat the second he lifted his head and saw who had just come in.

"Am I disturbing you?" Shelby asked,

walking toward him.

"No." Tucker stepped out from behind the counter. "Not at all." He pushed his hands into his pockets so she wouldn't notice if they trembled a little.

"How have you been?" she asked.

"I'm good." The lie wasn't meant to salve his pride, but to ease her mind. "How about you?"

"I'm okay." Her smile was several shades too bright. She wasn't anywhere close to okay. Why did they have to pretend?

"How's your mom?" Tucker asked.

"She's all right. Jack's making a good recovery, but he's living with his girlfriend now and wants to marry her. I don't think Mom's really grieving for him, but she does have a lot of anger. She's actually talking about seeing a counselor."

That was good to hear. But what about Shelby? When was she going to face *her* problems?

She cleared her throat. "Bryan's taking violin lessons."

"I know. He says you're a tough teacher."

This time her smile was genuine, but it didn't last. She peered at Tucker from underneath delicate eyebrows drawn to-gether by worry. "So you're really okay?"

Me? Oh, I'm just peachy. My chest has

almost healed where you reached in and snatched the heart out of my body. "I'm good," he said, nodding vigorously to shore up the lie. Her sad, fleeting smile made him ask, a little defensively, "Don't I look good to you?"

Her smile reappeared, wistful. "You always did look good to me, bear."

Pain spiraled through Tucker's chest. It had been hard losing David, but that kind of grief was bearable. *This* kind wasn't. It was one thing when loved ones went home to be with the Lord. Sure, you missed them, but you knew they were safe and happy, and you knew that one day, you'd be reunited with them. But this was different. Shelby wasn't safe and she wasn't happy. And as far as their ever being reunited . . . Tucker sighed.

He hadn't expected her today, but he knew exactly what she was here for, and he just needed her to get on with her business and get out of his shop before his heart imploded. "I suppose you've brought papers," he said, eyeing the leather handbag that swung from a strap on her shoulder.

"Papers?" She looked confused.

"Legal papers," he said flatly. "You want my signature."

Her gaze dropped to the floor.

She didn't have any papers? Why was she here, then?

"A-are you in a hurry?" she asked. "For a div—"

"No," he said quickly. "I'm not in a hurry for a —" He stopped and swallowed. Somehow, someday, he'd have to learn how to say the word. *Divorce*. Or *annulment*. He wasn't sure which legal term would apply in their situation, but in the end they both meant pretty much the same thing, didn't they?

Shelby looked nervous as she pushed her hair back behind her ears. "Because if you were in a hurry, I could go ahead and hire an attorney."

Tucker's heart tripped. "You haven't done that?"

She wrapped her arms around herself, assuming the defensive posture he'd come to know all too well.

"Why not?" he asked gently.

"No reason, really." Too casually, she lifted a hand and studied her fingernails. "It's just that I'm feeling a little fragile right now, so I'm not eager to tell everything to a lawyer and admit that I've failed at marriage, on top of everything else."

"What do you mean, 'on top of everything else'? What do you think you've failed at, honey?"

She hung her head. "You know what I've failed at."

Why was she still doing this to herself? Inside his pockets, Tucker's fingers curled into fists. "Not the baby," he managed, his voice trembling only a little. "That wasn't your fault."

"I don't know if it was or not. But there shouldn't have been a baby in the first place." She looked up. "That part of it *was* my fault."

Dismay unclenched Tucker's hands. "You thought you were in love. You anticipated your wedding night. Honey, if God has forgiven you for that, you've got no business holding on."

He didn't understand. She wasn't sure God *had* forgiven her. Because if He had, would everything still be going wrong? "I just wish —" She cut off her sentence and banished the thought just as ruthlessly. If God didn't see fit to answer her prayers, what was the point in wishing for anything?

In the brown depths of Tucker's eyes she saw hope flare like twin matches catching fire. "Do you want to come home?"

"No," she said wearily, hating to disappoint him. "I don't even know why I came here." She shook her head, giving up every pretense of being in control. "It's just that I keep thinking about what you said about wanting to be the safe place I could run to when —" She stopped again and pressed her fingers against her temples, knowing she sounded every bit as crazy as she felt. "I want you in my life, Tucker. I know that's horribly selfish, but I —"

"We're married," he interrupted. "I'm *supposed* to be in your life."

She moved closer to him and leaned her forehead against his chest. He rested his hands on her shoulders, his touch feather-light, as tentative as her own. "I don't want a husband," she continued in a low voice. "But I really need a friend, and you're the only one who understands."

His hands tightened on her shoulders. "Honey, I don't understand anything. All I know is that we should be together, and we're not."

She raised her head and looked into his face. "Are we still friends?"

"Always. *Forever.*" He looked bewildered. "How can you not *know* that?"

How could she explain that after awhile, you just stopped believing that anything good could last?

"Come home, Shelby."

She stared at the shamrock logo on his T-shirt. "I can't."

"Then at least call me if —"

She put two fingers over his lips to stop his words. "No more promises." She drew in a shuddery breath. "I don't seem to be very good at keeping them."

His black-coffee eyes remained locked on hers as his mouth moved under her finger-tips, making the shape of a kiss.

"I'll never forget you," Shelby said.

It was one promise she knew she'd have no trouble keeping.

# CHAPTER NINETEEN

Poodles weren't very bright, apparently, because although Tucker had come home alone every day for the past twenty-two days, Roadkill was still looking expectantly past him. As Tucker pocketed his keys and pulled the front door closed, the poodle lifted his head and looked the same old question at him. "I *told* you," Tucker said irritably, "she's not coming back."

Belatedly realizing that a guy who kept electric candles in his windows for someone who would never see them wasn't being all that realistic, himself, Tucker leaned down to ruffle his pet's ears by way of an apology. But Roadkill snubbed him and trotted off in the direction of the master bedroom, where he still slept.

The small bedroom was good enough for Tucker. And sleeping there helped a little, because sometimes when he awakened in the night he could almost believe Shelby was right down the hall, sound asleep and safe, with her fuzzy footwarmer lying at the bottom of her bed.

He opened the French door for Roadkill and went to the kitchen, where he put out fresh water and dog food. Then he opened the refrigerator and stared unseeing at the full shelves, not interested in anything there. He hadn't eaten all day, but he was too depressed to chew, so he poured himself some milk.

Roadkill pattered back into the kitchen and was just addressing his dinner when he suddenly raised his head, barked twice and streaked toward the front door. Tucker's first impulse was to ignore the doorbell, but then he thought it might be Bryan, so he trudged out to see.

The middle-aged, strawberry-blond, blue-eyed man on the front step was big, an inch or two taller than Tucker, and at least fifty pounds heavier. He looked as solid as a nightclub bouncer, but he was dressed in a crisp blue oxford shirt and an immaculately creased pair of khakis.

"Tucker Sharpe?" His expression was oddly tentative for someone of his size. When Tucker nodded, the man shifted slightly, which allowed the slanting rays of the late-afternoon sun to hit him full in the face, illuminating his eyes, which were not blue at all.

They were violet.

"I'm Phillip Franklin," the man said. "I'm Shelby's —"

"I know who you are." Tucker felt his blood chill. "She told me you were dead."

Surprise and hurt flickered in Phillip Franklin's eyes, but Tucker didn't feel the slightest desire to put the man at ease. He tilted his chin to an unfriendly angle and waited.

"I deserve to be dead," Phillip said quietly. "You have no idea what I did to her. And to her mother."

It wasn't the low, bright sun that narrowed Tucker's eyes. "Oh, I have an idea," he said nastily.

"Is she here?"

"No," Tucker snapped. "And you stay away from her. The last thing she needs —"

"Wait." Shelby's father lifted one hand. "Please. I came to see *you*. I made sure her car wasn't here before I rang the bell. Is she due back soon?"

"No." As he uttered that small word, the fight drained out of Tucker. "No, she's not coming back."

Phillip arched a tawny eyebrow. "She's left you?"

"Yes."

"I'm sorry. But could we talk?"

The man didn't deserve a hearing, but Tucker was eager to learn more about Shelby's past, so he stepped aside. Reaching the living room, he gestured to the sofa.

Phillip sat. "Whatever they've told you about me is true. I was a monster. And nine years ago, I left them." He closed his eyes briefly, appearing to summon the strength to continue. "I was an alcoholic. I didn't drink every day, and I managed to hold it together around the people I worked with. But whenever I drank, I usually ended up slapping my wife around. And if Shelby got in the way . . ." His gaze dropped to the floor.

The last thing Tucker wanted to hear was a recitation of this man's sins. "Get to the point," he growled, flinging himself into his leather armchair.

Phillip nodded. "Five years ago, I became a Christian. It's still hard for me to understand how God could have reached my cold heart, but He did. He forgave me and made me a new man." Phillip's gaze sharpened on Tucker. "Do you understand what it means to be 'born again'?"

"Yes. I'm a believer." Tucker knew he should be glad about Phillip's conversion, and he was honestly trying to be, but something deep inside him longed to see the man suffer.

"I wanted to beg their forgiveness," Phillip went on. "But it had been several years since we'd had any contact, and I was afraid of ripping open old wounds." He stared down at the hands he'd clasped between his knees. "*Should* I have contacted them?"

Compassion tugged at Tucker's heart. "I don't know." He opened his left hand, palm up, and absently studied the tiny reflection of his face in his gold wedding ring.

"Diana wouldn't accept anything from me," Phillip said. "No child support, not even birthday or Christmas gifts for Shelby. She refused all contact. So from time to time I've hired private investigators to give me reports."

Tucker's head jerked up. So someone had been watching her. That certainly explained a few things.

"I just wanted to know Shelby was okay," Phillip said. "I didn't plan to come forward unless she needed me."

"So where were you when her fiancé died?" Tucker couldn't keep the bitterness out of his voice.

"Brazil," Phillip said. "Filming a documentary. By the time I found out about her fiancé, you had already married her."

Tucker gave him a pointed look. "I suppose your detective checked me out?"

"Naturally." Phillip's steady gaze held no apology. "I couldn't understand why she married *you* so soon after your brother died."

"We weren't involved, if that's what you're wondering," Tucker said flatly. "She was going to have David's baby."

"She's *pregnant?*"

"Not anymore," Tucker said, feeling his shoulders bow under the weight of his grief. "She miscarried a month ago."

"Oh, that's awful," Phillip said.

Tucker rubbed a hand over his face. "She was already struggling with her faith, and losing the baby sent her into a tailspin. Now she's shutting everyone out."

"Should I contact her now?" Phillip asked. "Would that upset her, or might it help her find some peace?"

Tucker was fast losing his grip on his animosity toward Shelby's father. "I honestly don't know."

"I've been afraid she might blame herself for what I did to her and her mother," Phillip said. "Victims often do that, you know — find a way to blame themselves."

"She does. She says —" Tucker's voice

broke, so he swallowed and started again. "She says she's 'bent.'"

Phillip bowed his head. "Then maybe she needs to hear it from me. That it was all *my* fault and never hers or Diana's."

"I'm not sure it would be good for her to see you right now," Tucker said. No, he wasn't sure of *anything* these days.

"Are you a praying man?" Phillip inquired.

Tucker dipped his head in sober acknowledgement.

"Then I'll ask you to pray about this with me. My instinct is to go straight to my daughter, but that might not be the best thing for her. So I'd rather rely on your judgment."

"You don't know me," Tucker pointed out.

"Actually, I know quite a lot about you. You're highly respected in this community. You own a nice chunk of your father's business and your personal finances are in good order. I've just learned for myself that you're a Christian who understands the power of prayer. And from the way you talk about my daughter, I'd say you're deeply in love with her." He raised his open hands. "You might hate me for what I've done, but I don't believe you'll let that get in the way of what Shelby needs."

Tucker gave him a rueful smile. "I hated

you for about two minutes, but I couldn't hold on to it."

Phillip smiled back and drew a pen from his shirt pocket. "I have a family in L.A. My twin boys are about to celebrate their second birthday, so I need to fly home tomorrow. But my wife knows about my past, and she's eager for me to make things right. So if you call, I'll drop everything and come."

Phillip produced a small gold case from his pants pocket and extracted a business card. "Here's my cell phone number," he said as he wrote on the blank side of the card. "My flight doesn't leave until tomorrow afternoon, so I'll be available tonight and in the morning." Handing the card to Tucker, he added, "I'll be praying for you both."

Tucker saw him to the door, but when Phillip stepped outside, he turned abruptly and laid a broad hand against the edge of the door. "There's just one more thing."

Tucker lifted his eyebrows and waited.

"Maybe it's none of my business," Phillip began slowly. "But if you and Shelby weren't involved, why did you marry her?"

"I owed her." When Phillip's eyes asked a silent question, Tucker explained that Shelby had wanted the baby but lacked support. Then he confessed his role in promoting David's reckless lifestyle.

"But that's crazy," Phillip protested. "You weren't responsible for your brother's actions. He knew right from wrong, same as you."

They talked for another minute, then Phillip left and Tucker went back to the living room and dropped into his favorite chair, thinking about David. He had been reckless, but he'd never meant to hurt anyone, and it had always been easier for Tucker to shoulder the blame for his brother's mistakes than to watch him face unpleasant consequences. But Phillip was right. A man was responsible for his own actions, and Tucker had been staggering under this burden for too long.

"Father, help me turn loose of it," he said aloud. "My own mistakes are heavy enough without carrying David's."

He spent the next thirty minutes at his desk, seeking comfort and direction from the Scriptures. When he closed the soft leather cover of his Bible, his heart was quiet and he knew what to do.

He picked up the phone. "It's Tucker," he said when Diana answered. "I need to see you and Shelby right away. It's about —"

"Tucker." Diana's tone was far from

friendly. "I don't know what you said to her earlier, but she's in her room now, crying her eyes out. Can't you just leave her alone?"

Tucker squeezed his eyes shut, but when his heart finished its painful spasm, he made himself go on. "This isn't about Shelby and me," he said, wondering how best to unload this shocker on Diana. "This is something else."

"I told you, she doesn't —"

"Diana," he cut in. "It's about her father."

"Phillip Franklin is dead," Diana insisted in an icy tone.

"He's not dead." Tucker waited a couple of heartbeats before adding, "He's here in Dublin."

Beyond Diana's stunned silence Tucker heard Shelby's voice, worried and high-pitched: "Mom? What's wrong? Is it Jack?"

Did Shelby know her father was alive? Tucker held his breath and waited for her mother's reaction.

"I guess you'd better come over," Diana said, and hung up.

# CHAPTER TWENTY

"We are definitely not going to see him," Diana fumed. We don't owe him that. I can't believe he had the nerve to ask."

Why was the Lord doing this to her? Shelby wondered bleakly. She was trying so hard to hold on to her faith, but He kept sending wave after wave of trouble to buffet her. Did He not see that she was losing her grip, or did He just not care?

They were seated around the breakfast table in her mother's kitchen. Across from Shelby, Tucker sat tall and still, his gaze carefully fixed on the ceramic pot of English ivy in the center of the table. When Diana finally brought her tirade to a close, Tucker's alert eyes rose to meet Shelby's, and she knew he was waiting for the answer to a question he had not asked out loud.

"I'm sorry I lied to you," she said in a tiny voice. His eyes softened, but he said nothing, so she gave him more. "I was fifteen when we moved here from California. Everyone knew Jack was my stepfather, so when they asked about my real father, what was I supposed to say? That he had abused us and abandoned us? Jack said it would be easier if we told people he was dead."

"We *wished* him dead," Diana declared.

"No," Shelby protested. "We just wanted to move on with our lives. That was all."

"Well, we're not going to see him." The look Diana directed at Tucker was as cold and hard as marble. "You tell him that, and tell him if he tries to contact us again, I'll get a restraining order."

"No, Mom." Shelby had made her decision. "I understand if you don't want to see him, but I —" She shivered, then plunged ahead. "I need to."

Tucker still hadn't spoken, but there was no mistaking the approval and support in his steady gaze.

"Out of the question," her mother decreed, then leaned back in her chair as if she had just settled the matter. "You are not going to be alone with that man."

"She won't be alone," Tucker said. "I'll be there."

"This is none of your concern," Diana whipped out.

Tucker didn't appear fazed by her withering look. "It's very much my concern," he contradicted quietly. "You may recall that I have made certain promises to Shelby."

Not *that* again. "Tucker," Shelby said evenly, "I have released you from those promises."

He dipped his head slightly, returning her exasperated look with one of unflinching determination. "You don't have the right to release me. We were joined together by God."

Shelby sighed. It was easier to drop it than argue about it, especially in front of her mother. "Let's go to your house and call Phillip."

Diana huffed out an angry breath and pushed her chair away from the table. "This is *not* a good idea," she said darkly.

Tucker's face was impassive as he watched Diana storm out of the kitchen. Shelby covered her nervousness by collecting the coffee cups and carrying them to the sink to rinse them.

Tucker followed. "You've been crying," he accused.

"Nothing gets past you, does it?" she grumbled, acutely aware that her eyelids resembled fat pink marshmallows.

He moved to stand directly behind her as she rinsed the cups. He was too still and too close, and she had to do something before he put his arms around her and made her forget why she didn't want him to do that ever again.

"Let's go," she said abruptly, shutting off the tap and turning to face him. "Let's get this over with."

"I won't leave you alone with him," Tucker promised. "And if you feel uncomfortable, I'll make him leave."

She managed a quick, tiny nod. The movement caused one of her curls to flop over the corner of her left eye, but she didn't brush it back because Tucker was still too close, looking at her too intently. Hiding behind her hair seemed like a smart thing to do.

What she hadn't counted on was Tucker seeing it as an invitation to touch her. He captured the errant curl and tucked it back. "Don't worry," he whispered.

She was strung even tighter than her violin, but she almost laughed at those words. If she lived to be a hundred, she'd hear them in her mind every time she thought of Tucker Sharpe.

*Don't worry, Shel.*

She was trying not to. But all this pushing and pulling had to stop. She'd lean on Tucker one last time, and then tomorrow morning, she would stop making excuses and *finish* this. First thing tomorrow, she would hire an attorney.

Shelby had insisted on following Tucker home. He'd given in because he didn't want to upset her any more. But what did she think he was planning to do — kidnap her? Keep her prisoner in the little stone house?

Okay, maybe the thought had crossed his mind.

He sighed and checked his rearview mirror again. She was still right behind him as he swung the SUV onto his street and headed down to the river. At least she had agreed to come.

The sky darkened and the wind kicked up as an early-fall storm approached. Tucker didn't drive around to his garage, but parked in front of the house. When Shelby pulled in behind him, he strode to her car and opened her door.

Slowly, slowly, she extended one leg, followed ages later by the other. Ignoring the hand Tucker offered, she grasped the door's edge and hauled herself up, her movements as sluggish as if she were swimming in a pool of honey. And all the while she stared, slack jawed, at the house. "Candles," she whispered.

"They're electric," Tucker apologized. Did she hate them?

"When did you . . ." She made a vague gesture with her hand.

"The day you left," he said. She hated them.

She blinked. *"Why?"*

"To light your way home." So much for his grand romantic gesture. Why had he ever imagined that a bunch of Christmas decorations would mean anything to her?

The first sprinklings of rain had arrived, but Shelby, still staring in fascination at Tucker's Folly, was oblivious to them. "Come on," Tucker urged, slipping an arm around her shoulders. "It's getting wet out here."

She didn't respond. She couldn't seem to tear her gaze from the glowing lights, so he guided her up the walk. She stumbled once, but he didn't let her fall. "You don't have to do this," he said, guessing it was second thoughts about seeing her father that had made her freeze up like this.

"Yes, I do," she said, coming out of her trance.

When Tucker turned his key in the lock and heard a joyful bark, he felt a pang of dismay. Don't get excited, he wanted to tell Roadkill. She's not staying.

"Hello, baby!" Tucker barely had the door open before Shelby was on her knees, cooing at the wriggling dog as she gathered him into her arms.

"He misses you," Tucker said. "I really wish you'd take him, Shel."

"I couldn't." She stood, hugging the poodle, smiling as she whipped her head back and forth to avoid the long tongue that was trying to swipe her face. "He's your dog."

"That is not a dog," Tucker said automatically, then he met Shelby's eyes and his breath hitched in his throat. "We had some good times, didn't we, Shel?"

She looked away from him and it was a long while before she answered. "Yes. I'm sorry we don't have a future."

They'd barely had a past, he thought bitterly. Why couldn't she have given their marriage a fighting chance?

Outside, rain began to hammer the house as a roll of thunder rumbled over their heads. Normally, Tucker loved a good storm, but this one just seemed to underscore his hopelessness.

"I guess you should call my father," Shelby said.

As Tucker reached into his pocket for Phillip's card, he caught himself hoping the man would get here quickly. Tucker didn't know how he and Shelby would pass the time, otherwise. Because it was clear they had nothing left to talk about.

Phillip Franklin looked different from the way Shelby remembered. His face was thinner, the lines on it had deepened, and his strawberry-blond hair was turning gray. But his eyes were the same shape and color as her own, and maybe that was why she hadn't been able to forget him. Because every time she looked into a mirror, she saw her father's eyes.

Tucker had told her about Phillip's conversion. She wanted to trust this remade man, but her old resentment bubbled to the surface and she held out her hand as coolly as she would have to a stranger. "Hello, Phillip."

To his credit, he didn't hold her hand too long or squeeze it too hard. "Thank you for seeing me," he said, wiping the bottoms of his wet shoes on the rug beside the door.

She felt a gentle pressure in the middle of her back as Tucker silently urged her toward the living room. He steered Phillip to the leather recliner before taking Shelby's hand and pulling her down to sit beside him on the sofa.

Tucker had recounted to her his earlier conversation with her father, but Shelby had some questions. "A couple of months ago, did you call me and then hang up?"

Phillip bowed his head. "I'm sorry. I was in South America then." He scooted forward in his chair, as if he wanted to be closer to her. "I came down with something and was sick as a dog for three days. And at one point I had such a vivid, disturbing dream about you that I just had to call and hear your voice. I shouldn't have done it the first time, let alone the second, but I just couldn't stop myself."

She absorbed that in silence. "Tucker said you hired a private investigator," she said after a moment.

He nodded. "I just wanted to know you were safe."

"A couple of times, I had a creepy feeling that somebody was watching me," she said. "And once, somebody in a black Lexus followed me home. Was that you?"

"Yes. You might have spotted the detective when he was checking up on you, but I was the one who followed you home. I had business in Columbus, so I drove over to Dublin to see where you lived. I told myself that was all I was going to do. But then — I don't know, but I like to call it divine intervention — you pulled up right beside my car."

She felt her eyes narrow and made no effort to hide her skepticism. "And you recognized me after nine years?"

"Baby, I would have known you anywhere. I knew the make and model of your car, and the detective had sent me pictures of you, one of them a close-up that was good enough to frame. It's sitting on my desk at home."

She let that go as her mind went back to the spooky feeling she'd had in the parking lot the day he'd followed her home. "You were at the grocery store," she accused. "I . . . felt it."

"Yes. When I first saw you, you were just turning into the parking lot. I waited for you to come out of the store, then I followed you home. I knew it was a bad idea. But I just kept hoping for one more glimpse." His mouth twisted as he shook his head in apparent self-disgust. "When you passed your own driveway, I knew you'd seen me."

"You *scared* her," Tucker growled.

"I know." Phillip lowered his gaze. "I'm sorry."

Outside, the rain was coming down hard, and Shelby's heart was pounding just as violently. She had no idea how to manage the emotions that swirled inside her. Turning her head, she caught Tucker's gaze. She willed him to read the turmoil in her mind, to tell her what she ought to do next. He watched her steadily, communicating without words that these weren't things she had to settle now. She could have all the time she needed.

As if he, too, had interpreted Tucker's silent message, Phillip pushed up to his feet. "I know this is a lot for you to deal with, Shelby. I'd better give you some more time."

She objected for the sake of politeness, but she was relieved when both Tucker and her father insisted. It was true; she'd had enough for now.

"I haven't hugged you since you were a little girl," Phillip said when they again stood beside the front door.

Shelby caught her breath and was aware that Tucker shot Phillip a warning glance and gave a slight shake of his head.

"Never mind," her father said quickly, backing up a step to show he meant no harm. "I guess it's too soon for that."

"I'm not really much of a hugger," Shelby said, afraid that she'd hurt his feelings. "I never was."

"You were, once." Phillip's gaze, suddenly

misty, shifted to Tucker, then back to Shelby's face. "A very long time ago, you *were*." He looked down at his shoes.

A lump in her throat prevented Shelby from replying. She edged closer to Tucker, and a strong, protective arm was immediately draped around her shoulders.

Phillip gave her a wistful smile. "I'll go now. I just want you to know this, Shelby. Whatever you're feeling, it isn't wrong. My pastor always says we can control our actions, but not our feelings. So if you hate me, that isn't wrong. Do you understand, baby? Whatever you're feeling about me, it's okay."

What she was feeling wasn't hatred, but a sense of loss so profound she wanted to weep. Tucker must have guessed that, because his arm suddenly tightened around her. "Daddy, I'm sorry," she said in a little girl's voice.

"Baby, *no*." He looked devastated. "I didn't expect to come dancing back into your life and get a hero's welcome. I hurt you, and I'm ashamed. But don't you ever be ashamed. It wasn't your fault, baby. None of it was ever your fault."

She shifted her weight, easing away from Tucker. He withdrew his arm, reading her as perfectly as he always did, allowing her the space she needed.

The men exchanged a silent handshake, then Phillip turned to go. He was on the bottom step when he stopped suddenly. Pivoting to face Shelby again, he smiled broadly and pointed at the sky. "Look at that!"

The rain had stopped and the world was now bathed in a lovely pink-tinged light. It was past seven o'clock, so the sun rode low in the sky, but against a soft gray background of retreating storm clouds it projected a vibrant rainbow.

Shelby recalled sharing another rainbow with her father; a spectacular one seen from a California beach when she was ten. They'd tried to photograph it, but the snapshot hadn't turned out. Did he remember? Eagerly, she turned to ask.

But he was walking away, and as she watched him retreat she remembered the last time he had walked away. She wrapped her arms around herself, but it was too late to protect her heart. He had crushed it years ago.

Tucker was admiring the largest, showiest rainbow he'd seen in years when Shelby turned suddenly and brushed past him like a frightened animal. He quickly stepped back into the house. "Shel?"

She stood at the far end of the hall, wild eyed and trembling, breathing much too fast. Was this some kind of panic attack? Tucker had no experience with those, so he panicked, too.

Instinct warned him to give her time. Tucker ground his teeth together and, although every cell in his body was straining toward her, his feet didn't move.

"He came to my violin recitals," she said, wringing her hands in her agitation. "He told me I was beautiful and brilliant and talented. How could he have been such a good father and then hurt Mom and me that way?"

"Honey, he wasn't a good father," Tucker said gently. "But I think he did love you. And you loved him, in spite of the awful things he did when he was drinking."

"Is he really different now? How can I know that he's different? How can I trust him?"

"Just take it slow, honey. Give him time to prove that he's changed."

"He was always sorry. He used to say he'd quit drinking, and he promised he'd never hurt us again. But he always *did.*"

Tucker's right foot lifted, but he pulled it back down, forcing himself to wait. "I know.

But this time, I think it might really be true that he's changed."

"Yeah." The word came out on a pathetic little sigh. "I wish he hadn't gone so soon. I wanted to —" Her chin jerked up as she swallowed. "I really needed a hug."

He could still see her shaking, but she'd pulled back from the brink of hysteria. Tucker exhaled and felt the tension in his shoulders ease. "Well, if you still want to hug someone, I'm standing right here, and I'm not busy." He opened his arms and she surged forward, hitting him so hard his breath whooshed out. But he made a good recovery, and as her arms locked around his waist, he folded himself around her.

"Hold me tight," she pleaded. "I need to *feel* something."

Squeezing the woman he loved was no hardship, and Tucker gave it his full attention. She was still shaking, but even as he ached for her, he rejoiced over this breakthrough. She had finally set foot on the road to healing. He stroked her hair and murmured soothing words. And when she raised her head, he kissed her very softly — and briefly — on her full, warm mouth.

He drew back and was just about to apologize for his impulse when she whispered, "Do it again."

He did, lingering perhaps two seconds longer, afraid to push her.

She gave a small, nervous laugh. "I seem to remember you being a more enthusiastic kisser than this."

Hope filled his heart to bursting. "I'll show you enthusiasm." He snuggled her more securely into the crook of his arm and bent down to kiss her the way he'd dreamed of kissing her. Her eager response thrilled him, but after a moment he loosened his hold because he needed to gaze into her sweet face.

In the soft glow from the crystal lamp she looked bedazzled and beautiful, with pink cheeks and glowing eyes and a satiny, cherry-red mouth that possessed an astounding talent for making the whole world cease to exist.

"Oh!" She whispered. "That was —"

"Devastating," Tucker agreed, nodding furiously. "Let's do it some more."

"No." She eased away from him. "I should go."

"No, you shouldn't." Tucker pulled her close again. He wasn't about to let her go, not now. They were finally getting this right, and he would hold her, now and forever. "This is where you belong," he insisted. In his house, in his life, in his arms. "Stay."

She shook her head. "No. I can't think when you kiss me, and I have to think. Besides, my mother needs me."

"Maybe *I* need you," he said, exasperated. "Maybe I lo—"

"I have to go." She tore herself out of his arms and backed away, her eyes full of confusion.

He stepped forward and reached for her, but she spun away, eluding his grasp. And Tucker let her go.

Stay because I need you? What had he been thinking? He didn't want her that way. Nothing would be right unless and until she stayed because she wanted to be here and nowhere else.

The world outside lightened suddenly, drawing Tucker to the open doorway and out onto the steps. The dying sun was making one last effort, intensifying the colors of the rainbow. Tucker's wondering gaze slid from the red band on the outside of the arc and skimmed past the orange, yellow, green and blue. As his searching eyes came to rest on the curved streak of violet, his new favorite color, he felt his agitated heart grow still.

This wasn't over. She was at least half in love with him, and one day she would realize that. All Tucker had to do now was pray and wait patiently for God to open her eyes.

One day she would stop running and come home. First to God, and then to Tucker.

Scared mindless, Shelby ran, desperate to escape the confusing, conflicting emotions that stole her breath and set her heart thrumming. She reached her car and wrenched open the door, but then she stopped suddenly.

*Candles.* Her gaze flew to the window closest to her. He had put candles in the windows. *Why?*

His deep voice rumbled in her mind. *To light your way home.*

Why hadn't Tucker given up on her? She'd done everything she could think of to make him let go. But he hadn't.

And God hadn't, either.

She saw that now. Why had she never realized that her favorite story, the one about the man putting a candle in the window to light an errant girl's way home, was strikingly similar to the Prodigal Son parable Jesus told his followers to illustrate God's unconditional love?

Eager to share her discovery, she turned to look for Tucker. He stood on the doorstep, staring hard at the sky, and something told her he was praying. Her heart swelled suddenly, and as it crowded the air out of her lungs she felt her world shift and knew that everything had just changed.

She slammed her car door and hurried back up the flagstone walk, answering Tucker's questioning gaze with a breathless announcement. "I want to stay. Please. I want to."

Surprise widened his eyes. "Don't think I'm trying to dissuade you," he said cautiously. "I'd just like to know what's different now."

*Everything* was different. *She* was different. Completely unafraid, she laid her heart at his feet. "I love you, Tucker."

He closed his eyes.

"It's okay," she said quickly. "Don't say anything, just let me talk." It was all right if he didn't love her yet. He would love her one day. "I've been nothing but trouble to you," she said as his eyes opened and he gazed at her in perfectly understandable amazement. "And you've been right all along. About everything."

He stepped down to stand on the grass beside her. "Oh, Shelby, I —"

"No." She put her fingers over his mouth. "Please let me say this." She attempted to moisten her lips, but her parched tongue stuck to them. "I was a hopeless tangle of doubts and fears, but you were always there for me, no matter what, even when I thought I didn't need you."

His lips moved, tickling her fingers. "But Shelby, I —"

She shifted her hand to make a more secure seal over his mouth. "I wasn't even trying," she said. "You always insisted that if we made an honest effort, it would happen, but I never really believed that, so I didn't even try. But it happened, anyway, and now I'm in love with you. I don't know why I fought it so hard. It's not like you ever did anything to hurt me."

His face glowed with tender amusement as he caught her wrist and pulled her hand away from his mouth. "You were never this chatty before."

"I'm almost finished," she assured him. "It was the candles that made me understand. I realized you still hadn't given up on me, and somehow that made me think of God. He's been waiting for me to stop feeling sorry for myself and realize that He *has* been taking care of me. He sent me a wonderful husband, didn't He? And He's brought Mom and me closer together. And He saved my father and brought him back into my life. He must love me an awful lot to have done all those things, don't you think?"

Tucker opened his mouth to answer, but she rushed on. "I still don't understand about David and the baby, but everybody has trouble in life, right? And God has allowed *good* things to happen to me, not just bad ones. I see that now. And another thing. About our marriage. We got off to a rocky start, but I want you to know that from now on I am fully invested, absolutely *in* on this partnership. And —"

"Honey," he interrupted. "Come up for some air."

"I'm sorry," she said, embarrassed. "You can talk now."

His eyes sparkled and one corner of his curvy mouth lifted, drilling a dimple into his cheek. "I love you," he said. "Now let's get back to the kissing." He grasped her shoulders and pulled her to him.

After a minute, Tucker raised his head. "Come home," he urged in a deep voice that rippled with emotion. He captured Shelby's hands, pulling her up the steps and into the house. He closed the door and kissed her again, and everything in the world was right.

Almost.

When he began to kiss her in a new and

deeper way, she stiffened and eased away from him.

"What's wrong?" He looked down at her, concerned.

"Tucker, we have to get married."

"We *are* married," he said, going for her mouth again.

She turned her head, avoiding his kiss, unsure how to explain what she needed and why.

Understanding dawned in his dark eyes. "This is about your wedding vows."

"I didn't mean them," she said, praying that he would accept her need to make this right. "I said the words, but I didn't *mean* them."

"Then we'll get married again." His voice turned husky as he captured both of her hands in his. "We've done so many things wrong, Shel. We need to make this right."

He was doing it again, expressing her thoughts before she could even open her mouth. She smiled. "I love how you read my mind."

# CHAPTER
# TWENTY-ONE

They had gone to see Pastor Dean, so just before he concluded Sunday's church service, he invited Tucker and Shelby to join him at the microphone. Tucker stood and extended his hand to Shelby, and together they climbed the steps at the front of the church. When they reached the lectern, Shelby grasped the wooden structure's edges so hard her knuckles turned white.

It had been her idea to do this, and Tucker knew that as nervous as she was, she wouldn't back down. When she twisted around to look at him, panic in her beautiful eyes, he slipped an arm around her, wishing he could somehow absorb all of her fear. "Do you want me to start?"

She flinched as the microphone picked up his question and broadcast it to the church, but then she shook her head and leaned toward the microphone. "You all know that we got married recently," she began in a shaky voice. "But we . . . um, we didn't . . ."

Tucker squeezed her shoulder and moved his head next to hers. "We didn't do things God's way. We've asked the Lord to forgive us, and we've forgiven each other, but —"

"We need to ask for your forgiveness now," Shelby said.

"Because you're our family," Tucker added. "And we haven't set a godly example before you, especially the younger people."

Shelby's chin jerked and Tucker knew she had just swallowed hard. "You all know I was engaged to David Sharpe," she continued in a clear voice. "After he died I found out I was pregnant, and that was why Tucker married me."

"Pastor Dean advised against it," Tucker said. "He knew how torn up we both were after losing David, so he advised us to wait. But I thought I knew better, so I pushed Shelby to go through with it. And then —"

"Then I had a miscarriage. And somehow I convinced myself that God didn't care about me." When she glanced up at Tucker he sent her a silent "I love you" with his eyes. She turned back to the mike. "But I was wrong about that. God finally got through to me, and that was when I realized Tucker and I had fallen in love. So now I want us to get married again. Because this time I want to say the vows and really *mean* them."

"Will you marry us?" Tucker directed a look of appeal to Pastor Dean. "Here in the church?"

During their confession their pastor had stood to one side, arms folded, his expression unreadable, but now his craggy face spread into a smile as he stepped forward and held out his right hand to Tucker. "That would give me a great deal of pleasure."

As the congregation burst into spontaneous applause, Tucker heard his father and one of the other men boom loud "amens." But the best part came when the service ended and a tiny, blue-haired lady approached Tucker and Shelby.

"Will you have your reception in the fellowship hall?" she asked in a high, paper-thin voice, her watery gray eyes fixed on Tucker's. "I've already spoken to two of the ladies, and we'll recruit some others. We'd like to show our love and support by providing the food for your reception."

A pair of soggy violet eyes appealed to Tucker. He nodded. *Absolutely.*

"Oh," Shelby breathed, turning back to the woman. "That would be just . . ."

"Perfect," Tucker finished as her voice faded away. "That would be perfect. Thank you. We'll bring the cake."

The industrious little woman gave him a satisfied nod, then lifted a wrinkly hand to cup Shelby's cheek. "It took courage to say what you did, dear."

"I needed to do it," Shelby murmured.

"Yes. It's always a great relief when we cast our burdens before the Lord."

As the blue-haired lady disappeared into the crowd of well-wishers surging around him and Shelby, Tucker read his wife's glowing face and knew that for the first time, she was truly feeling that she *belonged* to these people. She was finally part of a family.

"We don't deserve this," she said a few minutes later as Tucker handed her into his SUV. "We don't deserve any of it."

"I know." He brushed the corner of her mouth with a kiss. "But maybe part of the reason God worked everything out this way was to give us a story to tell."

She blinked up at him. "A story to tell?"

"About His mercy and grace. About how He takes care of those who love Him, even when they don't deserve His blessings. People need to know this stuff, Shel. And we're in a position to explain it to them."

Understanding smoothed the lines from her forehead. "Maybe we could talk to the teenagers."

"You're reading my mind," he said, grinning.

There was just something about a tall man in a tuxedo. Or at least, *this* tall man. Resting one elbow on the table, Shelby leaned her chin on her palm and watched Tucker fork up the last bite of wedding cake on his plate and look around for more. She nudged her own plate toward him and sighed happily.

He smiled down at her. "Well? Did it 'take' this time?"

She grinned at his reference to the renewal of their wedding vows just an hour ago. "It took." She had finally made it right with God and with Tucker, and if the joy swirling around and through her right now suddenly turned to liquid, she would surely drown in it.

"I love you in that dress," Tucker commented as his dark gaze slowly swept her from head to toe.

She'd balked at wearing the gown she'd bought for David, but he had insisted. "You looked so beautiful in it," he'd told her. "I wasn't even in love with you, but that night you took my breath away. Please wear it, Shel. Wear it for *me* this time."

Their dress tonight was formal, but the ceremony had been simplicity itself. The only flowers were Shelby's small bouquet of red roses, and there had been no candles and no string quartet. Wasn't it odd that a woman who had always dreamed of the perfect wedding with all the trimmings could be completely satisfied with a brief exchange of vows followed by a couple of hymns played on a church organ?

No. She'd been stupid to believe it was the wedding frills that made a woman feel like a princess on her special day. It was the bridegroom who did that.

Tucker laid his fork across her empty plate and wiped his mouth on his napkin. "Are you ready for me to come home now?"

"It was *your* idea to stay at your dad's until the wedding," she reminded him.

He looked at the ceiling. "Honey, please don't say you need me to explain that again."

She chuckled and gave his arm a playful smack. "All right. Let's say our goodbyes and get out of here."

"Yes. And then tomorrow, let's go to Hawaii."

Shelby's heart tripped. "Hawaii?" she asked, afraid to believe he could be talking about a real honeymoon. She'd managed to clear her schedule and take a week off from school to spend this special time with Tucker, but after all he'd spent on their first wedding, the last thing she expected now was a honeymoon. "Why Hawaii?"

"Because," he said, leaning back in his chair to reach inside his tuxedo jacket. He extracted two small folders and slapped them on the cloth-covered table. "We have tickets."

*They had tickets.* Shelby held back a giddy squeal and posed a cautious question, instead. "Can we afford that?"

He gave her a dimply, heart-melting grin. "Not really. I'm afraid we'll be eating a lot of peanut-butter sandwiches in the coming months." His chair scraped a shrill protest on the tile floor as he pushed it back. He stood, tucked the airline tickets back inside his jacket pocket and held out a hand to his wife.

She took it, ready to follow him anywhere.

# EPILOGUE

"You need to sleep." Tucker's deep voice vibrated with loving concern as he smiled down at Shelby.

No, she couldn't sleep. Not just yet. She smoothed a wrinkle from the stiff white hospital blanket that covered her, then she held out her arms. "Come on, Tucker. *Please.*"

"No." He lifted his blue-wrapped bundle higher, until he was nose-to-nose with his newborn son. "David and I have things to talk about. Guy stuff. You wouldn't understand."

"*Steve.* Give me my baby."

He strolled to the window. "You got to carry him for nine whole months. It's my turn now."

Watching him marvel at their child filled Shelby with such a sweet ache, she sighed. "I love you."

Tucker swayed toward her, then checked

the movement and lifted one dark eyebrow in pretended disdain. "Nice try, honey. You almost had me that time. But it's still my turn."

She patted the edge of the bed. "Come sit beside me, then. You can hold both of us."

"And that's the problem with loving a woman," Tucker told his son as they moved away from the window. "She gives you That Look, and suddenly you're incapable of saying anything at all but, 'Yes, dear.' About three decades from now you'll know exactly what I mean. Don't say I didn't warn you."

Shelby suppressed a grin and rolled her eyes.

With one hand Tucker hooked the back of a chair and pulled it next to the bed. He settled his precious burden in Shelby's arms and then leaned forward, folding himself around his family. "Sleep now," he urged. "After twenty-three hours of labor, you've earned a rest."

Her body was tired, but her mind was too busy to sleep. Besides, she still hadn't finished saying her prayers of thanksgiving; the list was long.

Tucker touched the tip of his index finger to the baby's palm. "I love this," he said as David's tiny hand captured his finger. "The book says it's just a reflex, but it has to be something more." He lowered his head and kissed the baby's fist.

Shelby extended her free hand to caress her husband's stubbly cheek. He looked terrible this morning: unshaven, uncombed, exhausted, still wearing the wrinkled scrubs a nurse had given him last night. He'd probably go home today and write a column about how harrowing childbirth was. For the husband.

Shelby held back a smile. There had been something profoundly endearing about the terror she'd read in his dark eyes early this morning when her pain had reached its crescendo. Right at the end she'd forgotten the breathing exercises they'd practiced so faithfully and had actually screamed. Then she'd watched a fat tear roll down Tucker's ash-white cheek. Maybe it *was* harder on the husband.

He was still staring in unabashed wonder at the tiny fist that clutched his fingertip. "It's more than a reflex," he insisted. "He feels our love, Shel. He knows."

It was an easy thing to believe. Shelby felt a wild spinning in her body and imagined her heart twirling as she smiled into Tucker's wonderful brown eyes. "I never even dared to dream of happiness like this," she said.

"Me, either. But when I told Dad he was a grandfather, he said I should brace myself for unspeakable joy. I thought I already knew about joy, having spent this past year with you, both of us growing closer to the Lord, but what if this is only the beginning, Shel? What if it gets even better?" He stroked her hair, smoothing it away from her face again and again, until she closed her eyes.

Where would she be without him? He had refused to give up on her, and his loving touch had healed her heart. After they'd renewed their wedding vows he had encouraged her to get counseling and deal with her past. But although Dr. Stauffer had helped tremendously, even *she* had admitted that most of Shelby's healing had been wrought by the love of a remarkable man who took his promises seriously.

Tucker had been understanding with Diana, too, and just three months ago he had talked her into giving Dr. Stauffer a try. It had hit Diana hard when Jack married his nurse, but she was learning that she could live a full, rich life as a single woman. She had even gone to church a few times with Shelby and Tucker. And although she wasn't quite reconciled to the fact that Phillip had become an important part of her daughter's life, she and Dr. Stauffer were working on that.

Shelby couldn't think of her father these days without smiling. His loving wife and their three-year-old twins had tied his heart in knots, and he was so happy it almost hurt to listen to his voice when he phoned every week. He concluded every call with, "I love you, baby," and he was making plans right now to come and have a look at his first grandchild.

And then there was Bryan. He'd be sixteen on Friday, and this weekend he was planning to make a public declaration of his newfound faith in Jesus Christ by being baptized.

Could life *get* any better?

Tucker brushed her cheek with the back of his hand, and Shelby felt him lean close. "Unspeakable joy," he whispered in her ear. "Just think of it, Shel."

Her body felt as limp as a mass of overcooked pasta, but she had never been so completely happy. She wanted to sob out her thanks to God, but weariness was claiming her now. She teetered on the brink of slumber, and her last thought before she tipped over the edge was that her family was arranged like a set of Russian nesting dolls. Little David was safe in Shelby's

arms, and Shelby was secure in Tucker's.
And God was holding them all.

DEAR READER,

At times during the writing of this very emotional story, the character of Shelby Franklin became so real to me that I found myself in tears over her troubles. That was especially true toward the end of the story when Shelby, staggering under the weight of her grief, feels that God has abandoned her.

Have you or someone you care about ever felt that way? Our Lord promised never to leave us, but sometimes we hurt so much that we forget — and then we turn away from Him. But He is still there, right where He has always been, and He is keeping a candle in the window for each of us, waiting for us to come home.

I'm praying that *A Family Forever* will entertain you and encourage your heart. It has done both of those things for me. On the day I finished writing it, the Lord gave me a lovely gift; a spectacular sunset rainbow just like the one Tucker and Shelby see at the end of this story. I had just enough time to grab my camera and squeeze off a photo, which now sits on my desk to remind me of the joy I felt that evening when I finished this story and knew it was my very best work.

If you enjoy my writing, I'd love to hear from you. You can find me online at www .BrendaCoulter.com or you may direct a letter to me in care of Steeple Hill Books, 233 Broadway, Suite 1001, New York, NY 10279.

Trusting Him,
Brenda Coulter

# ABOUT THE AUTHOR

**Brenda Coulter** started writing an inspirational romance novel the same afternoon she finished reading one for the first time. Hopelessly addicted from that first hour, she had a complete manuscript and an interested publisher less than a year later. Although that first book went on to win both a HOLT Medallion and a *Romantic Times BOOKclub* Reviewers' Choice Award, it took three rejected manuscripts before Brenda figured out what she had done right the first time and did it again, resulting in a second sale to Steeple Hill Books.

Married for more than thirty years, Brenda and her husband, a mild-mannered architect, have two otherwise charming sons who torment their parents by interspersing requests for college money with harrowing tales of their latest daring adventures.

The employees of Thorndike Press hope you have enjoyed this Large Print book. All our Thorndike and Wheeler Large Print titles are designed for easy reading, and all our books are made to last. Other Thorndike Press Large Print books are available at your library, through selected bookstores, or directly from us.

For information about titles, please call:
    (800) 223-1244

or visit our Web site at:
    www.gale.com/thorndike
    www.gale.com/wheeler

To share your comments, please write:
    Publisher
    Thorndike Press
    295 Kennedy Memorial Drive
    Waterville, ME 04901